D1528718

They All Fall Down

A NOVEL BY

J.A. Blake

AND

Nick Moccia

For more information about J.A. Blake and/or Nick Moccia, go to www.theyallfalldown.net

Breakdown
Words and Music by Nick Moccia
Copyright © 2013 NICK MOCCIA
All Rights Reserved Used by Permission
Reprinted with Permission of Nick Moccia

Come Sail Away
Words and Music by Dennis DeYoung
Copyright © 1977 ALMO MUSIC CORP. and STYGIAN SONGS
Copyright Renewed
All Rights Controlled and Administered by ALMO MUSIC CORP.
All Rights Reserved Used by Permission
Reprinted with Permission of Hal Leonard Corporation

Over the Rainbow (from "The Wizard of Oz")
Music by HAROLD ARLEN Lyrics by E.Y. HARBURG
© 1938 (Renewed) METRO-GOLDWYN-MAYER INC.
© 1939 (Renewed) EMI FEIST CATALOG INC.

Opening quote from *Beyond Good and Evil*, translated by Walter Kaufmann, New York: Random House, 1966

ISBN 978-0-9892926-1-0 (ebook)
ISBN 978-0-9892926-2-7 (paperback)
Printed in the United States of America, 2013

Cover design: Blake Communications, © 2013.

Acknowledgements

From J.A. Blake: Thanks to my brave and trusting co-author, Nick Moccia, whose story inspired this literary pilgrimage and whose friendship has taken me on a journey of self-discovery. Thanks also go to Kai Schulz, husband extraordinaire, for his support and patience over three years of brainstorming, talking ideas out loud, and nights without dinner so I could write. I love you. My heartfelt and never-ending gratitude to my parents, John and Agnes Blake, for instilling in me my love of writing and for teaching me that family always comes first. And to my sister, Vicki, for always being the trusty sidekick whose resilience and kind heart inspire me to be a better person. Finally, I am grateful for the friends who continued to ask about this book and who, when it was needed, put their money where their mouth is.

From Nick Moccia: My thanks to my parents, Joanne and Dan Buscarini, for believing that I was always capable of more. Mom, whenever I wonder where I learned my inner strength, I think of you and I remember. To my father, Jerome Moccia, I am grateful for the gifts you handed down to me. Although you are not physically here, I feel you looking down on me and smiling. Thanks to the Moccia, Bevinetto and Sollitto families for understanding my need to tell this story even though they may not have agreed. To Jennifer Blake, thank you for opening my eyes to a new me. I have learned so much about myself since we started writing this book; things I would have never learned without London Drake. You have my love and respect always. Deepest gratitude to my oldest and dearest friend, Tim Cook, and his wonderful parents, Gail and Bill, who never turned their backs on an 11-year-old boy when the easier choice would have been to do just that. To Nancy Valente, Andrea Fanelli-Nola, and Angela Clack: you have forever touched my heart. Thank you for your work to guide me on my journey of self-acceptance. And finally, I say thank you to Nick and Adele Moccia. I have learned that a person should not be judged by a moment in time, but by a lifetime of moments put together. Forgiveness is a choice. I love and miss you both. I hope you now rest in peace.

About the Music

They All Fall Down is not just a novel; it is a multi-sensory experience. Every purchase of the book is complimented by a series of original songs by Nick Moccia that can be downloaded via the link offered below.

Many of these songs are referenced in the novel and help bring to life the feelings and sentiments of the book...its excitement, energy, heartache, and hope.

TRACK 1	Free
TRACK 2	My Reality
TRACK 3	Breakdown
TRACK 4	Found
TRACK 5	Longing for Monday
TRACK 6	Remember Me

Download the music from They All Fall Down at:

www.theyallfalldown.net/audio

Longing For Monday (They All Fall Down Soundtrack Version), Nick Moccia, © 2013.

*Whoever fights monsters should see to it that
in the process he does not become a monster.
And if you gaze long enough into an abyss,
the abyss will gaze back into you.*

~Friedrich Nietzsche

PROLOGUE

Please know that I love you all very much...her the most. I don't expect you to like the decision I've made for us. You may think I have just become a crazy man. I could see how you would think that.

I do not want to be remembered as a pathetic, withered version of myself. I will not be a victim of a failing body and a mind filled with desperation and sadness.

Today I take back control. I look at the disappointment in her eyes...the fear about a future she can't predict...there are no answers here anymore...

I am making a choice...one that frees us from a world that has just become too difficult. I offer us up to the angels and hope the promise of our faith is realized. I hope you can understand and that you'll remember me...us...with love...for always.

Goodbye.

Part One

MY REALITY

ONE

When the train rambled by his window at 5 a.m. – as it did every morning – London Drake was finally asleep. The small one bedroom apartment took the tremor of the passing locomotive bravely, picture frames rattled on their hangers from the bare white walls. Cocooned in blankets, London had only just fallen asleep an hour ago and was in the middle of a familiar and haunting dream.

> *A boy of eleven is dressed in a school uniform, carrying a backpack of books. He is walking down a tree-lined street on his way home from school. The air is warm with the smell of spring, tiny daffodils just poking up from flower beds. London sees the street through the boy's eyes. While other children run past him in playful groups, the boy walks alone. London feels anxiety growing inside the boy's tiny chest.*
>
> *"Decided to be a big boy and walk home alone today?" one of the other boys teases. "If you don't get lost, tell your granny I said hi when you get home," he said and spun away on a bicycle.*
>
> *In front of a brick house, the boy pauses at the bottom of four cement steps. One car sits in the driveway. The heavy wooden door is closed. London's own heart beats heavy, mimicking the pulse of the boy. One step at a time, the boy climbs the steps. At the top, he pauses in front of the locked door, bends to retrieve a key from under the doormat, and turns the latch.*

London propelled forward in his bed, gasping for air. Drenched in sweat, the images from his dream burned into his brain. His heart pounded.

"Fuck," he mumbled, as he reached to turn the clock on the bedside table. He made his way into the bathroom and fumbled in the medicine cabinet for a prescription. The mirror revealed his stubbled face, the dark circles under his eyes, and his messy hair. He decided not to dwell on the reflection. Instead, he turned on the spigot and cupped his hand under the running water. The cool wetness pooled in his hand; the other hand now held two sleeping pills. He splashed the water on his face, popped both pills into his mouth, dry swallowed hard, and then made his way back into bed.

When the phone on the bedside table vibrated, it was dark in the room. The brightness of the day was gone and indicated that he had slept away the entire day. He tried to recall the day of the week and quickly thought of the schedule book left on the kitchen table the night before. "Where tonight?" he mumbled, as he pushed fists into his tired eyes.

Again the phone vibrated, face down on the night stand. Reaching across the bed to switch on the light, he saw the time: 8 p.m. When he flipped the phone over to see its face, Cassandra's name lit up the screen.

Cassandra was a 28-year-old barista that he had met on a Sunday afternoon in his favorite coffee shop. He was drawn to the way her dark hair curled down over her back, stopping right before the spot where her back ended and the roundness of her bottom began. And when she turned to greet him at the coffee counter, her green eyes seemed to look right into his soul. The slightly southern twang in her soft voice was a remnant of her Virginia upbringing and made her even more attractive to him. He'd ordered his coffee, said something flirty, and sat by the window. Every once in a while, he would look up at her and smile with a grin that bore more innocence than it deserved. When her shift was over, he took her to his apartment and they had sex on every flat surface they could find. Now, four months later, she still called regularly as if she hoped that would imply some kind of steady relationship with him. And once out of every six or seven times she called, he answered. Today was not one of those times.

Instead, he uncurled out of the sheets and moved into the kitchen, opened his schedule book on the table and found the date. What the hell is today? he thought and then found the month of May. His thick finger traced the outline of the days...moved to May 7. He was booked at an acoustic show with his friend Jon at a local bar not far from his apartment. Then he noticed the start time: 9:30 p.m.

"Guess I better get moving. Wouldn't want all my fans to have to wait too long," he said sarcastically to the small cat that was curled up on the end of the sofa.

When he pulled into the parking lot of Whiskey Walkers, he took note of the parked cars. He could count them on one hand if he tried, but instead decided to attribute the lack of a crowd to the early hour. Plus, it was a Wednesday night. Not the busiest night of the week, but usually better than a Monday or Tuesday. He was grateful for the mid-week work. Not a lot of money, but 50 bucks in his pocket was better than nothing, he thought.

He and Jon were long-time friends and often joked that their friendship had survived for 15 years because they did not play on stage together regularly. Instead, once a month for the past three years, they did an acoustic show at Whiskey Walkers. Each of them played guitar and took turns singing the same set list month after month. Once in a while someone in the crowd would make a special request and they were usually able to accommodate it. No doubt some drunk guy at the bar would call out, "Stairway to Heaven," a joke that lost its humor years ago. But he always liked when someone requested something special. That way, he knew that at least one or two people in the small crowd were paying attention to the music, as opposed to just tolerating it while watching a game on the TV above the bar. He knew that most times the people in the bar were not there to see him and Jon. Instead, they just sort of happened upon the duo during a midweek outing. Sometimes, though, one or two of those people did decide to come back to see them again.

He parked his car by the back door of Whiskey Walkers just as it began to drizzle. It was a warm night for early May and in the distance he could hear the rumble of thunder. He hurried to pop open the trunk and began unloading...his guitar...his monitor.

"Hey, man," he heard, as Jon emerged from the propped open door.

"Been here long?" he asked Jon.

"Nah. Maybe 15 minutes or so. Not much going on in here. But Tony wants to see you."

Tony was the manager of Whiskey Walkers. From what London could gather through their conversations, Tony had graduated from college with a business degree, worked as a bartender for a year, and then came home looking for a job. When he wasn't able to find something on his own, his dad – the owner of the bar – offered him the management position as a place to "spread his wings." It was Tony's idea to bring live music in during the week. London and Jon were one of his first duos.

"Go take care of it, man," Jon said. "I got this shit. He's in the back office."

The door to the office was open just enough for London to see Tony inside. The boss was seated behind a desk that was covered in receipts. A girl on his lap – one of the waitresses –was kissing him.

London paused. As he turned, a squeak in the floor revealed his presence.

Tony pushed the girl aside to look around her. "Jesus, London. Come on in," he called and pushed the waitress off his lap. "Get back to work," he said to her, smacking her bottom.

As she passed London on her way out, she fastened a few open buttons on her white blouse.

He smiled at her, a smile not too wide, but enough to convey that he was sorry for the interruption. "Hey, Tony," he said as he entered the office, not offering an acknowledgement of the indiscretion he just witnessed. "Jon said you wanted to see me. What's up?"

"I wanted to talk to you about your music," Tony said. "I want to know if you want a solo gig here a couple times a month."

London's mind went quickly to the extra money a solo gig would bring in for him. "Hell, yeah," he responded.

"Great," Tony responded. "I'm glad to hear it. I was afraid you'd have a problem with dropping Jon and playing solo."

"Dropping Jon?" he asked.

"Yeah, man. What I want to do is have you play alone...every other Wednesday night. I'm looking to keep you on at your current rate. But instead of having one night a month, if you drop John and do the gig yourself, I can bring you back a second night for the same money."

"Oh," he said.

"Oh? That's it? Jesus, London, I thought you'd be flattered. I mean, I could just drop you both and find another solo. There are tons of guys out there just itching for a regular spot in a bar. But I wanted to offer it to you first...being we've been working together so long."

"But that's just it, Tony," he said. "We – Jon and I – have been working with you for a while now. How do I tell him that you don't want him back anymore, but that it's cool for me to keep coming? It just doesn't seem right to me. It doesn't feel good."

"Fuck feelings, London. This is business. I need to add more nights of music. You need to make a paycheck. If you want it, it's yours. If not, let me know. I'll find somebody else."

London stood still in the open doorway, not sure what to say.

"We're good as is until next month, London. But you gotta make a decision. Come July, it's either you alone, or neither one of you. You let me know."

"I gotta get out there," London said. "It's almost 9:30. We should get started."

Tony was already moved onto other things. He shuffled a pile of receipts around on the desk and waved London out.

"It's nothing personal against Jon," he said, as London turned. "It's business, man."

TWO

London made his way to the small stage in Whiskey Walkers where Jon was already sitting waiting for him.

"Everything OK, man?" Jon asked.

London nodded his head.

"Yeah, fine. You wanna get this show on the road?" he asked Jon.

The two glanced around the bar and back at each other as Jon began to strum the strings on his guitar.

London counted 11 people seated around the bar. He followed Jon's example though, and sang as if the bar was filled with people who had come just to see him.

An hour later, Jon and London wrapped up their first set. Of the 11 people who'd been there at the start, about half were still there. Another 20 or so had wandered in somewhere between "Brown Eyed Girl" and "Message in a Bottle." Alex walked in a few minutes after London sat at the bar.

"Order me one, too," he heard from behind him. He didn't have to turn to see who it was. He held two fingers up to the bartender and smiled. "Hey you," he said, as he turned to look at Alex. "Thought you weren't gonna make it tonight."

"Yeah, well, I just couldn't stay away from all this," Alex replied sarcastically.

London could not recall the exact night that Alex had walked into his life. The time just seemed to melt away into years. He did remember that Alex came out a few times with her girlfriends before they were actually introduced. She would show up at Whisky Walkers right around 10. She and the girls would order some bar food, toss back some beers, and by midnight were usually dancing. If she was there with five other girls, at least three of them usually stayed until closing. Then, they would all post pictures on Facebook and Tweet messages about the good time they'd had. London figured it was good publicity

One night, Alex decided she wanted to meet London. She walked up to him between sets and asked if she could buy him a drink.

"Singing like that must make you thirsty," she said, sort of flirtatiously.

"Is that an offer?" he asked her.

"Only if you're gonna say 'yes.' Otherwise it was just an observation," Alex joked.

When he did say "yes," Alex invited him to sit at her table. Her friends were off in other corners of the bar and the table was wide open.

In the 15 minutes between the first set and the second set of the evening, London learned that Alex was two years younger than he, had a college degree, and worked in public relations. She also shared that she was in a relationship with a guy named George, but London surmised from her tone that it was not a relationship that was good for her.

"People get used to each other, ya know?" she asked him. "We just sort of settle in and get comfortable and before you know it, three years have gone by."

"Not exactly stimulating," he said to her.

"Yeah," Alex reflected, a deep longing in her eyes. "I could use stimulating."

London knew what she meant.

Two years after their first meeting, Alex still made it a point to come out and see him. But she was no longer just a "fan." She had become one of London's closest and dearest friends. They went to concerts, talked on the phone, saw movies together. He never pursued a physical relationship with Alex, but would be lying if he said he never thought about it. More than once, after swallowing one too many martinis, Alex had not been shy about flirting with him. And she was good at it. Her chestnut brown hair, fair skin, and freckled face portrayed innocence, but mixed with her uncompromising personality, she exuded an air of confidence that was sexy. This made her flirting seem even dirtier than it would have if someone more timid had been the aggressor. But to have sex with her meant that there would eventually be consequences...good or bad. He learned that every decision had consequences. This would be no different. He would either need to be in the relationship he thought Alex would expect afterward, or risk losing her friendship.

Not having sex with Alex was a heart versus mind struggle. The loss of Alex would mean the loss of one of the only people in his life that "got" him. He couldn't risk that. His effort in life to make true friends was not as successful as he liked. He connected with Alex on a deep and meaningful level. Some of that connection was from their mutual acceptance of each other's flaws; some was from shared struggles in life; some was just chemistry. Regardless of the reason, the two understood each other. And so, he refrained from venturing into the physical with Alex. As a reward, he enjoyed one of the most meaningful friendships of his adult life.

"I am so in love with you," Alex told him one night over vodka martinis.

The words always surprised him. He would wonder, How can you know me so well and still love me? But then he would count himself as grateful and just accept the gift of her friendship.

"I love you too, pretty girl," he told her. When he said it, Alex felt safe and loved. He knew her demons; she knew his. They both knew they'd be friends for life.

When Alex pulled the empty chair next to him away from the bar and shimmied in to take a seat, he noticed that she was still dressed in her work clothes: a pair of black dress pants, pin-striped blouse, and heels. If she had been home, she'd likely be in jeans and flatter shoes. She let out a long sigh as she relaxed back into the chair.

"Long day, huh?" he asked her.

"Too fucking long," Alex replied. "I needed a drink."

"That bad, honey?"

"London," she replied. "I need to make some changes. What the hell am I doing with my life?"

He smiled. They'd had this conversation before. He knew what to say to make her feel better. It usually just took him pointing out to her the good things in her life. Within minutes, she'd feel guilty that she had even been whining and cheer up.

"Jesus, Lex, how many times do we have to have this conversation?" he asked her. "We both know that you've got it more together than most people our age. You have a good job, a cool apartment, a nice car. What is it that you want?"

Alex turned and looked him in the eye. She was sad. Suddenly, he realized that this was different than other times. There was really something bothering her.

"Lex, what is it?" he asked.

Before she could answer, Jon was standing behind her.

"Hey, Alex," Jon said, putting his hand on her shoulder.

"Jon!" Alex exclaimed, as if she hadn't seen him in years. "How the heck are you, you sexy thing?"

Jon giggled, almost boyishly.

"Thanks for coming out tonight," he said to her.

"Oh, Jon, I've been coming for years. You can stop thanking me now," Alex joked.

She swiveled off the bar stool and stood to embrace Jon. She had been hugging him for years, but just never got used to how skinny he was. *Under his glittered shirt and studded jeans, he must just be a pile of bones*, Alex thought. Alex also wondered if she were smaller would he still feel so slight to her.

"So you ready to start up again, man?" Jon asked London. He turned to Alex again. "Sorry to steal him away. Are you gonna hang around?"

London interjected. "You're gonna stick around right?" He wanted to talk more with her.

"Yeah, I'll be here, guys," she said, smiling. She lifted her martini glass to suggest it would keep her occupied. "Not even wild horses could drag me away from the two of you."

London leaned over and kissed her on the cheek before following Jon back to the stage. He watched Alex from the stage, wondering what she was trying to drink away with the two martinis she enjoyed without him during his second set.

By the time London and Jon finished their third set and began packing up for the night, Alex was drunk. Even from across the room, London could judge her sobriety by the way she moved. Her careless flirtation with the man seated on the bar stool next to her was also a pretty good indicator. With her black eyes, she gazed at him as he talked. London guessed the conversation really wasn't that riveting. Every now and again, she'd run one finger along the side of her face to tuck a piece of hair behind her ear.

Her body was turned to face him.

As London approached Alex, he could hear the man asking her if she wanted to go somewhere a little more private.

"Hey, Lex," London said quietly interrupting. "I'm just about done here." He turned to the man at the bar.

"Hey, man, thanks for coming out," he said, extending his hand between the stranger and Alex.

The man turned to London, displaying a gaze that London couldn't discern as annoyed or confused.

Alex hopped off the bar stool and stood beside London.

"London," she said, "this is Brian."

Again, London greeted the man. "Nice to meet you, Brian," he replied, noticing the band on Brian's left hand.

Alex excused herself to go to the bathroom.

"You and your wife come here on the weekends?" London asked.

"No, man," Brian replied. "I actually work right up the street and just stopped in for a nightcap. Funny thing, I go by this place all the time but have never stopped in before."

"Oh, you should bring your wife here sometime for dinner. They have a great weekend menu," London replied.

Brian motioned the bartender for his check. "Maybe we will," he replied, half smiling. "Hey, tell Alex I said goodbye, OK? I gotta get out of here."

"Good to meet you," London said, patting Brian on the back. "Be careful going home."

When Alex came out of the bathroom, London was back with Jon, packing up the last bit of his equipment. She took her seat again at the bar before noticing Brian's paid receipt in front of where he had been seated.

London walked toward her. "You need a ride home, honey?" he asked.

"It appears so," she replied, swiping her handbag off the bar.

London left Alex standing inside the bar and went to get his car. The night's earlier thunder had turned into rain, and deep puddles were forming in the street. He had always been a fan of thunderstorms. Alex, too. That was one more thing they had in common.

"Come on, hot stuff," he called to Alex, pushing open the passenger side door of his car.

Alex darted out of the bar and into the car.

"Did you drive here?" he asked.

"Nope. Took the train from the city earlier," Alex replied. "My car is still parked safely at home from this morning."

"One less thing to worry about, huh?" he asked. "Wanna grab a bite to eat?"

"Sounds OK," Alex replied with a slur in her voice. "Maybe we can just grab a pizza and go back to your place?"

"You off tomorrow?" he asked, worried that he'd have to get up earlier than he was accustomed to drive her to work.

"No," replied Alex, "but I feel a sick day comin' on."

He smiled. It was a perfect answer.

Alex excused herself to the bathroom as soon as the two arrived back at his apartment. He busied himself with the pizza, searching the cupboards for the paper plates he knew he had. He also started a pot of coffee, although he suspected his offer for a cup would be denied by Alex. The entire pot had brewed and she was still not in the room with him.

"Alex," he called, "You OK in there?"

No answer. He waited 10 seconds and called in again.

"Lex...you coming? Pizza's getting cold."

Still no answer.

He moved into the hallway and noticed the bathroom door open. Alex was not inside. Instead, he found pieces of her clothing...shoes...pants...her striped blouse...strewn across the floor, creating a trail from the bathroom to his bedroom. Following the clues, he found Alex passed out on his bed. She was wearing only her underwear and a black camisole. Face down, drooling on his pillow, she was fast asleep.

He took a blanket from the closet and moved toward the bed. He paused for just a moment to look at her. As he did, Alex rolled onto her side to face him and opened her eyes. He stood motionless, not sure if she was really awake. When she rolled all the way over on her back, the loose black camisole fell low on her chest, her right breast now exposed. His eyes fell lower on her body.

"See something you like?" she asked him playfully.

Now propped up on her elbows, the light from the hall cast a shine on her body. He noticed that her exposed nipple was erect; the roundness of her breast excited him.

"Come get in bed with me, honey," she suggested to him and patted the mattress next to her. She fell back on the pillow and mumbled something he could not discern. He moved toward her with the blanket, paused, and then covered her with it. Then he took a pillow from the bed, closed the door, and settled on the couch in the living room to enjoy the pizza alone.

THREE

"London, London," he heard. A hand shook his shoulder gently. Opening one eye half-way, he saw Alex standing above him.

She was now fully dressed in the clothes she had been wearing the previous night. Her hair was a mess, her eyes smudged with black liner from the day before. She was holding a cold piece of pizza.

"Jesus, Lex, how can you eat that shit?" he asked. His voice was deeper than normal.

"Good morning, Mr. Morning Voice," Alex joked.

"What time is it?" he asked.

"Almost noon. And it's a bright sunny day," Alex replied. "I can't believe I passed out on you last night like that. Thanks for letting me crash here."

"Noon?" he asked. "That's all?" he asked, smirking.

"Rise and shine sunshine," Alex replied, the melancholy of the previous night now completely gone from her tone.

"When did you turn into a morning person?" he asked, rising from the couch and scooping up his pillow. He moved out of the room toward the bedroom.

"Where ya going?" Alex asked as the microwave beeped.

"Back to bed where I belong at noon," he replied.

"But I made you coffee," Alex petitioned.

He paused and looked back over his shoulder at her. "You did not," he said, laughing. "And if you think I'm drinking the left over sludge from last night, you got another thing coming."

"OK, I'll make you a deal," Alex bartered. "You shower and get dressed and I'll buy you a fresh cup on the way back to my place."

"Yeah, yeah," he mumbled, closing the bathroom door behind him.

Alex could hear the shower start and knew that her request would not go unanswered. She kept her promise and bought him a mocha latte in the Starbucks drive-thru on the way back to her apartment, arguing that she could simply not go into the store looking the way she did.

"I'm wearing yesterday's underwear for God's sake, London," she told him.

He knew better than to argue with that.

When London dropped Alex off at her apartment, it was 1:00 in the afternoon. He was not used to being up and out at this time of day and actually found the sunlight energizing. He also began to feel a little mischievous, like a boy cutting school in the middle of the week. He was looking for trouble.

Alex's apartment was not far from the little coffee shop he frequented; the one where Cassandra worked. He hadn't been there in a few weeks and although he had just enjoyed the Starbucks latte, he found himself yearning for something sweet. He wasn't sure if a cinnamon bun or a taste of Cassandra's lips would satisfy the craving and decided to find out. He wasn't sure if she'd even be working, but decided to take a chance. If nothing else, he'd get that cinnamon bun.

The bells on the café jingled when he opened the door. The man behind the counter turned from the coffee machine he had been cleaning and greeted London.

"Good afternoon, sir. Can I help you?" he asked.

London paused, disappointed. He wanted to say, "Certainly not in the way I hoped," but refrained. "Uh, yeah," he answered, swaying back and forth in front of the pastry display, hands in his pockets. "Gimme one of those cinnamon buns."

"You havin' a latte to go with that?" he heard from behind him. It was a woman's voice. It was familiar.

He turned and smiled at Cassandra. "Hey there, beautiful," he said.

The man behind the counter put the cinnamon bun in a pastry bag and laid it on the counter.

"I got this," Cassandra said, as she moved behind the register, never taking her eyes off of London.

"No coffee today," London said. "Gimme an unsweetened iced tea instead."

"Iced tea?" Cassandra questioned, still playing the game of pretending like they didn't know each other. "Who drinks iced tea with a cinnamon bun?" she jested.

"I'm in the mood for something different today," he answered playfully. The chemistry between them boiled. "Something a little out of the ordinary," he said.

Cassandra turned her back to him and scooped ice from the machine under the drink dispenser. She bent slightly at the waist, calling his eyes to move down her body. When she turned back to face him, she caught his diverted eyes as they jetted back up to her face.

"I've been trying to call you," she finally said to him. "I think I've got your voicemail greeting memorized by now."

"Sorry," he said, not even trying to sound sincere. "Things have been a little crazy with me."

She stood silent.

He could sense disappointment in her eyes. "Then it occurred to me that I haven't talked to you in a while," he continued, trying to sound sincere this time. "I missed you."

"Missed me, huh?" Cassandra asked, hoping he would say it again.

"Yes," he replied.

"I get done in half an hour," Cassandra answered glancing up at the clock. "If you want to hang around ..."

"Absolutely," he answered without waiting for her to finish her sentence. "I'm just gonna go sit and eat my cinnamon bun."

He smiled with a warmth that melted Cassandra's heart. Charm was something he had mastered years ago. Coupled with his dark eyes, he was unrivaled at invoking tenderness from women. He often found forgiveness much quicker than he deserved; devotion quicker than it was earned.

He took a seat near the window and unwrapped his treat from its wrapper. He couldn't help but relate his friendship with Cassandra to the bun. If the two were represented in the dessert, she would be the sugar...the thick gooey substance that coated the cake; the part that made it work. He, on the other hand, would be the topping – either nuts or raisins, not because of any metaphor of what they represented, but because sometimes they would be on a cinnamon bun; sometimes not. You could never really count on them being there until they actually showed up. And, as in the case of most richly sweet desserts, a little taste every once in a while was all one needed to feel full.

He ate half of the bun and then pushed it aside. Cassandra was no longer behind the counter. He had missed the moment she disappeared, but guessed that she was in the back restocking the napkin dispenser, or refilling the creamer. His fingers sticky, he himself disappeared into the bathroom to wash his hands.

He was still drying his hands on a paper towel as he exited the men's room. He walked down a short hallway and past the ladies' room, just as the door opened and Cassandra emerged. She was no longer in the black pants and apron she had been wearing. Instead, she wore a denim skirt and scooped t-shirt. Her hair was now down, cascading curls over her shoulders.

"And there you are!" he exclaimed.

"Oh, did you miss me?" Cassandra asked again playfully, smiling at him.

"Of course I did," he replied.

"I just have to punch out and I'm ready to get out of here," she told him.

He followed her to the front of the café, watching how her hips swayed with every step. When she was ready to go, he held the door open for her. When they were finally out in the parking lot, he took her hand, pulled her toward him, and kissed her gently on the lips.

"I did miss you," he said and melted her heart.

FOUR

A tiny pink tongue licked London's cheek and stirred him to alertness. Yawning, he opened his eyes and saw the ceiling fan spinning above his head. Seated on his chest was a fluffy white Yorkie whose dangling name tag read "Zeus." He was naked and alone in Cassandra's bed. From the living room, he could hear soft music playing.

Pulling the bed sheet around him, he rose from the bed and moved into the living room. Cassandra was seated out on the floor in a cobbler's pose on her yoga mat, eyes closed. A Frangipani incense stick burned on the coffee table, the sweet smell of plumeria filling the room. He stood quiet and watched her for a moment before clearing his throat to announce his presence.

Cassandra opened her eyes and smiled but remained silent.

He smiled back and disappeared into the bathroom.

When he returned to the living room, he was fully dressed and Cassandra was no longer in her yoga pose. Instead, she was seated at the kitchen table, sipping a cup of organic red raspberry tea. The newspaper was spread out on the table before her; the small white dog seated at her feet.

"Hey, sweetie," he said.

"Hi," she replied. "Enjoy your nap?"

"I enjoyed what happened before the nap," he said.

Cassandra turned in her chair to look at him. He was still standing, indicating to her that he didn't plan to stay much longer. She sat still at the table, carelessly flipping a page of the newspaper.

"So, I gotta get going," he said, after a moment of silence. The pause was long enough to impose a sense of guilt on him. He knew she would like if he stayed for dinner. He knew he should offer to take her out to eat. Yet, he also now itched to move on with his day.

"OK," said Cassandra hesitantly.

He could sense her disappointment. "So, come give me kiss," he said to her. "Something to hold me over until next time."

With the promise of a future date, Cassandra rose from the chair and met him across the room. "Didn't I give you enough today?" she asked playfully.

"Never enough," he replied, glad that the tone had turned back to lightheartedness.

Cassandra leaned into him.

He kissed her gently on the lips. "See you soon?" he asked her rhetorically, knowing that was completely up to him.

"I hope so," Cassandra replied, walking him toward the door.

With one final kiss, he opened the door and turned to leave Cassandra's apartment.

She waited for him to say something else; a memento that he would call or be in touch with her again soon. He said nothing, but left. She closed the door behind him and stood for a moment, her forehead pressed against the dead wood of the door and feeling as if she had just given up yet another piece of herself.

FIVE

As London buckled his seat belt, his phone rang. It was his mother. The time was 4:00 p.m.

"Hey, Momma," he said in greeting to his caller.

Almost surprised that he had answered, his mother greeted him in return. "I'm surprised you picked up," she joked.

"You want me to hang up?" he questioned.

"Of course not, silly," she told him. "How are you? What's going on?"

"I'm fine," he told her. "Not much of anything going on. Just dropped Alex off at home."

He omitted the part of the afternoon he had spent with Cassandra. He had learned years ago not to tell his mother about the women in his life. It only strengthened her belief that one day he'd be married and she would be a grandmother; two things London himself was not convinced would ever happen. But his mother loved Alex. He always earned points for having spent time with her.

"Oh?" she questioned. "And how is Alex? She's such a nice girl."

He smiled. He had grown so used to hearing that from his mother. If she didn't say it, he would almost be disappointed.

"She's fine, Ma," he replied. Again opting for the less complicated story, he said "We were just out running a few errands."

"Well, good for her to be able to get you out of the house while the sun is still up," his mother joked.

"So what are you doing?" he asked.

"Just put on a fresh pot of coffee, threw in some laundry; not much," she replied.

"Can you wait to pour that coffee until I get there?" he asked. He knew his question would get an immediate response.

"Of course, dear. Are you serious?" she asked hopefully.

"Yeah. I was thinking about swinging by to see you. I have another appointment at 7, but I thought it might be nice if we visited for a while. That OK?" he asked.

"Sure is, babe," she replied. "See you in what...half an hour?"

"See you soon, momma," he replied and disconnected the call.

His mother was standing at the front door waiting when he pulled into her driveway. When he pulled the keys from the ignition, she pushed open the door with one arm, her body spilling into the open entryway.

"What a treat!" she said, as he approached. She smiled, but also silently worried that something was wrong. A mid-week visit like this was not a regular happening.

"Hey, momma," he said, wrapping his arms around her. She was half his size in stature. Even from her elevated position on the step, she was shorter than he was.

"So what's going on, honey?" his mother asked, as the two made their way through the living room and into the kitchen.

"Nothing really. I just wanted to visit a little," he replied.

"OK, then," his mother said, "what a nice surprise this is."

She retrieved two cups from the pantry and placed them on the round wood table where he was seated. She turned again to pull a carton of milk from the refrigerator and then a caddy of Sweet and Low from the counter.

"Coffee smells good," he commented as his mother pulled the pot from its holder.

After both cups were filled, his mother took a seat at the table with him.

"So how you doin', honey?" she asked. "Everything going OK?"

"Nothing really new," he replied with little enthusiasm. "Jon and I are still playing at Whiskey Walkers...."

"And how's that going?" his mother asked.

He gave his mother the abbreviated version of what had happened with Tony the night before. He could feel his anger growing as he spoke.

His mother sat and listened, waiting for him to ask for her opinion. When he finally did, the question was more about him than the situation.

"Mom, am I a failure?"

"What?" his mother asked, confused by the question.

"When you used to come and listen to me play, did you ever think I'd still be playing these little rinky-dink bars all these years later? Didn't you envision more for me?"

"Oh, London," she replied. "Your father and I always believed in you. I still do. I hope you know that."

"It just really annoys the hell out of me that I am still here...in this small town, playing these small gigs in places that no one gives a shit about," he replied.

"Are you doing what you love, London?" his mother asked.

"I don't know anymore, Mom," he replied. "There are nights when I go home feeling like that big break is about to happen at any moment...that I won't have to play someone else's songs anymore and that I won't have to hope anymore that I can pay the rent that month. And then there are nights like last night when some piece of shit club owner reminds me that I'm still not the one in control of my life. I'm tired of playing by someone else's rules, Mom. I wanna be the one calling the shots."

His mother smirked, but her amusement was not at what he had said. Instead, it was because she believed that most people felt that way. "Don't you think most people are frustrated, London?" she asked. "Don't you think we'd all like for things to go the way we planned? But life's not like that, honey. Life deals us the cards. It's our job to make the best hand we can and keep playing the game."

He sat silent, pondering what his mother had just said. "Do you remember when I was in high school?" he finally asked. "Do you remember how when all the other kids went to football games and parties, I was in my room playing guitar?"

"Of course I remember, honey," she replied. "I also remember how you struggled – even then – with the rules."

"And then on the weekends, you would drive me to all those gigs we managed to get." He smiled at his mother. "I was seventeen years old, sitting on a bar stool in front of a crowd of people, playing that guitar."

"I remember like it was yesterday," his mother said, now smiling herself.

"And do you remember that black leather jacket you always wore?" he asked, now chuckling out loud. The memory lifted his spirits.

"Jacket?" his mother questioned, knowing all too well the one to which he referred.

"Oh, come on," he chided. "There you were, dressed up like a biker babe, drinking your Diet Coke, and watching your kid sing to a bunch of people old enough to be his parents. Funniest thing was that no one even realized you were my mom!"

"I didn't want to embarrass you," his mother said.

"Oh, the guys hitting on you were enough to do that," he joked.

His mother reached across the table to place her hand on his arm. The two laughed out loud, remembering the days when they were both younger; both a little more naive.

"And do you remember how we'd come home, middle of the night, and dad would be sitting up waiting for us?" he asked.

His mother's eyes filled with tears. "Oh, honey, he was so proud of you," she said. "Even though his job kept him out late most nights and he rarely made it out to see you play, we would stay up for hours – even after you went to bed – talking about your night," his mother told him.

"You did?" he asked. He'd never known that.

"Your father had so many questions," she said. "He wanted to know what songs you played, if you got that chord you were struggling with just right. But the thing he wanted to know most is if you looked happy. That was really all that ever mattered to him."

He sat and listened. A tear rolled over his cheek. "I miss dad," he said.

"Me too, honey," his mother said. "Me, too."

SIX

The conversation with his mother had exhausted London so he was less than enthusiastic when he walked into Patricia's office at 7 p.m. But he also knew the time with his therapist would help him to process some of the feelings that were stirred up inside of him.

"Good evening, London!" Patricia said as she opened the door from her office and welcomed him inside. "How are you? How was the week?"

He took his usual spot in an oversized arm chair. Patricia's office was cozy. The orchestrated design made clients feel at home and comfortable. Patricia took her usual spot as well, in a matching arm chair on the opposite side of a mahogany coffee table.

He made small talk to begin the conversation. He always did. Casual comments about the weather or a movie he'd recently seem helped to ease him into a conversation with Patricia. He had seen a number of therapists in his life; men and women, middle aged and older. But to date, Patricia was his favorite. Not because she entertained his need for a light opening, but because she seemed to understand why he needed it. Despite the professional nature of their relationship, he also needed to trust the therapist. If she needed to engage in small talk to build that trust, Patricia was willing to do that.

After several minutes of discussing the afternoon traffic, London eased further back in his seat and bent his leg to place his right ankle on his left knee. Patricia took that as a sign to move forward.

"So, London," she began. "Last time you were here we were talking about the frustration you're feeling about your career. How would you rate that frustration today?"

He exhaled audibly.

"OK," Patricia led. "I'll assume we can continue on that topic."

"I just left my mother's house," London told her, leading Patricia to think he was shifting to another topic.

"Oh?" she asked. "Then let's talk about that. How was your visit?"

"It was nice," he replied. "It's always nice. She's always happy to see me."

"And so why do you sound disappointed?" Patricia asked, prompted by his tone.

"Well, that's the big question, isn't it?" he asked, more to himself than anyone. "I asked my mother if she thought I was a failure."

Patricia sat silent, waiting for him to offer more information. She did that intentionally at times when he offered up something deeply personal. She let him expel it – as if it were a demon inside him – and then let it just lie, out in the open, breathing in the air. The pause gave him a moment to catch his own breath so that he could move forward.

"I don't know what I expected her to say," he finally offered. "I mean, what's a mother gonna say when you ask her something like that?"

"And what did she say?" Patricia asked.

"She said that she's always believed in me; that she still does."

"I'm sure she does, London," Patricia replied. "Did she say anything more than that?"

"We talked about my dad."

His father had been a topic of conversation between the two in the past. Patricia knew that London's father had struggled with a gambling addiction; that when it came to home finances, he was careless, often leaving his family struggling to pay the rent or fill the oil tank for the furnace.

"I guess I'm just left wondering what the hell he really ever thought," he offered.

"Thought?" Patricia asked. "Thought about what?"

"About anything," he replied. "I mean, here I am living a life in which I miss him. I miss him all the time. But if you were to ask me what I miss, I'm not sure I could really tell you. I mean, it's not like he was around a lot when he was living."

"Did you talk with your mother about that?"

"Yeah, I did," he answered. "But she's full of shit about it sometimes.

She makes excuses...he was working, he was looking for a job...he was... he was...he was."

Again, Patricia waited to respond.

"He was out buying lottery tickets, is what he was doing," he continued, now with some anger in his voice. Those fucking lottery tickets that never won a god damned thing."

"And what about that bothers you, London?" Patricia asked. "Is it the addiction that bothers you or is it something more?"

"It's all of it," he replied. "It bothers me that he invested all his hope in something so random. It bothers me that he never kept a real job for any amount of time to be deemed responsible. It bothers me that my mother had to pick up the slack and do the job of two parents. It bothers me that he proclaimed love, but I have no idea what he meant by that sentiment. It bothers me that after my grandparents died it all just got worse...at a time when I needed it to get better. And it bothers me that I can't let any of it fucking go."

Trying to refocus London's energy, Patricia interjected. "And what can we do with those emotions, London? How can they help you now in a more positive way?"

"If I could answer that question, I wouldn't be here with you," he replied, chuckling. He paused. "I think the thing that really gets me is that here I am, hating the qualities that made my father my father. And at the end of the day, I am just like him."

Patricia leaned forward in her chair, intrigued. "Explain to me what you mean," she petitioned.

"The bottom line is that my father never lived an adult life. Sure, he had a family. But he was never able to provide for that family. His life was ridden with money troubles. He lived paycheck to paycheck...sometimes not even making it that long. He was a dreamer, putting all his hopes and dreams in a lottery that never paid off."

"And how do you see yourself in that, London?" Patricia asked.

"I'm just like him. While I don't play the lottery, I have invested my life in an equally silly dream of a music career. And, in the meantime, I'm just as financially unstable; just as unable to get my shit together and be a man."

"A man?" Patricia questioned.

"Yes, a man," he replied. "A grown ass adult who can step up and provide – for myself and for others; someone who can demonstrate control. Someone who knows how to look tragedy in the face and say 'Fuck you...I'm better than you.'"

"And why do you think you are unable to transition into this definition of manhood?" Patricia asked.

"I don't know," he replied. "I wish my father had been more present. I wish he had been more of a role model of the kind of life I think I want to live. Wish he had been there to support me after our family shattered into a million bloody pieces all over the news. That might have helped."

"But you also say that you loved your father, London," Patricia reminded him. "What did you love about him?"

He sat in silence. Tears began to roll over his cheeks. "I don't know," he finally replied.

"Well, then," Patricia responded. "How about if you and I work on that a little more and try to reconcile some of those feelings?" she asked.

He nodded.

"In the meantime, I want you to work with one premise, London," she said. "Can you try and do that?"

Again he nodded. He was willing to trust in the process.

"I want you to assume that your mother and your father loved you. It may not have looked like you needed it to. It may have fallen short for you. But I want to work from the premise that they did their best. They, too, were suffering. And while they were busy coping with the tragedy and struggle in their own lives, they didn't realize that you needed support, too. But their neglect was not intentional. Are you comfortable working from there, or do we need to assume otherwise?" Patricia asked gently.

"I'm OK with that," he replied. "It's a good place to start. I am tired of letting people who are dead ruin my life...my living. I need to let go and move forward."

"I think you are deciding today that you want to live, London," Patricia reassured him. "I hear you say that you want to move beyond just breathing to really living a life. To do that, we're going to have to work through not only your feelings about dad, but also what happened to your grandparents. That's gonna be hard work, London. But I promise it will be worth it."

He shook his head in agreement.

"Then let's work on that together. Let's not let the memories of dead people make you feel dead. I want you to live...and to love. But you have to decide not to be a prisoner to the memories. Do you think you can do that?"

"I am willing to keep trying, Patricia. That's why I am here."

"OK, then," Patricia said, moving the conversation forward in a positive tone. "That's enough for today. Are you in the book for next week yet?"

"I am," he replied. "In fact, I think I'm back again on Monday."

"Well that's great," Patricia replied. "I'm glad it's soon. Enjoy your weekend. And we will pick this up again on Monday. You made a good start today."

SEVEN

Ten feet from the surface, London struggled at the bottom of a pool. Flailing arms and legs in an effort that proved fruitless, he gasped for air, the chlorinated water filling his lungs. Above, he could see the glassy skin of the water's surface, reflecting light. He felt anchored, tethered to the bottom by invisible cinder blocks linked around his ankles and pulling him into blackness. He floundered, like a fish pulled from water and cast into the open air, unable to breathe. Struggle, he thought. Push! Swim harder! Hold your breath! But to no avail. The harder he fought, the heavier the pull from below became. Finally, resolved to his fate, he closed his eyes and gave up his struggle. The water enveloped him, cool and soothing and the light above doubled in distance. His muscles relaxed and he drifted weightless to the bottom of the pool.

From the edge of unconsciousness, a voice broke through the silent lull of the water.

"Son! Son!" another man's voice beckoned. "Son, I am here."

Without understanding exactly how, he was being pulled up, breaching the surface in rebirth. Hesitant to once again try breathing, he felt the tug of a man's arms pull him completely from the water. His wet body now lay on the hard tile surface next to the pool. He opened his eyes only wide enough to vaguely make out a face above him. The room around him blurred. He still did not breathe. From his haze, he recognized the crystal blue eyes peering at him; they were the color of a warm June sky.

The man sensed the confused recognition in London's eyes.

"Yes, son, it's me," he said. "Your father."

London suddenly became very aware of his environment. He was naked and wet, his body cold and shivering. The room was silent, except for the sound of his father's voice that echoed off the tile around him. Am I dead? he thought. Is this the end?

"We don't have much time, son," his father beckoned, refocusing his son's attention back to him.

London blinked his eyes, clearing the water droplets that had gathered on his long eyelashes.

"I need you to know something, son," his father said. "You have so much to live for...so much talent, so many possibilities...don't give up on all that yet. Live your life, son. Let go of the past and just live. Live, son, live."

With a deep gasp, like a child emerging from the womb, London woke up violently from his nightmare. He was drenched in sweat, clothes wet as if he had really been in that pool. He scanned the room for his father. It had only been a dream.

He beckoned for Chloe, who was sunning herself on a window ledge. In a scamper, she hopped up next to him, purring softly. Her fur was warm from the sun and soft under his rough hands. As he stroked her back, the small cat purred in contentment. Her affection calmed his nerves. In a show of gratitude, he rose from the bed and moved to the kitchen. Chloe wrapped herself around his ankles as he poured cold milk into a bowl and placed it on the floor for her.

He paused for several moments to watch the cat, hoping that something would soon bring him the joy she found in that tiny bowl of milk.

EIGHT

The tap on his front door at 4 a.m. annoyed London, who had just gotten in from his Saturday night gig. The bar tonight was not one of his favorites. Nor was it all that crowded. It was a night of work and he was tired. He ignored it, thinking it to be a person wandering home to the wrong apartment. When the tapping turned into a full knock, he went to the door. Squinting one eye through the peep hole, he saw Alex standing on the other side. She looked a mess.

He unchained the door. Before he could extend a welcome, she was already in the apartment. He could smell that she had been drinking, maybe smoking. Her black liner was streaked down her flushed cheeks.

"Alex..." he began.

Before he could say anything else, she was already in the living room, her coat flung carelessly on the floor.

"Don't talk to me, London. I don't want to talk," she said, angrily.

He was confused. Had he done something to invoke this emotion from her?

"I'm so sick of talking, of trying to make sense of these fucked up emotions inside me," she continued. "I'm so tired of being the responsible one who has all the answers all the fucking time."

"Lex..." he tried again.

"When is enough? When do I become good enough to deserve the things I want? How much fucking more do I have to give?"

Finally, he interjected. "Stop yelling at me, Lex. Talk to me," he said. "I need to know what's going on because you're throwing a boatload of shit at me and I really don't understand what it's even about."

"Do you love me, London?" she asked.

He grew annoyed that she had to ask that question. He had never been shy about his deep affection for her.

"You know the answer to that question, Alex," he said.

"Yeah, well maybe I wanna hear you say it. Maybe I need to hear someone say it to me tonight." Her arms were flailing.

He had never seen her quite so frustrated. "What's going on Alex?" he asked. "Where were you?"

"The question isn't where I was, London," she replied. "The true question is why I am here with you – at four o'clock in the fucking morning? Why am I dressed like this and standing here with you?"

He hadn't noticed what she was wearing until then. She was in a grey and black skirt, a black sweater, and grey heels. She looked pretty.

"It's kind of important that I know where you were," he joked, "since I obviously have no idea where you're going with all this."

Alex collapsed on the couch. A silence filled the room.

"Is it just that you've had too much to drink, honey?" he asked. He already knew the answer since Alex's words were slurred and sloppy.

"Yes, London, I've had too much to drink. And while you might think I'm strong and stable, my crazy little brain is swirling."

He moved to join her on the couch. "Tell me where you were," he whispered to her, brushing the hair away from her face.

She shifted her body to face him. "It doesn't matter. What matters is that I'm here now. I need you to see me."

"I see you, Lex," he said. "I don't understand you at the moment, but I see that something is obviously wrong. What do you need me to do?"

Alex reached for his hand. She guided his arm around her shoulder and folded into him as if he were a warm blanket. "I need you to say you want me here with you. I need you to let me be here."

London remained quiet. He was still very confused.

Alex leaned up into his face.

He pulled back from her.

"Let me, London," she pleaded.

He relaxed.

She closed her eyes and kissed his cheek, moved her lips to his ear, kissed down his neck. Then she found his warm mouth and kissed his lips.

He kissed her back. "Lex," he whispered. "What's going on honey?"

"Damn it, London," she replied in a quiet frustration, "I'm just looking for some connection with another human being who knows who I am – who I really am. Someone who knows all the bullshit that makes me me and isn't scared to death. Can't you just kiss me and say how nice it is?"

"I did just kiss you," he replied. He could tell there was really no making her happy tonight.

"Wow," Alex replied, with a tone of revelation in her voice. It was as if, for the first time since she arrived at the apartment, she could see how she was acting. "I'm so sorry." She jumped up from the couch. "Jesus, London. I'm sorry. You don't deserve this shit storm." She turned her back to him, embarrassed by her own behavior. "I shouldn't be here – not tonight. I'm really, really sorry."

"You don't need to apologize, Lex," he replied. "I still have no idea what brought you here, but it's OK that you're here. It's always OK that you're here."

Alex was quiet now, calmed down from the rage she was in just twenty minutes prior.

"Why don't you just crash here tonight," he offered. He could tell by her swaying that she was still too drunk to drive safely home.

"Thanks," Alex replied in low, sad tone. "Mind if I jump in the shower? I must look a mess."

"Help yourself," he said, extending his arm toward the hall bath.

While she was in the shower, he piled a few blankets and his best pillow on the couch for her. Then, he went into his own bed to try and sleep. From the room next door, he could hear her sobbing in the shower. He still had no idea why. When she finally emerged and fell asleep on the couch, he went out to check on her. He tucked the fleece blanket around her and said a prayer that the demon filling her with such sadness and frustration would leave her. He bent and kissed her cheek.

She opened her eyes only slightly and whispered a thank you.

Not convinced that he had helped at all, he at least felt good knowing that Alex was safe.

NINE

The Sunday morning sun broke through the curtains in London's bedroom and stirred him to alertness. The clock on the table indicated that it was early afternoon. He lay quiet in his bed, listening for the stir of Alex in the other room. Minutes passed. Hearing nothing, he rose from the bed, pulled on a pair of sweatpants and ventured into the living room. The sheets he had left for Alex were neatly folded and stacked on the couch, crowned with the pillow he had left her. On top of the stack was a piece of paper, folded. His name was written on it.

He reached for the paper and unfolded a note from Alex.

> *Dear London,*
> *I'm sorry for the way I showed up here last night. I dumped a boatload of shit on you that you didn't deserve. I'm a mess...but I'll figure it out. Don't worry. Oh...and thanks for the good pillow. I slept like a rock. I love you.*
> *Alex*

Just as he finished reading, his cell rang from the other room. He darted in to catch the call, hoping it was Alex with more of an explanation. It was not a number he recognized.

"Hello," he answered, annoyed that it was not the call he anticipated.

"Is this London?" a man's voice asked on the opposite end of the call.

"Who's calling?" London asked in return, sensing an irritation in the caller's voice.

"London, knock off the shit. This is George, Alex's boyfriend. Would you put her on the god damn phone? I know she's there with you."

"Oh, George, hey man," London answered calmly and in a tone more friendly than he had received. "I'm sorry, Alex isn't here."

"Knock off the shit, London. I know she's there. She's always fucking there."

London grew annoyed. Suddenly, the drama of the night before began making sense.

"I said she isn't here, George. Did you call her phone?"

"What the hell kind of question is that, London? Of course I called here phone. And you know what happened when I did?"

London stood quiet. He wasn't in the mood to guess.

"I heard it fucking ringing from the backseat of my car. I guess she left it in my car last night when ...." The caller paused.

"So you got my number from her phone?" London asked.

"Well, it wasn't hard to find since almost every call from her phone has gone out to you in the last two days."

"She's not here, man. Sorry."

George exhaled deeply on the other end.

London was tempted to mention that she had been there, but then decided that it was up to Alex to let George know where she was. If she wanted him to find her, he would. Instead of offering any information, he instead issued what he considered a warning. "George, Alex is an amazing woman...she's resourceful and smart. I'm sure she'll figure out soon enough where she left her phone. I'm sure she'll be in touch."

"I don't need you to tell me how wonderful she is, London. I don't fucking need you to point out any of her qualities to me."

London grew angry. If George knew how amazing Alex truly was, why did he continue to treat her like a trinket? So many times, London had bitten his tongue when Alex complained about George's behavior. He had trusted that she knew what was best for her. But after last night – and now guessing that something had happened between them – London struggled to remain quiet. "Well, if you're so aware of how awesome she is, then I don't need to tell you that she deserves to be treated right, George. Stop fucking with her. When you fuck with her, you fuck with me. You got it?"

George laughed, inciting even more anger in London. "I'm scared London. Really, I am. How valiant of you. Just tell her to fucking get in touch with me."

Click.

"Fucking asshole," London said out loud. "Fucking stupid asshole."

TEN

London resisted his sudden urge to drink something alcoholic and decided on a cup of coffee. As he stretched into the refrigerator for the milk carton, a brush of soft fur caressed his ankles. Chloe, his brown speckled cat, wrapped herself over his feet.

"Good morning, Lil Momma," London said in salutation to the cat. "How's my favorite little pussy cat in the whole world today?" he asked in a tone one might use to address a baby. The cat stared up at him, leaving him half expecting she would answer.

Just as the coffee brewer spit out the last drops of water, his phone rang. He guessed it was George calling back.

"This fucking guy just doesn't quit" he said out loud to the cat, which moved out of the way. Without checking the number, he answered. "Listen bro, I can do this shit all day, but the story ain't gonna change," London barked into the receiver. "Alex isn't here!"

"Well, it wasn't really her I wanted to speak with," the caller answered. It was Nathan, who continued without pause, "I was actually hoping to speak to the guy who will be playing at a Del Record Showcase in two weeks. Know where I might find someone who wants to do that?" he asked jokingly.

Nathan Brandt had been London's agent and manager for the last three years. Short in stature, Nathan was full of character and was often perceived as abrasive by the people who worked with him. His North Jersey dialect didn't help soften his tone, but he was focused on his business and dedicated to the talent he represented. London had first met Nathan in Whiskey Walkers, on a night when he was playing an acoustic set with Jon.

After the second set, Nathan had approached London, extended his hand, and said, "Why the hell are you wasting your time?"

"Excuse me?" London said with a strong tone of defensiveness, ignoring Nathan's outstretched hand. "Who the hell are you?"

"Nathan Brandt," he said. "I own an entertainment management company. Are you represented by anyone?"

"I represent myself," London told him, full of confidence and vigor, his guard still up.

"Well, you are obviously not doing a very good job, are you?" Nathan replied, chuckling. "I mean, why the hell are you playing in a place like this with the voice you have?"

London's face softened. Suddenly, he was listening. "Go on," he said.

Nathan reached into the pocket of his sports jacket and handed London a card. On it was Nathan's name and contact information. "Give me a call on Monday," Nathan said. "Maybe we can work on getting the world to hear that voice of yours."

London pocketed the card, almost discounting it. He knew of so many musicians who were struggling just to pay rent or put food on the table. Guys he knew – with better voices than him – were intentionally dropping cans in the grocery store so that they could be sold as "damaged" at a reduced price. Why would he deserve any better than they did?

But he'd called Nathan that following Monday and three years later, Nathan was still loyal to him. He had managed to get him booked in bigger clubs and casinos than Whiskey Walkers. Although he was still working as a cover band artist playing other people's music, London at least had a steady, although meager, income. And Nathan still worked hard all the time to get him better exposure and better crowds.

London's hostility subsided. "You've got to be kidding me, Nate," he replied with enthusiasm.

"I kid you not," replied Nathan. "I played him the unplugged recordings of 'Free' and 'Alive' and he loved them. I actually even played him that slow song in G Minor with no lyrics yet and he enjoyed it as well."

London was surprised. "Nate, neither one of those songs is complete... just my voice and a guitar. They are not ready for human consumption," he protested in jest.

"Well, kid, that's the best part. When I played them for Tommy, his exact words were: 'a great song is a great song whether it's played by a full band or just a guitar and a voice...and those are great songs.'"

London hung up from the call, after agreeing to get to Nathan's office first thing the next morning.

"We have quite a bit to do in a short amount of time, but I want to strike while Tommy's iron is still hot," Nathan had told him.

Then London remembered the appointment he had the next day with his therapist. He fumbled with his phone another time, but not to cancel with Nathan. When the phone rang on the other end, he was surprised when the call was answered instead of the more usual transfer to voicemail.

"Patricia Leonard," the voice said. "Good afternoon."

"Hi, Patricia," London answered, with the tone of a teenager calling home to say he'd be late for dinner. "It's London. Why are you answering the phone on a Sunday?"

"Well, hello, London," she replied with a chuckle. "What can I do for you?" she asked, never answering his question about her work hours.

He explained to Patricia that he would be unable to make their Monday appointment, offering more information than was probably necessary given the fact that he was, after all, paying her for the time. But he felt an affection for the therapist that made him want to include her in the day's news.

Patricia reciprocated the admiration by noting her pride in London's success. But she also stayed true to her role as therapist. "Let's just be careful not to lose sight in all this craziness, London," she cautioned. "We still have a lot of work to do."

A pregnant pause was again followed by Patricia's voice. "Unfortunately, I am booked the rest of this week. But there's some homework I would like you to do for the next time I see you."

"Homework?" he questioned, feeling even more like that teenager.

"Yes," she answered. "I want you to start carrying a notebook with you, London," she told him. "Whenever you start to feel overwhelmed by feelings or anxiety, I want you write down in that notebook exactly what's on your mind. It can be a full blown novel or chicken scratch...I just want it to reflect in real time what's on your mind." With her directions complete, Patricia wished London good luck in his meeting and hung up.

He immediately pulled an empty journal from his desk drawer and put it in plain sight on the desk.

"Now is not the time to lose focus," he said out loud.

ELEVEN

You would think that the rocking of this boat would soothe me. But it doesn't. I feel anxious, nervous, agitated.

London reread the words he'd just written and then scratched them out. He repositioned his pen again on the paper and tried again.

I feel like a man on an island. I feel cut off from the world.

Again, he paused and read the words scribbled on his paper. His reflection was interrupted by a man's voice over a speaker.

"Attention passengers, please use caution while moving around the ferry. Deep swells today are causing a bit of rocking. Please take advantage of the handrails should you need to move around on deck."

The slow rise and fall of the ferry on the water could not be ignored. An uncomfortable quivering in his belly made him queasy. He rose from his seat at the front of the ferry and repositioned to a mid-ship position where the rocking was a little more neutralized. He continued to write.

I have to wonder how I got here. How did I lose track of my life...How did I get this old so fast? Why don't I have more figured out by now?

He lifted his eyes and gazed out on the ocean. Melancholy began to grow in his chest.

I'm struggling to be happy. Even with the promise of something positive on the horizon, I can't help but wonder what will go wrong. All around me are families...young girls being watched by protective fathers...those dads working to preserve innocence as long as possible. The simplicity of youth is mesmerizing to me. Maybe because I didn't know it long enough.

Again, he paused to reread the words he wrote.

Maybe I have it all wrong. Sometimes, when I watch the world around me, I see a herd of people conforming to what society tells them is right. The whole white picket fence, job in an office, 2.5 kids at home notion of security. I never thought that was for me. But maybe I'm wrong. They look happy. They seem content with their 'normal' life. Why can't I want that? Why can't I just be like everybody else? Why do I have to pursue something that brings me so much struggle? Do I have a choice? Have I ever had a choice about what happens to me?

Again, the voice over the speaker interrupted London's thoughts. "As we dock in Cape May, please be sure all of your belongings are secured for your departure. Those who have a vehicle on board are asked to please make their way to that vehicle. On behalf of the Cape May-Lewes Ferry, thank you for traveling with us today."

He pulled off the ferry and made his way to the Garden State Parkway. At Exit 13, he exited toward a private yacht club perched on the inlet. His gig was scheduled at 4 p.m. And he was surprisingly on time. As he pulled into the parking lot, the sound of Biggie Small's "Big Poppa" blared from the speakers of a party boat. Two 40-year-old men dressed in white pants and captain's hats walked past his car. Two girls, half the men's age, followed shortly behind. When a "Gin and Juice" remix started to play, the two girls ran ahead to catch up with the men. He watched the women grind up against their dates. One of the men scooped up his leggy blonde and carried her toward the yacht. The other couple veered off in the opposite direction.

He pulled the keys from his ignition and stood in the parking lot laughing to himself. A woman's voice caught him off guard.

"Something funny?" she asked.

He turned to face a woman dressed in plain black clothes. She wore little makeup and her hair was pulled into a tight bun at the back of her head. He guessed she was a member of the catering team.

"Too funny," he replied.

"What?" the woman asked. "The rich assholes bumping and grinding to rap music, or their indescribable fashion sense?"

He laughed again. "Well," he said, "Now that you mention it, I guess both!"

"I'm sure Snoop had these exact people in mind when he wrote this song," the woman said to London. "I mean, I'm sure they can totally relate to those lyrics, don't you?"

"Well, I'm sure they are drinking gin," he joked. "And I'm pretty sure at least some of them have money on their mind."

The woman laughed out loud. "Good point," she said offering kudos to London's quick thinking. "Hey, have a good night. Thanks for the laugh."

He finished gathering his gear from the trunk and moved toward the dock. His short conversation with the caterer left a lingering impression on him. He began to think about his own music and wondered how people would relate to him. He ached for opportunities to sing his own songs, to create connections with people based on his music. He was tired of the cover band scene. Then, remembering the upcoming showcase with the record executives, he thought of one word: faith. To have faith meant that he would have to trust, that he'd have to have confidence in himself and in forces outside of himself. Nothing terrified him more.

TWELVE

Two police cruisers sped past London's haggard Oldsmobile, shaking the glass windows. He was relieved when they continued past Whiskey Walkers and turned left down Raymond Boulevard. The drama of a police bust in the bar parking lot was not something he needed tonight. Even though it was still an hour and a half before his scheduled set, London hoped for an easy set-up and a very cordial meet and greet with the record executive from Del Records.

Jon, as usual, was already at Whiskey Walkers and was setting up for the evening's showcase performance. Tony was positioned behind the sticky pine bar.

"Hey there, Rock Star," Tony called as London entered. A couple of patrons turned to look at London, curious about whether he was already famous.

"Hey, Tony," London replied with the eagerness of a child's first trip to the dentist. He raised his hand in an unenthusiastic wave and continued toward Jon.

"So buddy, you ready for this?" Jon asked, extending his arms open in an embrace.

"I think we're both ready for this, my friend," London replied, smiling.

Just over an hour later, Nathan arrived at Whiskey Walkers. He was accompanied by a man who resembled Harrison Ford, although slightly shorter and younger. While London was surprised by the man's unassuming demeanor, he had learned a long time ago never to judge a book by its cover. In the music business, that man held power that London could only dream of having.

London rose and walked toward Nathan. Jon walked slightly behind London.

"London Drake, I would like you to meet Tommy Jenkins from Del Records."

London shifted his body to face the record exec head on. He extended his hand and shook with confidence.

"Thank you for coming out tonight, Mr. Jenkins. It is a pleasure to meet you," London told him.

"Please," the man responded with a smile, "Call me Tommy."

"Well, OK, Tommy," London replied. "This is Jon Keebler. Jon co-wrote some of the songs we are going to play for you tonight. He's a hell of a guitar player, too."

Again, the record exec extended his hand. This time, Jon returned the greeting.

"So let's sit and talk a little," Nathan suggested, pointing to an open table to his right.

"I'm gonna finish setting up a few things," Jon said, excusing himself from the conversation.

A waitress immediately appeared at the table to take drink orders. After a few minutes, London leaned forward in his chair to address the man seated across the table from him.

"So, Tommy, what are you interested in hearing tonight?" London asked.

"Based on the demo Nathan shared, I'm really interested in 'Free'," Tommy told London. "I am also curious about one other track..." Tommy continued, looking at Nathan for help with the title.

"Tommy liked 'Alive' as well, London," Nathan interjected.

Tommy shook his head in agreement, now sipping his vodka tonic. "And I thought maybe he'd be interested in the last song...the one with no name at the end of the disc. How's that one coming along?"

Nathan knew how it was coming; he knew it wasn't yet finished.

"To be honest, guys, that last song is a work in progress," London replied. "I need to really feel a lyric for it and it's just not there yet."

Nathan shifted nervously in his seat.

London felt slightly annoyed that Nathan would suggest a song he knew wasn't ready.

"A man of musical integrity," Tommy said, swallowing his vodka. "I like that."

London exhaled.

"How about you just go up there and be you?" Tommy suggested.

'That's a deal," London replied. He stood and extended his hand again to both men before joining Jon on the stage.

Once seated behind his guitar, London finally noticed the crowd that had apparently wandered in during his conversation with Tommy and Nathan.

For the two weeks leading up to the showcase, Alex and her girlfriends had posted news of the showcase all over Facebook. She tweeted constantly about it. London judged that her efforts were a success.

At promptly 9:30, London struck the first chords on his Ovation acoustic guitar. His fingers moved over the strings as if he were touching a lover he would never forget. "My Realty" earned favorable response from the crowd and London expressed gratitude for their applause. As he moved into his second song – "Free" – London noticed Tommy stand and move away from the table where he was still seated with Nathan. Tommy held a cell phone up to his ear and eventually exited the bar, still talking to the caller on the other end. London shared a series of glances with Nathan, an expression of worry in his eyes. Tommy had specifically asked to hear "Free," and yet was absent from the bar for three-quarters of that song and most of the remaining set. Tommy finally reappeared as London began his last song of the 25-minute set.

London played the last chords of "Found" and thanked the audience for their support. Lifting the acoustic guitar up and over his head, he placed it in the guitar stand to the right of his stool and approached the table where Tommy was again seated with Nathan. He struggled to hide his disappointment at Tommy's prolonged absence.

Almost immediately, Tommy spoke. "I'm sorry I had to step outside, London. I was thinking about something while you were in the middle of 'Free' and didn't want to lose the idea. I had to make a call to see if I could get something rolling with that song. I hope you didn't misunderstand my actions as rude."

"Idea?" London asked, now eager to hear more.

"Yeah. I was listening to you sing that opening song and all of a sudden, I had some ideas," Tommy continued. "I wanted to talk to Tyler about it."

London sat waiting for more details. "Tyler?" he asked.

"Tyler Schramm," Tommy replied. "He's a producer. Maybe you know his work?"

"Know his work?" London asked sarcastically. "Hell, yeah. He produced some of my favorite records from the last decade."

"Well then, I think you'll like my idea," Tommy replied. "I've asked Tyler to come in and listen to the songs you have down on tape already."

London tried to restrain his overwhelming enthusiasm, but was thrilled beyond even his own expectations. "That would be amazing, Tommy. Really amazing!" he said, turning with a wide grin to look at Nathan.

"So, we'll be in touch then," Nathan interjected, bringing a sense of business back to the table. "Thanks so much for meeting with us tonight. We'll look forward to working with you."

Tommy stood up from the table. His rise was met by both London and Nathan, who once again shook his hand and thanked him for his time. "I'll be in touch once Tyler has had a chance to listen to the demos," Tommy told London. "Pleasure to meet you."

"Let me walk you out," Nathan offered to Tommy. "London you better get back up there and finish the night," he said, winking at London.

In the few minutes before the next set, London filled Jon in on the conversation with Tommy. Halfway through the set, the packed club began to thin out as people remembered that it was a Wednesday night and they'd need to get up for work the next day. By the time London and Jon finished at 1 a.m., only a few people remained at the bar.

"Alright, gentlemen," Tony exclaimed. "Shots on the house for my boys! What'll it be?"

Jon waved his hand in protest, saying that he had already had enough.

London moved over to the bar and took a seat. "Tequila," he told Tony.

As Tony poured the cold Patron into London's shot glass, Jon tapped London on the shoulder to say good night.

London turned and hugged his friend. "Be careful, man," he told Jon. "Great job. Thanks for tonight."

London turned back to the bar and swallowed the cold shot. "I'm outta here, too," he told Tony and turned his back to walk away from the bar.

"Night, man," Tony said. "See you next week."

London paused, and turned again to face Tony. "Yeah...about that Tony," London told him. "Tonight is going to be our last Wednesday."

"What do you mean, London?" Tony asked, surprised. "Tonight was packed! Things are changing for the better...you and Jon are welcome here as long as you like."

Trying to quiet the irritation that filled him, London spoke calmly in reply. "Jon and I spoke about what is best for us and our careers, and you're right...things are changing."

Tony tried to speak, but London cut off his words.

"It's nothing personal against you Tony," he said, again turning his back to leave. "It's business, man."

THIRTEEN

When the phone rang on Friday morning, London had only been sleeping for a couple of hours. The first few rings went unnoticed. When the call went to voicemail, the caller hung up and rang again. This time, he heard the chime and stirred only slightly under the covers that enveloped him. Again, the caller rang back. Now annoyed, he reached across the bed to the phone on the night stand. His hand reached beneath a Rolling Stone magazine that had helped ease his mind into sleep. He had been reading an article about a celebrity who was a more apparent mess than London even believed himself to be. Somehow, the fact that the celebrity had overcome both drug and sex addictions to reach stardom made him believe that there was hope for himself. And, the fact that the guy was still pretty much a mess – getting thrown out of sporting events and making inappropriate remarks to waitresses – made London feel like his own imperfections would not prevent him from having the things in life he really wanted.

When he was finally able to feel the phone in his hand, he raised it to his ear and mumbled an abbreviated hello.

"London." It was Nathan's voice. "London, Jesus Christ. Wake the hell up."

"What the fuck time is it, Nathan?"

"I don't know what time it is...early. But you gotta get your shit together. I just heard from the record company, London. They want to sign you."

Could the dream the two of them shared finally be coming true? Would his voice finally be heard by the world?

London's eyes opened wide. He lay silent in his bed, waiting for the punch line to reveal a joke.

Nothing.

He pulled the phone back from his ear, double checking the caller ID. He was not sleeping. This was not a dream.

"London. London. Are you there?"

"Yes, Nathan, I'm here. Let me call you back in two minutes."

"Get it together, man," Nathan warned. "This is no joke, London. You gotta get into the office. This is your shot."

When Nathan hung up, London lay still in his bed, staring at the white popcorn ceiling. So many times he had lain in this same bed at night, staring straight up, wishing on the popcorn as if each fleck of texture was a star in the sky. Now, with the call from Nathan, it was as if the ceiling had opened, revealing a sky full of wishes about to come true. Inside, he felt anxious. He jumped out of bed, ran to the bathroom, and threw up.

Part Two

FOUND

FOURTEEN

London stood in front of an open closet door, wondering what attire most clearly said, "Hello, dreams. It's about time you're coming true." He pulled his best and only black suit from the assortment of linens hanging before him. With more consideration, he decided the suit jacket was too formal and opted only for a perfectly pressed, white button-down shirt. Wrapped around his body, the crisp white cotton looked smart and pulled together. Paired with the black pants and newly shined shoes, London was dressed to impress.

He spritzed his neck with his favorite Issey Miyake scent and made his way toward the door. He crouched for just a minute to say good night to the cat and grabbed the keys to his 79 Oldsmobile from a cracked dish on the hall table. Seated behind the steering wheel, London thought of his father. The car had been his dad's; it was the only inheritance London received. Complete with an eight-track player and whitewall tires, the car did not imply finesse, but it ran with a strong engine. It was reliable. In his mind, you couldn't ask for much more than that.

Thoughts of his father and the car quickly shifted to memories of his grandmother. He closed his eyes and could picture her, dressed in a housecoat and seated in a lawn chair in the family's garage. The joy on her face was as real in the memory as it had been in real time. She would come out to the garage when London's band practiced. The group was called "Silent Fury," although there was not much silent about them. They were a group of young musicians, striving to make it and making a lot of noise in the meantime. Despite their novice approach and missed chords, his grandmother would remain, listening. Sometimes, she would get up and dance, right there in the garage, the motion of her wide hips oblivious to the mistakes in the music. At the end of every song, she would clap, looking at London with pride in her eyes. His own eyes teared up at the memory. He missed her.

The chime of his cell phone brought him back to the present. Nate barked from the other end of the receiver. "Where the hell are you, man? Our meeting is in 20 minutes."

"I'm on my way, Nate," he replied. "Can you take a deep breath or something? You're making me nervous as hell. I'll be there with 10 minutes to spare."

Half an hour later, he shifted back and forth in his seat in Nathan's office as Tommy Jenkins explained the breakdown of numbers for a typical Del Records label deal. Tommy was negotiating a $125,000 advance with Nathan and a two album deal. The tentative agreement was sweetened with a $10,000 signing bonus that would be used to pay for the recording. The record label would do the typical promotion for his release.

In the end, the deal meant that London needed to sell more than 200,000 records and have a successful promotional tour before he would see one cent from royalties. The label would recoup all their expenses and the producers would be paid before London saw a dime of profit. But for him, this wasn't about money. He'd finally get to make a record to be heard by the world. To him, that was a priceless opportunity.

"Are you OK with all of this?" Nathan asked London, when Tommy excused himself to use the bathroom.

"OK?" he asked in return, overwhelmed by the experience. "We're talking about $125,000, man. Thirty minutes ago, I was digging in the ashtray of my car to find four quarters for the meter."

FIFTEEN

London was slightly drunk when he returned home. He and Nathan had enjoyed a celebratory drink after their meeting and now Nathan accompanied him up to the apartment. The jingling of his keys in the lock was returned with the quiet meow of Chloe from the other side. When he pushed open the door, the cat scampered across the linoleum entryway and into the kitchen.

"She's no dummy," he remarked to Nathan, raising the brown paper bag he held in his left hand. "Here you go, lil girl!" he called out to the cat. He reached into the bag to retrieve a can of tuna. "As promised!" he told her, crouching down to place a bowl on the floor.

Nathan remained in the living room, peering out the small window. "So London, don't ya think it's time to consider a move across the bridge?" he finally asked. "I mean...not for nothing, but the next three months of your life are going to be spent in the studio." He paused. "Don't ya think it'd make more sense to just live in the city?"

London joined Nathan at the window. His view of the go-go bar on South Broad left a lot to be desired.

"You want me to leave all this?" London joked in reply. He turned to the cat, still busy at her bowl. "Chloe!" he demanded. "Are you ready to tackle the big bad city?"

"There's no turning back now, kiddo," Nathan said, placing his hand on London's shoulder. "No turning back!"

"I know," replied London, with childlike enthusiasm. "Isn't it fucking amazing?"

Nathan took a seat on the couch as London disappeared down the hall toward the bathroom.

"So, Tyler Schramm will be naming the players for the record soon," Nathan hollered to London. "They are sure to be some great NYC session players."

London returned to the living room, wiping wet hands on a towel. "What?" he questioned. "Wait..."

"Sorry, man," Nathan said. "I thought you could hear me from in there."

"I heard you, Nate," London replied in a more somber tone. "But I don't like it. You mean session players for everything except guitar, right? What about Jon?"

Nathan's eyes diverted to the floor and then back to London. "I'm sorry, London...their money, their rules," he said.

"Nate, that's bullshit and you know it," London said, more forcefully. "Jon and I have been together on this from the start. I can't do this without him. It wouldn't be the same."

"I know, kiddo, but we're playing by their rules," Nathan said, figuratively throwing his hands in the air. "When this record takes off, there will be more leeway to negotiate with Tommy. We know the record is gonna be a success. We just gotta show them. Then, we'll get Jon out on the road with you."

London sat on an ottoman positioned in the center of the room. Chloe jumped onto his lap, still licking tuna from her delicate whiskers. The cat purred and rubbed her head against his chest, almost as if she were trying to soothe him. As he stroked her smooth orange fur, his heart slowed again to even measured beats.

"Would you like me to talk to Jon?" Nathan asked.

"No, Nate," he replied. "It has to be me."

"If he's your friend, he will understand, London. I mean, this is a big deal shot at what you've always wanted."

"Of course, he will understand," London said, interrupting Nathan. "That will make this even harder."

The next evening, London met Jon at The Belmont Tavern, one of the friends' favorite Italian restaurants in Newark. The sweet scent of garlic, olive oil, and basil pumped out of the brick oven chimney, perfuming the surrounding neighborhood. The smell inside was even better. When he entered, he found Jon sitting in the corner of the bar, squeezing lemon into a glass of ice water.

"Hey buddy, thanks for coming," Jon exclaimed, standing up from his bar stool.

"Of course I came," London joked. "Wasn't I the one who invited you?"

"Uh, yeah. I guess you did," Jon laughed. "Hey, where's Alex? I thought she was coming and she usually beats you."

"Alex isn't coming until eight," London replied. "I wanted to speak to you alone for a little while before she joined us."

"OK," Jon replied, confused. "What's up?"

While London had clued his friends into the meeting with the record company, they still knew none of the details. Both Jon and Alex assumed that the dinner was to celebrate what had resulted in a successful deal for London.

London and Jon sat back at the bar and London told Jon about the record executive and about the deal he was offered. He spoke with enthusiasm, but he tried hard not to seem too excited. He didn't want to build up any of Jon's hopes. Then, London moved into the hard part of the conversation; the part he had rehearsed over and over again in his own mind. It was an obvious struggle for him.

"So, I have to talk to you specifically about the album and the tour," London said hesitantly. "I need to tell you something..." London's voice trailed off.

"I hope you're not expecting me to go with you," Jon interceded.

London lifted his eyes from the table to stare at Jon.

"It's OK, man," Jon continued. "I called Nathan this morning. Honestly, I had a feeling it would be like this after that guy from the record company was only interested in talking with you at Whiskey the other night. I wouldn't want you to lose a deal because of me."

London's head began to throb. He rubbed his own temples with pointed fingers. He lowered his chin, shaking his head with eyes closed.

"It's OK, brother," Jon finished. "Don't sweat it. I know in my heart that if you make it, I will make it, too. I know this isn't your doing. And as soon as Nathan can get me out there, I know he will. Really, London. It's OK. I'm happy for you."

With tears now pooled in his eyes, London stood from his stool and pulled Jon up next to him. Just as the friends embraced, they heard Alex's voice behind them.

"What have I always said about starting the party without me?" she joked. "There should never be hugging without me. Come on, now." Her smile was a welcome interruption. "Always room for you, Lex," Jon replied, as London wiped tears from his cheeks and opened the hug to welcome her into the circle.

SIXTEEN

Five months later, London was in the middle of the small scale publicity tour planned by his record company. It consisted of concerts in small venues and some record signing events in local music stores. He had already performed a dozen times in cities like Farmington, Maine; Ithaca, New York; and South Bend, Indiana. He had signed autographs in Hard Rock Cafes and a slew of FYE record stores.

Out on the road, the reception to the album was good. But with that good reception also came some outside pressure to keep the momentum going. There was already talk of a sophomore album and Nathan was working harder than ever on publicity. It was all a little overwhelming for London, who hadn't even wrapped his own head around the public's acceptance of his work.

While he was adjusting to his new small scale fame, he was also dealing quietly with more frequent nightmares. His sleeping had grown more sporadic than ever. When he did sleep, he was often startled awake by a darkness he struggled to understand. Like scenes from a movie, memories of his childhood would play in his sleeping brain. He struggled to understand why the nightmares came so frequently now. In his awake life, his best dreams seemed to be coming true.

The publicity tour landed him in a hotel just outside the Pocono Mountains in late October. Drawing back the curtains in his room, he admired the scenic view of the autumn trees. His schedule had been tight – every moment booked in the past few days –and he was enjoying the stillness of five minutes alone. He gazed out the window, daydreaming. He wished his family could be there with him. Despite the amenities of fine hotels and chauffeured cars, he missed the dynamic that was his family: Dad always telling dirty jokes, Mom smacking him in the arm, his grandmother cooking up her many delights, and his grandfather watching M.A.S.H. on the tube. It wasn't a perfect family, but it was his family. Now, in strange cities with strange people, he often craved the comforts of home; comforts he had not really thought about in years.

A light tap on the door pulled him from his daydream. He ignored it and went back to his window view. Another tap. Another.

Annoyed, he made his way to the door and peeked one eye through the peephole. A maid stood waiting next to her cart. He opened the door.

"Excuse me sir," the maid said. "Is there anything you need...towels, shampoo?"

"Uh, no. No thank you," he replied to the young woman. "I just checked in, but everything seems to be fine."

"Are you sure, Mr. Drake?" the woman asked, lingering by the door.

He nodded and motioned to close the door.

"You are London Drake, right?" the woman asked, already knowing the answer. "I am a huge fan!" she exclaimed.

"You are?" he asked, as he reopened the door. He was no longer annoyed at the interruption.

"Yeah, man," the woman replied. Her speech grew faster and excited in tone. "My name is Sophie. I could so totally get fired for this. But I saw you come in earlier today and I just had to take a chance at meeting you."

"You're a fan?" he asked. "You have tickets for the show tonight?"

Sophie frowned.

"You're not coming?" he asked.

"I have to work here," she said. "Tried to get the night off, but couldn't swing it. You know how it is...real life sucks sometimes."

"Well, I'm disappointed, Sophie," he said. "I will miss you at the show."

"Oh man," she replied. "You don't know how bummed I am. But this... this rocks. I can't believe you didn't slam the door in my face!"

"Why would I do that?" he asked.

"Cause you're a rock star and I'm just a maid?" she replied.

"Let me tell you something, Sophie. Knocking on the door the way you did takes balls. I admire that."

"Really?" she asked.

"Really," he replied. "Why don't you come in for a minute? I want to give you something." He turned and made his way toward his briefcase.

Sophie entered his room and stood hesitantly just inside the door.

Retrieving a CD from the front pocket of a briefcase, he turned back toward her. He pulled a pen from the desk drawer and scribbled on the CD cover:

To Sophie...no guts, no glory. London Drake

"Oh my God," she exclaimed. "This is so amazing! Thank you so much."

"It's a CD of live recordings," he told her. "We've been putting it together as part of the tour. You get an advanced copy."

"I can't believe how nice you are!"

"Yeah, yeah. Don't spread that around," he told her. "And don't go posting this shit on the internet anywhere. The copy is for you."

Sophie launched forward and wrapped her arms around his neck.

He stood motionless while she hopped up and down, arms still around him. Then he kissed her gently on the cheek. "It was nice to meet you, Sophie," he said, motioning her toward the door.

"You too, Mr. Drake. Knock 'em dead tonight!"

A short time later, he glanced at the clock on the bedside table and noted the time: 7 p.m. From his window, he could barely see the Susquehanna River, now blanketed in twilight and dusted over with fog. He decided that a quick shower would help to move him out of his deeply reflective mood and into what he called "stage mode." That persona would serve him well in front of the large crowd. It would make him seem stronger than he was, more confident. It was the persona his fans paid to see, the one they believed in. It was the person he had been working to become his entire life.

When he arrived at the arena, he was greeted by a short, fat man who smelled of tobacco and mint gum.

The man extended his hand to greet London. "Hey man, you ready to get started?" he asked, his hand still extended.

London stared hesitantly at the man's chubby fingers, nails dirty with what looked like grease. On stage, a drummer was already beating a bass drum, vibrating noise through the room.

"Sounds like we're ready," replied London, avoiding the handshake. Instead he patted the man on his right shoulder and moved to the microphone already waiting for him. He smiled casually at a guitar player who was seated on top of a speaker, tuning his instrument. The musician nodded his head back to London, as if to say, "What's up?"

The sight of the strange guitar player thrust London back into a more melancholy mood. The unfamiliar face reminded him of the relationships he was missing on the road. He had asked Nathan at least three times now to bring Jon on the road with him. *These strange cities would somehow be friendlier if just one familiar face were here*, he thought.

Despite his sour mood, he was committed to delivering no less than perfect for his fans. He used the sound check to work out the bugs and build whatever chemistry was possible with the people on the stage with him. When the band wrapped up, he felt confident that the show would go well. Still, he used the time between sound checks and the concert to call Nathan.

"London, how's it going man?" Nathan asked, in answer to his ringing cell phone.

"It's going great, Nate. Nice venue. Great hotel. They tell me the show is sold pretty good for tonight."

"That's right, London," Nathan replied. "I talked to the events manager this afternoon. They're happy with sales."

'Glad to hear it, man," said London. He paused. "So Nate, since I seem to making people happy these days, I'm hoping you can do something for me...to make me happy."

"Jesus, London, when am I not working to make you happy?" Nathan joked. Sensing that a serious request was about to follow, Nathan pulled the chair from his desk and took a seat. "What's up?" he asked.

"It's not a new request, Nate. I'm just repeating it because it's important to me. I want you to get Jon on this tour with me..."

Nathan interrupted. "London, we've had this talk before. You're asking me to do something I'm not sure I can do."

"That's bullshit, Nate. I've seen you move fuckin' mountains. You can make this happen."

"London, this tour has a budget. It's cheaper to get local musicians to play with you."

Nathan let out a deep sigh.

London couldn't tell if it was a sigh of frustration or resignation, but he didn't hesitate to continue making his point. "This tour is great, Nathan. Don't misunderstand. I am grateful that it's happening. But there's something missing. That something is Jon. I'm starting to feel like an island out here in the middle of nowhere. I need just one rock to cling on to... something familiar. I won't ask for anything else."

Finally, Nathan replied in a way that consoled London. "London, I will call the execs over at the record company tomorrow afternoon," he said. "I can't promise you anything but I will do my best to get Jon out there with you. Maybe there's some wiggle room in the budget."

"Thanks, Nate," he said with appreciation.

"Now, don't you have a show to do?" Nathan asked diverting the somber tone of the conversation to a question filled with enthusiasm.

"That I do," he replied. "And it's gonna be good!"

"Of course it is," Nathan replied. "It's a London Drake show. They are always good."

The two shared a laugh.

"Listen, London," Nate said, in closing. "You're headed back this way next week. I think I'm gonna take some time to check out a few shows. You know...see what my money is paying for and all that."

"Sounds good, man," London replied. "Bring a nice bottle with you and we'll share it!"

When the call ended, London noticed that everyone but a couple of stage crew were gone. He wasn't surprised. The other musicians didn't know him. They held no real allegiance. If the next record stunk, they wouldn't need to stick around.

But he resigned himself to the fact that his career was filled with people who were there simply to be part of the show. He took it as an occupational hazard that he never really knew if people were there with him because they were really interested or because he represented a paycheck for them, a path to stardom. It was his own insecurity about people's motivations that left him with few intimate relationships. It was why having Jon on the road with him was so important.

As he packed a few things into his bag, he noticed a delivery guy carrying in a case of beer. He guessed that it was part of his own performance waiver; one that was simple compared to other he had heard about. All he requested was a case of light beer, a case of bottled water, a bottle of vodka, and a handful of lemons. The most important request, though, was that he liked to be introduced to the stage with a playing of "Somewhere Over the Rainbow." It wasn't the old Judy Garland version, but the more contemporary version, made famous by Hawaiian musician Israel Kamakawiwo'ole in the early 90s. London picked it for many reasons, but mostly because the song was considered by millions of people to be a pillar of hope.

The lyrics: *"Why, oh why, can't I?"* inspired people to dream, to want for more. London thrived on hope. He had spent his whole life clinging to it.

Two hours later, he was standing behind a black curtain, his nervous heart beating rapidly in his chest. He wore jeans and a dark t-shirt. Around his neck was a strand of red rosary beads. His mother had given them to him years ago. They had been his father's.

The arena was filled with people. From the rumble, he could hear a distinct scream or two. One girl shouted for him by name. "London Drake, I love you!" she yelled.

He smiled. He just never got used to the crowd's enthusiasm. Sometimes, he wished he could be out on the floor with them, screaming for his favorite band to play. The rush of that anticipation was something he would never grow tired of.

Then the sound of a ukulele began and the crowd screamed louder. A video of storm clouds clearing behind the stage played and then a rainbow appeared. The image faded to black and in white letters, the crowd could see four white letters appear, one at a time: H-O-P-E. They screamed louder now as the band took its place on the stage.

When the first bars of London's upcoming hit *Free* played, he kissed the cross that hung around his neck and moved to the front of the stage. "Hey, Pennsylvania!" he screamed into the microphone. Citing a song from his album, he asked, "Are you ready to feel ALIVE?"

SEVENTEEN

After almost two hours, London stood backstage in the dark. The cheer of the Pocono Mountain crowd called after him, beckoning for an encore. It was a sound that never tired him. The clapping and cheering resonated in his chest. It was as if he had taken a shot of whiskey on a cold day; the warmth of the crowd bubbled inside of him. When he finally answered their call and stepped back onto the stage, the crowd cheered louder as the first chords of his latest single filled the arena. The song "Found" had just started to chart in the top ten and was receiving regular radio play. It had become the regular encore song on the tour.

When the song finished, he lowered his guitar and took a final bow. He took once last glance across the faces of his fans and then disappeared again into a black background.

It was a ten-minute ride from the convention center back to his hotel. He slid the plastic key card into the door slot of room 618 and felt the rush of air condition greet him. He sat on the edge of the bed and called Nathan.

"Hey, kid, how was the show?" Nathan asked.

"Energy was amazing tonight, man," London replied. "I love this part of Pennsylvania."

His sentiment was sincere. His fans in the Lycoming Valley were always kinder than in other places and their support of him and his music had continued to grow. The affection was mutual.

After a few minutes, he finished his check-in with Nathan and decided he was thirsty. But rather than drink from the mini bar, he decided to shower and venture downstairs to the lobby bar in the hotel. He had noticed when he returned from the convention center that there was a decent crowd. Despite his fatigue, he was craving some company.

After a quick shower, he splashed cologne on his clean skin. Dressed in jeans and a white v-neck, he decided to forego underwear as a physical expression of the mischief he felt brewing inside of him. As he walked toward the elevator, he paused outside of a room just down the hall from his. The thumping of a headboard was echoed by the moans of a woman. His voyeuristic nature made him pause and listen a moment longer, but he quickly decided that neither participant really sounded all that interesting.

Once downstairs, he casually made his way into the bar. Scanning for an open seat in a place that would afford him a conversation with someone, he noticed an open chair at the bar. Seated next to the opening was a brunette whose sweater really could have been worn a size larger. She sat by herself, cleavage spilling out of the sweater.

Like taking candy from a baby, he thought to himself, as he moved toward the open seat. His cockiness was soon checked by a man who beat him to the available spot. The man kissed the woman on her neck and whispered something in her ear. When she raised her hand to cover a giggle, London noticed her wedding ring. He continued to watch the couple, who paid their tab and exited the bar together. He admired the passion that they displayed. It gave him hope that someday he, too, would find contentment in one woman.

One hour and two dirty gin martinis later, he noticed an attractive 20-something sitting across the bar alone. She was obviously staring at him, but was working hard to look inconspicuous. Medium chestnut hair framed her face that was characterized by striking, dark eyes.

London rose from his stool and approached her. "Hello," he said. "My name is London. Mind if I have a seat?"

"I thought it was you," she said with a coy smile. "London Drake, right?"

"Oh," he answered, a little flattered. "Were you at the concert tonight?"

"Yeah, I was," she answered. "I went with my cousin who is a fan of yours," she said, with more enthusiasm.

"Your cousin is a fan?" he asked, with expressed disappointment.

"I'm sorry! That didn't come out right," the woman replied instantly. "What I meant was that I didn't really know your music until tonight. I enjoyed it a lot." She began to fumble with her words and then stopped to take a deep breath. "Can we just start over and try this again?" she asked nervously.

He smiled.

"Hi, London," the woman said, with almost too much enthusiasm and an outstretched hand. "It is so nice to meet you. My name is Debbie and I'm a huge fan of yours."

With the tension broken, he and his new fan laughed out loud at the previous awkwardness.

London signaled the bartender, who placed another Malibu Bay Breeze in front of Debbie. London moved onto his third martini.

"So where is this cousin of yours and why are you here all alone?" he asked, hoping she was, in fact, without a man for the evening.

"My cousin is upstairs, passed out in our room," Debbie replied, "but she would just die if she knew I was down here with you." She wrapped her lips around the straw that poked out of her drink.

"Would you like to call her and invite her down?" he asked, hoping she would decline.

"Mmmm. I don't think so," the girl replied flirtatiously. "I think I want you all to myself," she said, giggling.

"Last call," said the bartender, who now stood behind the bar in front of the two.

"Would you like another drink?" London asked.

"Yeah, let's have one more and then go somewhere quiet," Debbie responded coyly.

Fifteen minutes later, Debbie slurped up the last of her drink and London decided to make his move. He moved closer to her and lustfully met his mouth with hers. "So, on my way down here, I heard the couple two doors down from me attempting to fuck," he told Debbie, her doe-eyes now wide and interested. "How about you and I go up to my room and teach them the right way to wake up the neighbors?"

When London woke the next morning, Debbie was already awake and was laying on her side, propped up on an elbow and staring at him. She didn't hesitate to talk at the moment his eyes opened.

"You were really great last night," she said, a little louder than he would have preferred after a night of martinis. "I am definitely a fan now!" she told him as she rose from the bed to slip into a pair of white mesh panties.

He watched her perky breasts bounce up and down when she moved. He wondered if she would join him back on the bed for another round. Before he could make the suggestion, she was in her clothes.

"I really have to get going," Debbie told him. "It's almost checkout time and I'm sure my cousin is wondering where the hell I am." She pressed her lips to his and kissed him softly. Then she handed him a business card. He squinted at the tiny print, trying to focus his tired eyes: DEBBIE KOUYOUMJIAN, *Fashion Consultant.*

"In case you want to give me a call the next time you're in town."

He lay speechless. It was usually he who was leaving so abruptly.

Debbie flipped open the dead bolt on the hotel door and paused. She turned back toward London as if maybe she had changed her mind about leaving. "Oh...can I get that autograph for my cousin?" she asked.

EIGHTEEN

London watched the signs on I-95 as the tour bus made its way south into Delaware. His stomach fluttered, not because he was particularly excited to be playing at The University of Delaware, but because he was expecting to see Alex. After a three month separation, the two of them were scheduled for dinner after that evening's concert. Now, he felt the kind of giddiness Alex always seemed to prompt in him.

Two hours and lots of adjustments later, the concert's sound check was complete.

"You headed back to the hotel now?" one of the stage musicians asked him.

"Not quite yet, man," he replied. "I gotta make a stop. But I'll see you in a bit so we can rock the shit outta this place."

"OK. Cool," the musician replied.

Twenty minutes later, London wandered somewhat aimlessly around the local mall. There was always the chance that someone in the mall might recognize him, causing a little commotion and delaying what he intended to be a quick trip, but he wanted to pick up a gift for Alex. The problem was that he had no idea what to get her. He wondered how to say, "I miss you all the time, I wish we talked more, and I'm trying to be supportive of you even from far away" all in one tiny gift. He decided to start in the card store.

Making his way to the friendship cards, he laughed out loud at some of the "Hallmark moments." He was sure that Alex would also laugh; they shared a sense of humor. But he didn't want his message to come off as too casual. He wanted her to know that he was sincere.

He moved to the "Someone Special" section of the aisle and began flipping open cards. None of them said what he wanted to say. They were too corny, too superficial for his liking. But the romantic love cards were also not what he wanted. He soon realized that his relationship with Alex was more unique than he had ever realized. He sighed and stood in the aisle with his eyes closed. He could see her smile, hear her laugh. He really couldn't wait to see her.

He plucked a blank card from the holder and made his way to the register. He would just write in his own words. He wanted Alex to have something to take home with her; a reminder that they were really only separated geographically. He always had her with him in spirit.

He got back to the hotel in time to shower and change his clothes. The phone on the night stand rang as he was pulling a t-shirt over his head.

It was Nathan. "You ready to rock Delaware?" he asked.

"Yep," London replied. "Just walking out the door. I'll let ya know how it goes."

He scrambled to grab a few last minutes things: a chain for his neck, his wallet, and the card for Alex. He paused to wonder if the words he had written were really the ones he wanted to say, but it was too late now to do anything different. He tucked it in his back pocket and left for his show.

Two small dressing rooms were reserved in the back of the arena. One was for him; the other was shared among the rest of the band. He still laughed a little every time he saw his name on the door.

Between the dressing rooms was a shared space where the crew could partake in snacks and drinks. London never ate before a show – he found that it affected his singing – but he more often than not enjoyed at least one drink.

He poured some vodka over ice, squeezed a lemon over the liquid, and moved to his dressing room. When he opened the door, he was startled by the presence of a woman.

It was Alex. She turned from the mirror to greet him. "Hey, Stranger," she said simply and moved toward him.

"Lex!" London exclaimed. He'd thought they were meeting for dinner; her presence at the show was a happy surprise.

The two friends embraced in a deep hug. The smell of Alex's hair was familiar; the way she folded into his body a nice reminder of the past. He really had missed her.

Still embracing, Alex spoke to him. "I couldn't come down here and not see you perform," she told him.

He pulled back from her.

"You're not mad, are you? 'Cause I didn't tell you?" she asked.

"Mad? At you?" he questioned. "Of course not. I'm so happy to see you!"

Alex smiled.

A knock at the door interrupted their conversation. "Five minutes, Mr. Drake," said a voice on the other side.

"So this is what it's like to be a rock star, huh?" asked Alex.

"Sort of," he replied.

"Well I'm looking forward to the show," she said. "Go rock my socks off."

"Rock your socks off?" he asked teasingly.

"You know what I mean," replied Alex. "Wow me."

She used to always say that to him. They could be in the biggest dive in town, five people in the whole place, and Alex would say that to London before he picked up his guitar.

"You're gonna watch from backstage, right?" he asked.

"Damn right," Alex told him. "Not every day I get a chance to do that."

He leaned over and kissed Alex on her cheek. "See ya in a bit, sweetheart," he told her and opened the dressing room door.

NINETEEN

"I'm so glad you drove down," London told Alex when the two were seated for dinner. He had already said something like that to her about 15 times.

"I can't tell you how proud I am of you, London," she said in reply.

He squirmed in his chair.

"I know, I know," Alex interjected. "Don't get sappy. I'll try not to do that. But I gotta tell you...watching you on stage is just magic. And the fans love you."

"They are what make this so much fun, Lex," he told her. "You know it's never been about money or even fame for me..."

"But it's nice to be able to pay the bills!" Alex joked. "And to be putting your name in the spotlight...you know...in a positive way."

"Amen to both of those things, honey," he said, raising his wine glass.

Alex raised her glass in response. "To old friends," she said. "And to new beginnings."

Each took a sip of wine and then greeted the server who stood before them.

"Good evening, Mr. Drake," the server said. "It is a pleasure to have you with us this evening."

London glanced at the name tag she wore and responded. "Well, thank you, Reds," he said. Then noting the vibrant red color of her hair, he joked, "Should I guess how you got that nickname?"

"I'll give you three guesses, just for fun," she replied. "But let me give you a minute to think about it and I'll be right back to take your order."

He and Alex smiled and thanked the server for the menus she left on the table. Through all of dinner and two bottles of wine, the two friends shared conversation. So intently were they fixed on each other that they failed to notice that the busy dining room had all but cleared out when Reds returned to the table to take their dessert order.

"Care for dessert?" she asked, pulling their attention away from each other.

"Wow," Alex said finally noticing that their candle was one of only four or five still flickering in the restaurant. "Is it still OK?"

"OK?" Reds asked, confused. "Of course. Whatever you like."

London ordered an after dinner cordial and Alex poured the last bit of wine into her glass. They also decided on a piece of chocolate lava cake.

"So, Lex," London said to her. "I got you a little something," he began.

Alex interrupted. "Oh, London. What the hell did you do that for? I mean...I didn't bring you anything."

"It's nothing really, Lex. Just a little something you can take home with you as a reminder that I'm out here."

"I've very well aware of where you are, London. How could I miss that you're not home with ME?" she questioned playfully.

"Well, that's the thing, Lex. No matter where I am, you're with me," he told her.

Alex sat in silence. Her eyes grew glassy from the sentiment on the table.

He pushed the card he had bought toward her. "See? It's nothing," he said. "Just a little something from me to you."

Alex smiled at him. Now was the time to share her news. She placed her palm over the envelope on the table and slid it toward her. Hand still flat on the card, she paused and looked up at him.

"I have something to tell you," she said.

"Don't you wanna open your gift first?" he asked.

"I do want to open my gift," Alex replied. "But I've been wanting to tell you something all night."

"OK," London said. "Let's hear it."

Without any sugarcoating, Alex blurted, "George and I are getting married."

He felt like someone just kicked him in the chest. It wasn't that he didn't wish marriage and a family for Alex, but the thought of her committing herself to someone who didn't seem to appreciate her really bothered him. And what would it all mean for him? George wasn't exactly comfortable with their friendship.

"Married?" he said, with laughter in his voice, noticing her naked ring finger. "Stop it."

"I'm not kidding, London," Alex replied.

"Really, Lex. Stop it," he said.

"London, I know you don't like him..." she began.

"You're serious?" he questioned.

"And I know you think I deserve better," she continued, "but we've really been trying hard to work out our kinks these past few months."

"Kinks? You don't have any kinks, Lex," he said sternly.

"London, I know you like to think I'm perfect, but I'm not," Alex said, emotion filling in her voice.

"You're a hell of a lot more perfect than the asshole you're planning to marry," he said more emphatically. "Jesus, Lex. Really?" His irritation was now obvious.

Alex paused and swallowed; she seemed unsure of what to say.

Reds appeared to place the chocolate cake between them on the table. "For the lovely couple," she said, as if she were trying to clear the tension. "Two forks."

Alex waited for Reds to be away from the table before she spoke again. "London, I just don't get it," she said, in a hurt tone. "All these years, I've watched you filter women – one after another – through your life." Her voice registered her confusion. "And all this time, all this fucking time, I've been right here to support you. Never did I push for anything from you but friendship. And quite honestly, you never demonstrated to me that I was ever good enough or hot enough to be one of your 'girls.' So, now I tell you one of the most important things to happen in my life and you can't even muster a little bit of fake enthusiasm for me? Am I supposed to live in an emotional vacuum with you, caught someplace in between friendship and a real relationship? Are you fucking kidding me?"

He was now grateful that the restaurant was practically empty. Alex's voice had risen above what he considered an acceptable tone. The words she spoke were ones that stabbed at him. How could she not know that he wanted her to be happy?

"Lex, calm down. We'll talk more about this later," he said, trying to pacify her. "Read your card," he petitioned.

"I don't want to calm down, London. What I wanted was to share some news with you and have you support me. But you can't even seem to trust me enough to know that this decision is one I made really carefully."

"It's not about trusting you, Lex," he said. "I just think your judgment is a little off. I don't want to see you get hurt."

"Well, isn't that the fucking pot calling the kettle black?" Alex asked in return.

Reds appeared one more time to leave the check on the table. Her visit this time was short. She said nothing.

Tears were now running over Alex's cheeks. "You know what, London?" she asked more calmly. "Of all the people in the world, your reaction about this meant the most. Do you get that?"

"Lex," he started. "I just don't know what to say."

"You don't have to say anything...it's what you haven't already said that speaks the most." She stood, dropping the napkin from her lap onto the table.

"Where are you going?" he asked, hoping it was just to the rest room.

"I'm going home, London," she replied. "There's really no reason to prolong this. It is what it is."

Still seated, he asked her to stay.

"It's just best if I go. I'll talk to you in a few weeks when you're home." The disappointment in her voice was really more than he could stomach.

The two met eyes one last time before Alex swiped her purse and the card he had given her off the table.

"Let me at least take you back to the hotel," he pleaded.

"Why, London? It's not like I'm gonna get lucky." She turned and moved quickly out of the restaurant.

He sat motionless at the table and then jumped from his chair to follow her.

Outside, rain pounded the pavement. Alex stood at the end of the valet drop-off with her purse over her head and her other arm raised to signal a taxi. Before he could reach her, she was in the cab. The door slammed shut and she disappeared into the distance.

TWENTY

London found it very difficult to sleep that night. After watching Alex disappear into the night fog and following several unsuccessful attempts to reach her cell phone, he ventured back to his hotel room and drank himself into a numb oblivion. In a restless sleep, still in the pants he wore to dinner, he was haunted by a dream.

He is sitting on a porch swing that hangs from a country cottage. It is springtime and the breeze is filled with the scent of daffodils. The warm sun peeks below the rafters and shines light on his face. His feet are lifted and he enjoys the gentle rocking of the swing. He is happy.

In the distance, he sees a woman approaching. She is dressed in a long, cotton dress. The light fabric flows carelessly around the curves of her figure. When the sun shines from behind her, he can see her silhouette perfectly outlined under the sheer fabric. Dark curls cascade down over her shoulders. Wisps of hair dance around her head in the breeze.

The woman approaches the porch and carefully steps up. She moves toward him and joins him on the swing. Resting in her lap is a bouquet of red daisies. Against the contrast of her white dress, they are vibrant and beautiful. He can smell her perfume, sweet and clean.

The two share the swing for only a few minutes before he rises and moves into the house. She follows him into the tiny living room, where he takes her hand, and leans in to kiss her cheek. When he brushes the hair from her face, he notices tiny freckles on her cheeks and the rosy glow of her complexion. She is beautiful.

The two move into the kitchen where a pitcher of iced tea waits for them at the round country table. He offers her a full glass and invites her to take a sip. She lifts the glass to her pursed pink lips and sips the sweet tea. She smiles at him with a child-like innocence he loves.

The woman in the dream again raises the glass to her lips to take another swallow of his cool, sweet elixir. This time, however, the glass slips from her hands and falls to the floor. It shatters around her, spilling liquid around her bare feet.

His heart began to beat faster in his chest.

He crouches to wipe the liquid. As he wipes, the watery substance grows thick and dark, like molasses. The woman finds her feet stuck to the floor. She is unable to move. The faster he wipes, the thicker the substance becomes. It is now like glue. The woman begins to react, scared and confused.

He stands up from the floor and turns away from the woman to wet his towel in the sink. When he turns back to her, she extends her arm toward him, offering the bouquet she carried onto the porch. The daises are now wilted, weakened stems, unable to support heavy blooms. Petals are gray and fall in clumps. She opens her hand to drop the dead bouquet onto the floor.

The woman bends at the waist, as if she might collapse. She moans a deep guttural sound and then stands upright once again, her arms clenched around her waist. Her dark hair is now gray. Her face is filled with wrinkles; the freckles of her youth gone.

"Oh, London," she mutters, dropping her arms to her sides.

Her dress is stained with blood, a vibrant red dye tainting the white fabric.

"How could you, London?" she asks through tear-filled eyes. "Why didn't you save me?"

TWENTY-ONE

On day 86 of the "Longing For Monday Tour," London and his band pulled into rainy northwestern Pennsylvania. Watching the grey scenery from the bus window, he wondered what the hell he did wrong to ever end up at the Williamsport Arts Center. He was still holding onto the argument he had with Alex a few days before and sleeping had become impossible for him. Although he had tried several times to call Alex, every attempt went to voicemail. Now the drab scenery only deepened his melancholy mood.

Welcome to the middle of nowhere, he thought to himself. *How prestigious.*

Within seconds of exiting the tour bus, he was greeted harshly by a passing street trolley that splashed water in his direction. The streets of the small town were narrow with cobblestone sidewalks the color of salmon. Street lamps imposed an antique quality, reminiscent of the early 1950s. While the simplicity of the town contrasted the complexity of his own life, he appreciated the romantic quality of a town such as this one, so unapologetically proud of its failure to embrace the current times. It knew who it was. He was envious of that.

While the road crew began its job of unloading lights and stage gear through the side-receiving door, he pulled open the front door of the theater and made his way in. As he moved down the center aisle, a voice called out to him. "You're late, Drake," he heard in a tone that was familiar.

He smiled. He'd know that distinctive slow drawl anywhere. He quickened his pace and took the steps on stage right.

"Jon, my friend! You are a sight for sore eyes," he exclaimed enthusiastically.

The two friends embraced in a long hug.

"Man, it's so good to see you," London said.

"All I needed to hear was that you wanted me here, London," Jon said. "When Nathan called a few days ago and asked if I wanted to come out on the tour, there was no way I was gonna say no."

"Jon, you don't know how long I have been trying to get you out here on the road with me," he told his friend. "I'm so sorry for the way things went down after I signed the deal. Please know that I wanted you here from day one, but those damn record company guys...they just wouldn't budge."

"London," Jon replied, "there is no need to apologize. I knew the deal from day one. I know how this business works. Nate always told me that he would get me on tour as soon as you picked up some steam. I knew we'd be doing this eventually."

London was grateful for his friend's understanding.

"But damn it, man," Jon joked. "You think you would have worked to hit the Top Ten a little quicker. I could have starved to death by now."

The two shared a laugh. Then Jon looked at London with a little more gravity. A serious inflection filled his voice. "Congratulations, my friend," he said. "You deserve every minute of this."

"I couldn't have done it without you," London replied. He checked his watch to realize they had a few hours to kill before sound check. "Wanna grab a drink?" he asked.

"Sounds great," Jon replied, "I could use a 20 ounce right about now!"

London again laughed out loud, knowing that Jon's 20 ounce referred to coffee and not to the libation he had in mind. "Jon, you never change," he said. "How the hell do you drink so much coffee and remain so fuckin' calm all the god damned time?"

After a ten minute walk around town, the two friends arrived at Julie's Coffee Bar. Tiny bells rang as London swung open the glass door. He ordered two Velvet Macchiatos, each with an extra shot of espresso, while Jon took a seat at a high-top in front of the shop window.

"So, London, are you still getting lucky in coffee bars?" Jon teased.

London smirked and whispered, "Are you still watching me get lucky in coffee bars, buddy?"

"You suck!" Jon blurted as he choked out a laugh. His next question assumed a more serious tone. "So, seriously, how are you doing out here, London?"

"I'm cool." London said, very nonchalantly.

"Nathan seemed...concerned...about you."

London shifted in his chair, but remained silent.

"Look, man" Jon said, "you can bullshit your friends and I can bullshit mine, but let's not bullshit each other. What's going on? Is it those dreams again?"

London was a little surprised at Jon's insightfulness. "Oh, Jon," he finally said, "I had one of those dreams the other night. It was so surreal, just filled with weird images...like a movie, but more personal." There was a sort of terror in his eyes.

"It started with me sitting on a porch swing sipping on iced tea," he continued. "No worries, ya know? There was even this woman with me. She was in a white dress. She was beautiful."

"Why was that disconcerting?" Jon asked.

"It wasn't. It was actually nice," London replied. "But then, the next thing I know, the woman is in front of me in the same white dress. But it's stained with blood and she's asking me why I didn't save her."

"Oh, man," Jon said. "That's tough."

"I don't know why they're happening so often now, Jon," London told his friend. "I just know that I feel lonely a lot."

Jon just shook his head, trying to understand.

"I needed you out here so much," London said. "There's just no one here who really knows me for who I truly am."

"Are you talking with Alex while you're on the road?" Jon asked, knowing that she always helped ground him.

London exhaled. "I actually saw her when we were in Delaware last week."

"Well that's cool," Jon replied.

London remained silent.

"Did something happen?" Jon asked.

He told Jon about the argument he had with Alex. "I guess I was just wrong to not be more supportive," London said. "That guy, though, he just doesn't deserve her. Why can't she see that?"

"I don't know," Jon answered. "I did just see her the other night. We bumped into each other in the Barnes and Noble."

"Oh?" London asked.

"Yeah. But it was just for a minute. She told me she was late for an appointment."

"Did she tell you about her engagement?" London asked.

"No, she didn't," Jon replied.

London looked away.

"Things will work out, London." Jon said reassuringly. "When the tour winds down at the end of next month, and you and I get back home to the city, everything will be like old times."

He was touched by Jon's sincerity. "I would really love that," he said, not convinced that he could ever muster a suitable apology for his reaction to Alex's news. Swallowing his sadness and the last bit of his coffee, he glanced at his phone. "It's almost five. We should get going," he said. "We have a tour to get ready for."

"And then an after party, right?" Jon asked.

"Oh, yeah," London replied. "Tonight, we're at a night club in the center of town. Rumor has that it used to be a prison and the state's last electrocution sentence was carried out there."

"That sounds cheery," Jon joked. "But I gotta tell you, London, there is just no place I'd rather be right now."

London believed him. And it felt good for him to be with a friend.

TWENTY-TWO

For two hours, later that evening, everything was perfect in London's world. He and his band played the entire "Longing for Monday" album, ending the night with two encores: a cover of Kiss's "Hard Luck Woman," and a song by London called "Found." The second encore was scheduled to be a single on London's sophomore album.

Despite his increasing fatigue from being on the road, London felt energized by Jon's presence. Having him there brought London both professional and personal satisfaction. Right before the stage finally went black at the Williamsport Arts Center, London and his band joined hands at center stage and bowed to the sold out crowd. Then London rushed backstage to change his shirt and gulp some water before fans came to the meet and greet that he always did after a show. While the time with fans usually meant that he had to hang around for a couple of hours after each show, it was the part of every concert he loved the most. To meet and connect with his fans was what music was all about to him.

After all the pictures were snapped and every CD was signed, he retreated back to his dressing room for a few moments of silence.

"Tap, tap," called a knock at the door.

"I need ten minutes," he called in response. He wasn't asking; it was more of a statement. He was tired.

"Um, OK buddy," he heard from the other side of the door. It was Jon's voice.

"Dude, what are you knocking for?" London asked as he opened the door. "Come in!"

"I just wanted to say thanks," Jon said, as he entered the dressing room.

"Jon, it was so great to hear you play lead guitar tonight."

"Hard to believe this all started at Whiskey Walkers, huh, London?" Jon asked with a giggle.

London paused in reflection for a moment, lifted his beer in a toast, and said only one word: "Amazing."

Minutes later, the two rode in a limousine en route to the concert's after-party. When the car approached the curb, the privacy screen lowered so that the driver could announce their arrival. "Alright gentlemen," he said. "Here we are. Welcome to the Cell Block."

Jon's eyes widened at the sight of the place. "Fuck, London," he said. "You weren't kidding. We're at a real fucking prison."

"Well, it used to be," replied London, stretching one leg out of the car. "Promises to be an interesting evening, huh?"

The Cell Block was indeed the former Lycoming County Prison, until it was converted into a night club in early 2001. Downtown Williamsport seemed to mostly consist of historical buildings made into businesses such as restaurants and tiny specialty shops. But when day turned to night, the town took on a darker side.

London and Jon scaled the cement steps up to the club's entry. Ten foot high double dungeon doors granted them access. At the right of the dungeon doors, a purple sign clung on to the stone prison's walls. It read: "London Drake: The After-Party."

Just inside the entry, London and Jon were greeted by an electric chair that held a makeshift prisoner in its clutches. Cold cement coated the floors and walls. Prison cells lined the corridor. As he and Jon walked up the metal gated stairs to the second floor of the club, London turned to Jon. "This is fucking nuts!" he shouted, with nervous enthusiasm.

The club was crowded with people who were downing shots and foam-headed beer. They gyrated to the house music pumping through the speaker system.

A tall man with shaggy black hair approached London with his hand extended. "London, welcome to the Cell Block," he said in salutation. "My name is Scott and I own this madhouse!"

London shook Scott's hand and thanked him for throwing the party.

"We're happy to have you here," Scott replied. "Make this place your home tonight...whatever you need. You'll find the main party downstairs in The Gallows."

"Did you say The Gallows?" London asked. "What the hell is that?"

Scott seemed to chuckle at the question. "Best if you see it," he said and motioned for London and Jon to follow him.

Scott flung open a second set of dungeon doors and London stood speechless at what he saw. People packed a room that was very obviously once a prison mess hall. Now transformed into a bar, it boasted a large round stage and a dance floor. The cover band on stage was pounding through their version of a Killers song, which seemed both ironic and perfect to London.

Scott reiterated his invitation. "London, make yourself at home and have a great time," he said. "My security team is here for when the craziness starts. If you need anything, just say the word."

London looked at Jon, who shared his expression. "Did he say 'for when the craziness *starts*'?"

TWENTY-THREE

"Somebody, anybody, everybody, scream!"

Those four words and the beating of his own heart resonated in London's ears.

"Somebody, anybody, everybody, scream!"

Ninety minutes after their arrival at the club, he himself felt like screaming. Three shots of Patron and six beers in, he was feeling threatened by the tightness of the club.

Again he heard: "Somebody, anybody, everybody scream!"

"Really?" he said out loud. "If this DJ says that one more time, I will fucking scream!" Motioning to Jon, he petitioned his friend. "Jon, this place is feeling way too closed in for me...we should get out of here soon."

"OK, pal," Jon replied. "I think slowing up on the beers is probably a good idea anyway."

London pushed his hand into the bottom of his jeans pocket, caressing a blister pack of Klonopin. Patricia had prescribed the drug for him earlier in the year as a method of helping him quickly calm his nerves before they prompted a panic attack. He pulled the packet from his pocket and cradled it in his fist.

"Hey, man! What is that?" Jon questioned with concern in his tone.

"It's for my panic attacks," London rebutted.

"What is it? Where did you get it?" Jon pushed.

"My doctor prescribed them for me," London replied, very matter-of-factly.

"Really?" Jon continued with sarcasm in his voice. "Did the doctor prescribe it with a half dozen beers?"

London did not appreciate the sarcasm or the implied judgment. "Hey Jon," he barked. "I had one father and he didn't teach me shit. I don't need another one!"

"London, that's not what I meant," said Jon, in a calmer tone. "All I'm saying is that maybe you shouldn't be taking those pills along with all the booze you've been downing tonight."

"Dude, I'm stressed. These are just gonna take the edge off!"

Jon reached for the pills, only to have his hand smacked away by London, who was now annoyed.

"Jon...how's the view from the fucking cheap seats, huh? If you were standing in my shoes, you would be popping these pills too! Now leave me the hell alone!" London yelled. He popped the pills into his mouth and swallowed them with a large gulp of beer.

An awkward moment felt like a lifetime between the two friends. London's chest grew tighter. Then, a voice over the club microphone offered some relief.

"Ladies and gentlemen, can I have your attention?" the voice asked. "Before we go into the next song, let's see if we can get our guest of honor up on stage!"

London's eyes darted from one side of the room to the other.

"You guys want to see London Drake get up here and jam with us tonight?" the voice petitioned.

London knew it was more of a statement than a question. Almost in rehearsed response, the crowd started chanting: "London! London! London!"

Jon stared at his friend with worried eyes. In response to the look, London leaned toward Jon to apologize for his earlier harsh tone. Jon raised his hand to stop London's words. "Go have a good time, London," he said. "I'll be watching right here from the cheap seats."

Color drained from London's face. He turned away from Jon and walked toward the stage.

The lead singer of the band on stage shouted to London, "Aerosmith cool?"

"Yeah, let's do it!" he shouted back, with more enthusiasm than he really felt.

The club went black...pitch black. A single white spotlight transfixed itself on London's silhouette. The air filled with the groove of bass. The opening to "Sweet Emotion" thumped its way through the club's huge speakers.

He looked out on the crowd. Colored lights danced off the people before him. He noticed a woman in the crowd—fake blonde hair, fake boobs, silly smile.

All these different faces...
screaming...
waving beer bottles...
more screaming...
cameras flashing...
even more screaming...

He began the song's first verse. His heart thumped in his chest. His vision began to blur. Blinking, he cleared his eyes and continued to sing, almost robotically. His gaze and attention fixed on something in the distance, hanging from high above the club. It was a makeshift prisoner, a mannequin. It hung from the rafters from a noose tied tight around its neck. Its legs swayed from left to right. Limp arms dangled at its side.

He tried feverishly to shake the vision from his eyes.

Was it the beer? The pills? The shots?

All of it pounded in his head and wreaked havoc on his system.

Blinking in rapid succession, he lowered his head to focus on the crowd. He could still feel the terror building inside of him. He tried closing his eyes to focus on the song lyrics. He continued to sing, but he felt like he was watching the scene from somewhere outside of his body.

He opened his eyes and fixed his gaze once again in the distance. Now he could see clearly. It was his grandfather hanging lifelessly from the club's rafters. He squinted, trying to make out the image more clearly. The limp body was cloaked in a white undershirt.

The hanging man's right arm rose up as he watched. With full intention, the figure's clenched fist stabbed at its own chest and then fell again to its side. He saw bright red blood drip from his grandfather's pale fingertips. The thick droplets fell slowly on the crowd below, and then rained more steadily down, staining the blonde hair he'd noticed earlier a bright red.

Suddenly, his moving lips yielded no more sound. Intense pain shot through his lungs like shards of broken glass. His body fell to the floor as fireworks exploded in his head. He landed face up on the beer soaked stage.

The club went silent as Jon rushed toward his friend.

The sound of paramedics caused London to reopen his eyes several minutes later. He knew they were there with him. He could feel them tugging at his clothes, but their words were muffled, as if they were in the distance. High above him hung the mannequin. It swayed in the breeze of the air conditioning vent, taunting him. As he was positioned on a stretcher and carried from the club, he swore he could hear the voice of his grandfather coming from the mannequin.

"London, my boy," the figure said to him. "Our family puts on quite a show."

TWENTY-FOUR

The hospital rang with chaos. From somewhere outside his own body, London could hear an orchestra of voices shouting around him.

"Attention: Code Blue, Code Blue. Crash Team, please report to room 327 immediately!"

"Dr. Graham, blood pressure is dropping!"

"Dropping – 110/75"

"Still dropping – 90/60"

"Dropping – 60/40; now – 50/33"

"Shit...we're losing him."

"Get me the paddles...clear!"

Whap!

"OK...clear!"

Whap!

"Come on, damn it...Come on!"

The voices grew less frantic, more solemn.

"We've lost him...he's gone."

"He didn't deserve to live anyway," a voice judged. "Time of death... eleven years old."

With a violent thrust forward, London woke up in his hospital bed on the third floor of Williamsport General. His gown and the covers around him were soaked in sweat. Startled to alertness, he breathed heavily, surveying the empty room with panicked eyes.

Alex entered the room carrying a fountain soda. "Look who's awake!" she exclaimed as she entered, happy to see his eyes open. "It figures that I leave for two minutes and you finally decide to wake up! I've been sitting here for hours waiting for you to open your eyes."

"Where am I?" London asked, not sharing her enthusiasm. "I had the most horrible dream."

"You're in the hospital, honey," she told him. "Don't you remember anything?"

He looked at her, confused and groggy. "Alex, what are you doing here?" he asked softly.

"What did you think, silly, that I was not gonna come when I heard what happened? Jon called me," she replied.

His head was a muddy mess of fractured memories from the night before.

"Where's Jon?" he asked. "I need to talk to him."

"He's downstairs in the lobby, waiting for Nathan."

"Nathan?" he asked. "Oh shit. Is he here?"

"Not quite yet," Alex told him. "But he should be here any minute."

In his car on Rt. 180, Nathan sped toward the hospital. He spent the time in the car recalling memories of his first meeting with London in Whiskey Walkers, of the struggle they had shared to get London signed and touring, of the friendship the two had developed. They were more than just talent and an agent. They were family.

Nathan reflected on the qualities in London that drew the two of them together. Nathan had himself been a singer. Now he saw in his friend the same fire he once had as a Doo-wop singer. Discouraged by his own parents to do something more "productive," he had never seen his own dreams realized. Now, he was getting a second chance at that dream through London's career. He took great pride in the contract he was able to secure for London and in the talent he saw growing in his friend.

When he finally pulled into the hospital parking lot, Nathan wiped tears from his eyes and raised a hand to greet Jon. The two hurried through the lobby and rode the elevator to the third floor. Just outside London's room, Nathan paused and took a deep breath. Exhaling, he turned to Jon.

"Hey man, you mind if I get a minute alone?" he asked.

Jon just nodded and made his way down the hall to the coffee machine.

"Hey pal, how are you feeling?" Nathan said, announcing his arrival to London.

"I feel like I got hit by a fucking freight train!" London replied.

Alex smiled at Nathan and excused herself, as if guessing that Nathan wanted to have a private conversation with London. "I'll just be out here keeping Jon company," she said.

Before Nathan could even begin to talk, a physician walked in and interrupted. "How are we this evening?" the doctor asked, extending a hand to London. "My name is Dr. Mathis. I'm the doctor on rounds tonight." The doctor paused and looked at Nathan, as if to question whether or not he should continue talking.

"This is my agent," London said. "It's cool to talk in front of him."

"Well, Mr. Drake, you gave us quite a scare last night," the doctor told him. "You put a really dangerous mixture of pills and alcohol into your body. You should consider yourself lucky that you were surrounded by people. If you were alone, this story could have had a much different ending."

London was embarrassed. "When can I get out of here?" he asked, diverting the focus of the conversation. "I have another show in three days and some press interviews in between."

The doctor paused, catching Nathan's eye, and then shifted his attention back to London. "We anticipate that you'll be released later today or tomorrow, Mr. Drake. But I'd advise you to take it easy for at least a couple more days. Your body has been through a lot. You may be pushing harder than we'd recommend as healthy."

London had no reply. The doctor again shook London's hand and left the room.

"So kiddo, we need to talk about something," Nathan said to him after a minute.

London was wiping tears from his eyes. He was so disappointed in himself.

"People are talking, man," Nathan told him. "There's video all over YouTube. Jordan from the record label has been blowing up my phone all day. London, it's not good."

"How bad is it?" London asked.

"I think we need to consider canceling the rest of the tour, London," Nathan said.

London protested. "Nate, we only have three more dates left. Please don't let them cancel this now. We have all worked so hard. And Jon is here now. I'll be..."

Nathan spoke firmly. "London, when I spoke to Jordan he was very particular in his instructions to me."

"OK, so what does he want? I'll do whatever he wants if I can just finish this tour," London pleaded.

"It's not about what he wants, kiddo. It's about what needs to happen if we're gonna see you continue as a successful artist after this tour."

London knew Nathan was serious.

"We're gonna cancel the last couple of dates, London." Nathan said.

"But..."

"Listen to me, London," Nathan interrupted. "Tyler Schramm is telling the label that he won't work with you again unless you get your shit together, man. We have to demonstrate that you're doing that. He's too big of a name to just let walk away."

"I don't want him to walk away, Nate," London said.

"He doesn't want the drama associated with him," Nathan said. "So, we cancel what's left, get back to New York, you start seeing that fancy therapist of yours again, and we plan next steps."

"I fucked up, man," London said, more to himself than to anyone.

"Come on, London," Nathan encouraged him. "I need you to refocus and get behind this plan. Besides, it's not like you are missing New York City," Nathan said, a little less seriously. "It's only fucking Cleveland." Nathan was now laughing.

London smiled too. He was grateful to have Nathan on his side.

"OK, I gotta get outta here," Nathan told him. "I have some calls to make."

Nathan leaned over the hospital bed to kiss London on the cheek. "I love you kiddo," he whispered in London's ear.

TWENTY-FIVE

London was released from the hospital later that afternoon. Nathan decided to stay behind at the hotel and catch up on some work, but London, Jon, and Alex opted to spend the day in town before London headed back to New York. When they returned to the hotel that evening, they ordered a pizza, and rented movies on the TV. Nathan, who fell asleep sometime around 8 p.m., was fodder for their jokes the rest of the evening.

"So, Jon," Alex questioned," you gettin' any out here on the road?"

"Getting' any what?" London blurted.

"Come on, now," Alex continued. "There must be some poor girl just longing to have you on top of her," she teased.

Jon stood up and walked toward his guitar case. Unlatching the clamps in one quick motion, he stood in the center of the room holding up his black Vintage '57 Fender Reissue. "I sleep with this sexy baby every night," he proclaimed in a drunken slur. "She's all I need!"

"Pfffft!" came from London, who thrust fists of popcorn at his friend. The three of them rolled in laughter.

"So, guys, can we talk about something?" London asked, in a more somber tone. He rose from his chair and stood before them.

Both Jon and Alex sat forward on the couch and watched London intently.

"Listen, I need to say something to the both of you," he said.

"Speech! Speech!" Jon called, still laughing and raising his beer bottle in the air.

London continued. "First of all, I couldn't ask for better friends," he said sincerely. "These last few days have been a real struggle and I couldn't have gotten through this without the two of you." He paused.

Jon, who had still been giggling, sat quiet.

"Jon," London continued, "I am so sorry for what I said to you the other night at the club." His voice cracked. "It was stupid and cruel. The truth is, I wouldn't be here today doing what I do if it wasn't for you. Sometimes, I take for granted the friend I have in you, and I promise that I will never let that happen again."

Alex shifted in her seat.

"And Alex," London said, turning to her, "I can only hope that you know how much I love you. There are so many times I just would have never gotten through without you. And while I don't understand your relationship with George, I really hope you are happy. I'm sorry I couldn't find these words at dinner. I hope you can forgive me."

He put his hands over his face and began to weep. He hated to disappoint his friends.

Jon and Alex stood from the couch and moved toward him. The three friends embraced in a hug that lasted long enough for their shirts to become damp with tears.

"Since we're being honest," Alex interjected, "you think maybe you can tell us what happened the other night? Jon and I watched a video from the club on YouTube. You looked like you saw a ghost."

London plopped backward into a chair. "I did see a ghost," he said.

TWENTY-SIX

Early the next evening, London was finally back in his New York apartment. Without even removing his coat, he fell into the end seat of a black leather couch, letting the softness of the fabric envelope around him. The leather was warm from the sun that shone through the large window behind it. That warmth mimicked the feeling he felt inside himself. It had been a long tour. He was tired, but he was also feeling very grateful for the fans that came out to see him, for the company of Jon on the road, and for his reconciliation with Alex.

He sat in silence for what had to be half an hour. He had no desire to put on the TV, to listen to music. He was content in the silence, his mind full of nothing. After some time, he rose from the couch and moved to the kitchen. A note on the refrigerator indicated that Alex had been there in earlier in the day.

"It's a good thing you have me," the note said, followed by a smiley face. "You might otherwise starve to death."

He opened the refrigerator to find a pan of lasagna, a case of Diet Pepsi, and a chocolate cake. The icing on the cake read, "Welcome Home."

He chuckled. He wondered when Alex had time to do this. She had left Williamsport only hours before him. Ignoring the lasagna, he reached for the cake and a can of soda and made his way back to the couch. He dropped his coat on the floor next to him and snuggled back in his seat with a fork and the entire chocolate cake.

Three bites in, he heard a tap on his front door. He thought for a moment about ignoring it, but then decided to see who was calling on him so soon after his arrival at home.

When he got closer to the door, he could hear the soft purrs of a cat from the other side.

Chloe! he thought and threw open the door. Standing opposite him was Alex. She was smiling wide and holding a cat carrier.

"I figured you missed your girl," she said and leaned in to kiss London on the lips.

"Oh, Alex, I did miss her," he replied, reaching to take the carrier from Alex's hand. "Thank you for taking her while I was gone." He quickly crouched down to open the door that was the cat's release. She emerged quickly, curling herself around his ankles. She purred loudly.

He scooped up the cat and lifted her above his head, her back limbs dangling. He lowered her face to his and kissed her head.

After a few minutes, Alex cleared her throat. "Nice to see you, too, Alex," she said sarcastically.

London lowered the cat to the floor. "Oh, Lex," he said, grinning wide. "Come here."

Alex reached toward London, lifting her hand to his face. "I see you found the cake," she said, wiping icing from his cheek. She pulled her hand back and licked her finger. "Is it all gone?" she asked. "I mean, I came all the way over here for a piece of chocolate cake for God's sake."

London stood with arms crossed, staring at his friend. "Just for cake, huh?" he asked playfully.

"Well, that and to return the cat," she replied.

Part Three

BREAKDOWN

TWENTY-SEVEN

The first few weeks of being home brought London time to relax. He met regularly with Patricia and he journaled his thoughts and feelings, as she had requested.

Nathan refused to even talk to London about resuming any kind of tour schedule. Instead, he wanted London to focus on writing in preparation for a follow-up album. "They always say that there's no such thing as bad publicity," Nate joked with him. "Might as well get a new album out there, while your name is still on people's tongues."

Since London had already written three songs for his sophomore album – two on the road and one left over from the first CD – he, too, was eager to move ahead. "If nothing else," he told Nathan, "a tortured soul is a hell of an inspiration."

But now, on a cloudy Tuesday, he sat uninspired and stared out his window onto the city below. He felt restless and bored, but too lazy to make any real effort. The dichotomy of his emotions began to irritate even him.

Blinnng, blinnng, his phone chimed from the bedroom. It was a text message. He ignored it, deciding he didn't want to move. *Blinnng, blinnng*, it chimed again.

"Go get that for me, would ya, Chloe?" he asked of the cat that was curled up next to him. Her energy level mimicked his, and she certainly did not care who the texter was. Blinnng, blinnng.

"OK, OK," he said and rose from the couch, curiosity getting the best of him.

Fumbling with the phone, he scrolled the message list down to the most recent noise maker. *"Hungry?"* was all it read.

A devious smile crept over his face. The message was from Samantha, a newly graduated coed he had met in New York right before he left for his tour. He'd known her only two weeks before he left, but he'd had sex with her at least as many times as there were days in that time period. The text suddenly infused him with a little more energy.

"My place or yours?" he asked in reply.

Twenty-five minutes and one crazy cab driver later, he exited the taxi in the neighborhood of Brooklyn Heights. He walked casually up a tree-lined street, noticing the beauty of the old homes and the old money that afforded them. Sam's apartment overlooked the park and was the latest "gift" from her dad. From what Sam described, her parents' divorce triggered a game in which affections were bought. Sam's dad thought the apartment was a fitting gift for his newly graduated baby girl on her 21st birthday.

London's nonchalant attitude had all but dissipated by the time he entered the lobby of the Archstone Apartments. He was now sort of giddy in anticipation of seeing Sam; not because he thought their relationship would turn into anything meaningful, but because he could have an afternoon of fun without thinking.

Sam did not disappoint. She opened the door to greet him in nothing but a very thin white t-shirt. Her caramel nipples poked through the cotton, inspiring him to grow hard inside his jeans. She said nothing, but smiled and extended her hand. She held his grip and guided him through the apartment and into the bedroom. Just inside the doorway, she let go of his hand and turned her back toward him, moving closer to the bed. He noticed the sway of her hips, the roundness of her backside. She crisscrossed her arms and lifted the shirt up over her head. Now naked, she sat coyly on the edge of the bed.

He stood watching.

"Come here, Rock Star," she cooed.

As he approached, Sam lay back on the bed, knees bent and legs slightly apart. She was naked and exposed to him. He unbuttoned his own shirt and unbuckled the belt at his waist. As he undressed, Sam began to explore her own body.

She started at her own neck, slowly running her hands down the sides of her body. She cupped her breasts, squeezing each firm nipple between her fingers. Then she opened her legs to reveal herself fully. Her fingers glided over her warm center and she arched her back in an offering of herself to him.

He hovered over her now, first kissing her neck gently. Her own fingers moved more aggressively beneath him as he circled her nipples with his tongue. She whimpered feverishly as he trailed kisses down her body.

The tease was always his favorite part of sex with Samantha. He enjoyed making her want him; he reveled in her soft moans and her pleas for him to be inside of her. But he took his time. He alternated soft kisses with gently flicks of his tongue as he moved between her breasts and her belly button. He tugged at her belly button ring with his teeth and traced the tattoo on her pubic bone with his tongue. The words were inscribed above a small mound of black pubic hair.

The curve of the R....

The stricter lines of the E ...

And again the swoop of the S...

Halfway through the word, he could no longer resist his own need to take her. He grouped the remaining letters and kissed them together...
PECT.

Two hours later, London was again hailing a taxi to return home. Nestled in the backseat, the smell of Samantha still on him, he accessed his voicemail to retrieve a message left while he was at Sam's apartment. He listened to Patricia's voice telling him of a cancellation that evening, in the event he'd like to take the now open appointment. Now 5:10 p.m., there was still time to make the open 5:30 appointment

"Excuse me, driver," he called from the back seat. "Change of plans... please go to St. Adele's Hospital."

"The hospital?" the driver asked nervously. "Are you OK?"

"Oh, yes," London replied in response to the driver's concern. "I'm fine. I just need to go there before I head home."

Patricia greeted him with happy surprise when he walked into her office a few minutes later. Since he hadn't returned the message she'd left, she had assumed he wasn't coming. London found her packing a laptop into a messenger bag when he arrived.

"London!" she said with surprise.

"Hope the appointment is still open?" he asked.

"It is. I'm just surprised to see you since you didn't call me back."

"Yeah, sorry about that," he replied. "I had...a lunch date with a friend."

"That's nice!" Patricia said and motioned for him to take his usual seat on the leather sofa.

London grinned.

"Oh," Patricia replied, familiar with the connotation of London's grin. "And do I already know about this particular young lady?"

"No," he answered, a little taken aback that a grin could imply to Patricia that he had been with a woman. But then again, he liked Patricia – trusted her – because she was intuitive. She could read him; sometimes better than he could read himself.

"So, how do you feel about this particular woman?" Patricia asked, not asking him to reveal the woman's name.

"I don't," he answered, matter-of-factly. Sensing Patricia's confusion, he reiterated. "Feel about her? I don't."

Patricia opened a note pad she held on her lap. "London, a few sessions ago you and I had talked about taking a step back from purely physical relationships."

"I know we did," he replied. "But I needed to have a little fun today. I needed some release for a few hours. I don't think that's unreasonable."

Patricia listened.

"What the hell is wrong with that, Patricia?" he asked defensively. "Do you think I'm addicted to sex or something? Jesus. It's not like that. I just wanted to be careless. And I mean that...care less...just shut it all off and enjoy an afternoon."

"Well, London," Patricia continued, shifting slightly forward in her seat. "I think you suffer from what therapists call PTSD."

"PTSD?" he asked.

"Yes. It stands for post-traumatic stress syndrome, London. It's an anxiety disorder that can develop after exposure to a terrifying event or ordeal. But there are other triggers too," Patricia told him. "Things like the loss of loved one, violent personal assault, or even something as simple as a car accident can trigger PTSD. Given all that we've talked about...the incident with your grandparents...the dynamic of your family...I think it's an accurate assessment."

He dropped his defense. He was interested. Could this be the answer he had been looking for his entire adult life? Had years of therapy actually offered a diagnosis? And more importantly, could it be "cured"? Still, he was confused at Patricia's approach.

"I'm not sure what that has to do with my afternoon," he said respectfully. "I wasn't hurting anyone and I didn't feel any anxiety. In fact, what I felt was relaxed. It was a nice break from my real life."

"Well, that's exactly it, London," Patricia clarified. "I think you're still in a place of escape. I think what happened to you that night in the club – the night that essentially ended your tour and distracted you from your work...your dream – I think it is related to stress and your inability to escape from that stress."

"I wouldn't argue that," he agreed. "But why it happened – and how it happened – still isn't clear to me."

"Well, London, it happened because your level of anxiety – mixed with the alcohol – got to the point that your brain couldn't turn it off."

He nodded in agreement. His heart was beating faster even just by talking about that night. "But we started this conversation because I told you that I spent the afternoon having sex. How does that make sense?" he asked.

"Let's think about it this way, London," Patricia suggested. "When you were a boy, you lived with your parents and your grandparents. And then something happened that pulled your grandparents away from you in a very violent way. Then, to use your own words, as a result of that event, you also perceived the loss of your father, saying that he was never the same again. Is that a fair recollection of what you said?"

"Yes," he replied, visibly shaken by the memory.

"Let's continue then," Patricia urged. "I believe that you have never rectified the loss of your grandparents...that you have not made peace with the events that took them from you. Is that fair?"

"Yes," he said.

"So, we now have a situation in which you never really dealt with those losses," Patricia continued. "Those unresolved feelings mix around inside of you all the time, London. They naturally cause anxiety for you. Now, take something like a record tour that adds additional stress. What you have is a recipe for disaster. What happened in the club that night was the result of that recipe."

He dropped his head.

"If we consider your father on top of all that, the disorder grows even more faceted," Patricia continued. "Again, someone you loved left you without any obvious choice in the matter because of his heart attack, right?"

He exhaled. A tear rolled down his cheek.

"And you told me, London, that your mother was so damaged by the death of your father that you felt like you lost her too. Can you see where the trauma exists in all of this, London?"

"I don't see trauma," he replied. "I see bullshit. All of it...it's just all been unfair."

"Well, London," Patricia replied, "life is not always fair. But neither is death. Unfortunately, in this case, that's not the lesson you were taught." Patricia paused and waited for him to look up at her. "I believe, London, that all of these events taught you that when you love someone, they get taken away from you, and that you're powerless to do anything about it. Would you say that's a fair assessment?"

He thought quietly for several seconds. "It makes sense," he said.

"Could you agree that it seems safer for you to not get too attached to people, London?" Patricia asked. "Could you agree that when you are out meeting these random women for casual affairs that it just might be because you crave a connection, but choose not to make any emotional connection? In that way, you will never have to deal with losing them?"

His face revealed some revelation. He ran over the pattern of women who ventured in and out of his life the last several years. Again, he exhaled.

"I know this is a lot to comprehend, London," Patricia said, "but I also think that if you can embrace the ideas I just laid out and own them, they will bring you closer to some resolution. You have to move away from seeing yourself as a victim, London."

"How do I do that?" he asked. "I am a victim. A lot of shit has happened to me."

"I don't deny that, London," Patricia reassured. "Our best effort needs to start with reconciling the emotions around your grandparents' death. We need to work on getting you to a place of forgiveness where you can acknowledge that you don't have to like what happened, but that you can forgive your grandfather for it. Much of that will be about forgiving yourself, too."

"So how many years is that gonna take?" he joked, trying to break the sobriety of the room.

"I believe you are much closer than you think, London. Besides, all of that is the easy part," Patricia told him.

"Easy?" he exclaimed, in disbelief.

"The hard part will be when I ask you to accept that you deserve to be happy," Patricia warned him. "Eventually, I am going to ask you to love yourself, London, and to open yourself to loving someone else and letting that someone else love you."

"I love people," he defended. "I love Alex...I love Jon...my mom."

"I know you do, London," Patricia replied. "But that's not what I mean."

He knew what she meant.

"You keep telling me that you're frustrated with your lack of intimacy," she continued. "If we are successful, you will know the intimacy of a truly loving relationship, London."

Both stopped speaking and sat in silence for a minute.

"Thank you," he finally said. "Thank you for seeing a future where all that happens for me."

"It's not me who has to see it, London."

TWENTY-EIGHT

It had just started to rain when London's taxi approached his apartment building. The driver pulled up along the curb and waited for his fare. After a moment of silence, the driver turned to face London.

"Is this the right address?" the driver asked.

"Oh, yeah. This is fine," London replied. "Good night," he finally said, tossing a $20 bill at the man.

The door slammed shut.

He pulled his long black coat up over his head to shield him from the rain which was now splashing heavily in the street. The sky rumbled with thunder in the distance. He dashed under the entrance overhang and into shelter. As he walked toward the elevator, he noticed every annoying squeak of his shoes on the terrazzo floor. The noise confirmed his own existence at a time when he just wanted to disappear.

He pushed the "UP" button and stood waiting for the elevator. He was still alone in the lobby when the doors opened and revealed an empty space. He was relieved. No company meant no stops on the way up to his loft on the 33rd floor. He entered and pressed his floor number. As the doors closed, he closed his eyes and exhaled, a deep sigh filled with frustration and sadness.

But then, a jerk. He opened his eyes. The doors to the elevator were open just enough for an arm to penetrate the space, causing the elevator to stop. The doors opened wider, revealing a woman in a short, strapless dress. Her hair was the color of a rich Merlot, slightly damp from the rain, and flowed down in casual curls that draped over her olive skinned shoulders. On any other night, he would have been happy to have this kind of company. Tonight, his only thought was on getting upstairs.

"Jeesh," said the woman. "I thought the darn thing was gonna take my arm right off." She smiled at him.

His first reaction was to tell her how dumb she was to even be sticking her arm in the space to begin with. But he refrained. Reactionless, he leaned his head back against the wall of the elevator, again closed his eyes, and stood silent.

The elevator did not move. He began to count the seconds in his head ....One...two...deep breath...three...four. Damn it, he thought. Just press your button.

"Man, I can't seem to find my key," said the woman, who was now fumbling through her purse. "I know it's in here somewhere." As she lifted her eyes to smile again at him, the bag slipped from her hands and fell to the floor. The contents were now spilled out...a small note pad, a lipstick, a checkbook, two credit cards, a smart phone, a three-pack of condoms. "Shit," she spurted as she squatted to gather the belongings closer to her. "I'm such a mess."

Yes, yes, you are, he thought. *A fucking mess in a dress*. Instead of saying out loud the words screaming in his head, he bent to help her. He reached for the cell phone, deciding it was the least personal of the belongings now laid out at his feet. As he clutched it, it began to play a musical ring.

"You're my brown-eyed girl..."

The display lit up with a name: Lucy.

He rolled his eyes. In his head, he thought, *Are you kidding me with this song?* He had heard it so many times at weddings and events. He had himself sung it on stage. But he was surprised that this was her choice. It annoyed him that of all the songs she could have chosen as a ring tone, she had committed to such a cliché. Yeah, she had brown eyes. *Big deal*, he thought.

Instead of commenting, he stretched out his hand, palm open and up, revealing the still ringing cell phone. "Here you go," he said, acknowledging the woman for the first time. When he stopped to really look at her, he noticed her eyes. *Better than brown*, he thought. *Deeper*.

"Oh, thanks," she replied, again smiling at him as the ringing stopped. "You'd think I'd be better at this whole thing by now." She rose from the elevator floor and curtly pressed the button for floor twelve.

He was puzzled by what she meant, but he related so deeply to her statement. "Better?" he asked.

"Oh yeah," she replied, "at this whole being an elegant, sophisticated adult." She snickered. "But I guess it's like they say, 'you can dress her up but you can't take her out.'"

He sensed a deeper frustration than just a purse falling open on the floor. "I'm sorry," he said, "I'm not quite sure what you mean."

"Oh, well, of course you don't," she replied. "I'm talking in riddles to a complete stranger. I'm sorry. Just ignore me. I'm sure you want to get home."

"It's OK," he replied, as the elevator halted to a stop on floor 12. The doors opened and she exited, without turning to say goodbye.

When the doors once again closed, he was left alone, except for the song now stuck in his head and the sweet, candy-like smell of sunflower scented perfume that wrapped around him.

TWENTY-NINE

London exhaled a deep breath that, when finished, found him on the 33rd floor. He was still thinking about the woman he had just met when the doors opened and revealed the hallway to his apartment.

When he pushed his key into the lock, he could already hear Chloe on the other side, purring to announce his arrival. Her greeting always made him smile, a reminder that some things were constant; that devotion really did exist in the world. He had gotten the cat when she was just a kitten. Now eight years old, she still greeted him at the door and waited impatiently to curl into his lap on the couch. Chloe had seen women come and go from his life. She'd witnessed friendships built and shattered. Despite those temporary relationships, Chloe made him believe that he was capable of love; capable of sustaining more permanent connections with people.

"Well, good evening, Miss Cat," he said as he entered the loft and threw his keys in a glass bowl on the hall table. "And how was your day?"

Chloe was wrapped around his ankles, purring.

"I don't know about you, but I need a drink." He glanced down at the cat, almost expecting her to say: "What else is new?"

He shed his coat and threw it casually on the couch as he made his way to the kitchen. He passed the long glass windows that lined his living room and paused for just a moment to look down on the city street

When he pushed on the light in the kitchen, he noticed the cat already up on the counter, next to the refrigerator. "Am I that predictable?" he asked her, as he opened the refrigerator door. Then he chuckled a little. "I guess I am," he said.

He tipped a pitcher and poured some lemonade into a bowl for the cat, before filling his own glass half way. Then, reaching into the freezer, he retrieved a bottle of Grey Goose and removed the cap. "When life gives you lemons," he said, tilting the now open bottle toward the cat. He filled what space was left in his glass with vodka.

Nineteen floors below, two sisters in apartment 1256 were also sharing a drink.

"I can't believe what an ass I just made out of myself," said Katorah Alexander to her older sister, Lucy. "Everything was all over the elevator floor" she said.

"Well, did he help you pick it up?" Lucy asked.

"Of course he did, Lucy," Katorah replied. "Although I was scrambling pretty good to get it all myself."

"You're being hard on yourself, Kat," Lucy replied, trying to calm her sister. "It's not like you're the first girl to drop her purse in an elevator."

"Yeah, I know, Lucy, but for God's sake. He was cute. And I was a bumbling idiot!"

"Well, at least the condoms were sexy!" Lucy interjected with some levity. The two women burst into laughter.

"Thanks," she said to Lucy. "I'm so glad I moved to New York so that you could have even more opportunities to tease me!"

"No problem, sis," Lucy replied. "I'm always here for you. Now, how about you get into something a little more dry and comfortable and I'll make us some tea?"

"That would be great," Katorah replied. "Gimme a quick minute."

In the spare bedroom, Katorah slipped out of her wet dress and into the silky pink pajamas. As she changed, she glanced around the bedroom. It was so cozy and warm. Lucy had lived in New York now for 17 years. Katorah could remember Lucy making the move the year Katorah entered high school. On summer breaks, Katorah would visit her sister for a few weeks at a time. It was then that she fell in love with the city. Despite its heat and its traffic, Katorah felt at home there. She loved the bright lights at night, the diversity of the people. It was very different from their childhood home in Westchester County. Now she, too, had made the move to the city. Only there for a couple of days, she had begun watching the rental listings months ago. Still, the perfect place seemed to elude her and her suitcases were still packed in the corner of her sister's guest room.

"You've made this quite a home," Katorah said to Lucy, as she took a seat on the couch next to her sister.

"Thanks, sis," Lucy replied. "Some days it amazes me that I've actually been able to survive here. And other days, it doesn't seem hard at all."

Katorah was surprised by her sister's stated struggle. "You make it all seem so easy," she said to Lucy.

Lucy laughed. "Easy? No," she replied. "Not easy, but worth it."

Back on the 33rd floor, London was questioning his own survival in the city. Now three drinks in, he lay in the darkness of his bedroom, propped up on pillows in the center of his large mattress. Chloe lay on his stomach purring. The two listened to an old Kiss record that was spinning on a turntable across the room. The old vinyl record was gritty and raw. He preferred it to the digital mastery of current CDs.

He sang along with KISS singer Paul Stanley. Between verses, he sipped his lemonade concoction; every sip eased his tension and helped clear his mind.

"Genius," he said to Chloe, recalling that this album was what prompted him to ever even want to make music. "Fuckin' genius."

He passed out on the bed just as the song concluded. The three remaining tracks lulled him deeper and deeper into sleep.

THIRTY

When London woke the next afternoon, he was immediately greeted by a throbbing pain between his ears. The sun pouring in through the large bay window made him feel as if he would disintegrate, like a vampire, at any moment. The thought made him chuckle a little to himself.

I could evaporate, he thought, and then said out loud, "Poof. Like smoke."

The thought of his own sudden disappearance stirred him to get up out of bed. Meandering into the kitchen, he popped a K-cup into the coffee maker and breathed in the rich smell of the brew. Despite its alluring aroma and soothing warmth on his scratchy throat, he wondered why the home brewed coffee just never tasted as good as the cup he'd frequently enjoyed in that little coffee shop, back before the success of his record. He guessed it was the atmosphere of the café that he missed, the scholarly nature of the people who often surrounded him, the view of Cassandra, the barista he once knew. It was all so simple and comforting.

The growl in his stomach soon announced his hunger. Settling on eggs and toast, he bent to retrieve the frying pan from the cabinet next to the stove. The change in position caused some dizziness that he attributed to the previous night's Vodka. His now pounding headache affirmed that diagnosis. He opened the bread drawer, took the last two slices of rye from a bag, and popped them into the toaster. He turned and moved to the fridge. The open doors washed a coolness over his face, causing him to pause. He closed his eyes and stood silent, still, letting the chilly air rest on him for a moment. It felt refreshing and clean. He breathed deeply.

The smell of burning toast propelled him back to his task.

"Shit," he said, and he turned to see smoke coming from the toaster.

"God damned thing."

He grabbed the egg carton, and moved back across the kitchen. He tugged at the toaster's electric cord, pulling it from the outlet, and forcing the toaster to eject his now darker than intended bread.

"Fuckin' thing," he said as he cracked two eggs into a pool of melted butter in the now warm pan. Letting them sizzle just long enough to firm up, he pushed a spatula under the eggs and lifted them out and onto a plate. He spread some butter on the crispy pieces of rye, and placed his plate on the kitchen table.

Before he sat, he refilled his coffee cup and put on the radio that was mounted under the cabinet, just over the kitchen sink.

He slurped some coffee, and pushed his fork into the sticky egg yolk. The yellow substance spilled out from the center, coating the white of the egg with its gooey thickness. He dipped in the edge of his toast and then took a mouthful. He wondered why people would ever scramble their eggs. To do so would mean that the distinct parts of the egg would be lost. He preferred to enjoy the firmness of the white and the juiciness of the yolk. *They complement each other perfectly*, he thought. To scramble them together only meant that each part was compromising the characteristics that made it unique.

THIRTY-ONE

London got into the shower at 5:30 p.m. He had just gotten wet when he heard the phone ringing from the other room. Deciding to ignore it, he leaned into the stream, bending his neck forward so that the water ran over his head and down the back of his neck. He stood with eyes closed, trying to anticipate how his interview with a SPIN reporter would go that night. If he had to guess, he would predict that it would be nothing out of the ordinary. Instead, he'd be asked the same routine questions; the ones normally covered in interviews:

Who were your musical influences?

Were you one of those kids who hated school?

How is your life different now that you have a hit record?

Do you have a girlfriend?

Blah, blah, blah, he thought, wondering if a magazine would ever step out of the template to write a really interesting article about someone famous. He abandoned those thoughts quickly, deciding that if the world knew his real story, they might not be so accepting. Templates were safe, he decided.

He wrapped a towel around his waist and stepped out of the shower. He opened the medicine cabinet to retrieve his toothbrush and a razor and wiped his hand across the mirror to clear the fog. As he ran the blade down his face, he noticed how the reflection reminded him so much of his father. His dark eyes were round and deep set like his dad's had been. The chisel of his jaw line was a paternal trait he now carried. With every passing year, he resembled his father more and more.

He splashed an Armani scent on his fresh shave and made his way into the bedroom. The light on his cell phone blinked with a missed call. He dialed into voicemail to retrieve the messages.

"Hey, kid, it's Nathan. Just calling to remind you about the SPIN interview. If you're sleeping, it's time to get up and get ready. Oh, and London, be nice to this one, please."

London grinned and shook his head. He loved that Nathan called him "kid." It made him feel like someone in the world was out to protect him, not that he'd ever admit that. He erased both Nathan's message and an earlier message from his mother reminding him to call her. Before he could redial Nathan's number, the phone rang again. He answered too quickly to take notice of the caller ID.

"OK, Nathan," he said into the receiver, laughing, "I'm way ahead of you, buddy."

The woman on the other end replied with confusion in her voice. "Mr. Drake?" she asked.

"Oh, shit," he answered, with equal confusion. "I'm sorry. I was expecting someone else. Who is this?"

"Mr. Drake, this is Michelle calling from SPIN magazine. I'm just confirming your 8:00 meeting with our reporter this evening."

"Yes. OK. I will be there," he said impatiently. He glanced at the clock: 6 p.m. He was still on schedule.

"I have the meeting location as Reflections on the Bay in Bayville, NJ. Is that correct, sir?"

"You got it," he replied. "I will be there at 8 p.m."

"Thank you, sir. I will relay the confirmation. Have a nice evening."

Before he thought to ask the reporter's name, the caller hung up.

"OK, Nathan," he texted, deciding to forego an actual conversation. *"I'm up, showered, and almost dressed. No worries, pal. I got this. Leaving soon. Oh...and I'm always nice."*

Within a minute, the phone chimed back with a text reply. *"I'm not worried,"* said Nathan, *"Knock 'em dead with your charm!"*

London smiled. Another text buzzed him. *"Don't forget to text me when you're done."*

He entered his large walk-in closet and began pushing clothes from one side of the rack to the other. He picked a black blazer from its hanger, a white button-down shirt, and a pair of dark washed jeans from the shelf. Grabbing a pair of black dress shoes from the floor, he plucked a white handkerchief from the blazer's pocket and threw it aside.

When he was dressed, he paused to look at himself in the full length mirror. He ran his fingers through his now almost dry hair, letting the tousled look fall freely in whatever direction it chose. He felt good; confident. It was 6:30 p.m. Time to get on the road.

He grabbed his keys from a glass bowl on the hall table and took the elevator down to the garage. With a click of the remote, the doors to his SL Class Mercedes popped open and London took his seat behind the wheel.

As he exited the garage, he cracked open the driver's side window. The heavy fog of Manhattan would soon be replaced by the smog-free air of the suburbs. He looked forward to the crispness of the autumn evening in his lungs.

It wasn't often that he had the chance to make the hour-long drive alone through the Lincoln Tunnel into New Jersey. When he did travel these days, he was often accompanied by Nathan, a record company exec he barely knew, or a fellow musician. The travel time was a chance to do business. The car rarely gave him alone time to think, to breathe.

He chose an Urban Elements CD from his console and popped it into the BOSE sound system. The modern jazz relaxed him and helped him to focus. He began to run interview responses through his head, anticipating how he might answer some of the questions he'd be asked. How would he make his responses interesting? What could he say that would make him different from every other musician interviewed by SPIN? What should he NOT say?

Normally, these kinds of interviews were set up in a New York office or in a busy downtown café at lunchtime. He had even done interviews over the phone; a practice he was not fond of, since he couldn't see the reporter's reactions to his answers. He gave every moment of silence too much thought. But tonight's location outside the city was negotiated by Nathan.

"Guess what?" Nathan had said to London in the studio a week earlier.

"What?" he had replied in question, anticipating that the answer would not be one he wanted to hear. Nathan always made questions sound more interesting if he anticipated sharing information London would not like.

"SPIN magazine wants to feature you, man," Nathan had told him.

"Oh, yeah?" he had replied again in question, taking pause from his task. "No shit."

"Yeah...no shit, London. This is big...the biggest interview that's been requested."

"Well, it's not Rolling Stone," he had said, with a coy smile.

"Jesus, man, you're never fucking happy," Nathan chided.

"Never will be," London replied. "But that's got nothing to do with SPIN," he laughed.

Nathan stood silent.

"So when do they want me to squeeze in this interview?" London asked.

"Actually, they don't want to squeeze you in at all. In fact, they've asked us to book at least 90 minutes."

London, who had his back to Nathan, now turned to face him. "What the hell am I supposed to talk about for more than an hour?" he asked nervously.

Nathan could sense anxiety in London's voice. He knew it was rooted in London's insecurities; his feeling that if someone asked too many questions, they'd eventually stop liking him. "I'm sure it'll be fine. You'll just answer some questions, London. They're the ones who will be doing the work...moving things along."

"And I'm just supposed to go sit in some noisy bar with a clumsy reporter for all that time while they run through the routine questions?" London beckoned.

"Yeah, man. You are," Nathan replied more firmly. "Jesus, London, give me a break here, will ya? You're always on my ass about publicity this and publicity that. Now I'm giving you SPIN magazine...SPIN fucking magazine...and you're gonna complain because they want too much time?"

Nathan was the one who now turned his back. For so long, he and London had worked to get this kind of recognition.

The reality of it was hard for London to believe. "I'm sorry, Nate," he finally said. "Of course, I'm happy about the interview."

"Yeah, I know," Nathan replied, without his earlier enthusiasm. "London, they want to do a feature story. It's not the cover, but it is beyond the bullshit questions you've gotten used to answering. This is about you and your music. For real." Nathan now faced London and looked him squarely in the eye. "Don't answer the questions you don't want to answer," he said.

"Yeah...OK," London replied, a tone of worry still in his voice.

"OK?" Nathan questioned.

"Yeah...I said 'OK.' So, OK. Set it up," London replied.

Three days later, Nathan called London to tell him about the out-of-town location.

"So, the SPIN thing is all set up," he told London on the phone.

"Oh, yeah? Great. Where and when?" London asked.

"Reflections on the Bay. 8 p.m. Friday night," Nathan told him. "Someone from the magazine will call the day of to confirm."

"Reflections on the Bay?" London questioned with surprise. "In Bayville?"

"Yep. That's the one...the little place you like, right?...on the Barnegat Bay?" Nathan asked.

"Yeah...the little place I like for special occasions, Nate," London answered. "Special occasions like dates and birthdays. Special occasions like when I wanna get laid," London laughed.

"This is a special occasion, London!" Nathan answered, in a celebratory tone. "This interview is a special occasion...it's gonna be a huge success and everyone is gonna know who London Drake is, man. People are gonna be lining up to buy your next record. You're gonna be headlining in big cities. And we're gonna fuckin' celebrate!"

London's heart filled with love for Nathan. He had been with him for so many years, sharing the same dream. All that time, Nathan always believed the day would come when London's name would be mainstream. Some of that recognition had started with the small tour for the first record, but Nathan always saw London's potential for more. And he always found a way to make London believe it, too.

"Thanks, man," London replied, chasing back tears. "That's perfect."

THIRTY-TWO

London barely gripped the wheel of the Mercedes as he made his way through the city toward the Lincoln Tunnel. In no time, he was approaching Liberty Street and the site of Ground Zero. He glanced in his rearview mirror and saw no one behind him. A line of cars were stopped at a red light down the block. He had a few minutes to slow down in front of the site. He still found it so sad. Like the rest of the world, he had watched in horror as 3,000 people and so many of their rescue workers died. Now, the site was dedicated to honoring the lives of those who were lost. Spanning more than 15 acres, the standing memorial transformed a place of tragedy into one of hope for the future.

His thoughts soon turned to memories. His heart grew heavy as he recalled how he had both witnessed the tragedy of the World Trade Center and suffered his own personal loss in the same week. While it was now more than ten years later, the pain of that week ripped at him like a new wound. His car was now stopped in the center lane. He sat motionless, and could hear his father's voice.

"My son," his dad had said to him, in a memory that placed him in a hospital room. The recollection transported London back in time.

"Dad? Yes, Dad. It's me. I'm here," London replied, popping up from the hospital chair he had occupied for three days in Room 1510 of Holy Name Hospital. He took his father's hand.

"Son, I had the most terrible dream," his father said. "I dreamt the Twin Towers fell down." The sick man's eyes filled with tears. "Son, it was so, so terrible."

London turned his head to glance out the hospital window.

In the distance, in the shadow of the George Washington Bridge, was the site of the World Trade Center. Had he been paying closer attention to the view, he would have realized sooner that the window truly was one to the world. The towers were gone. A haze of dust rose from where they used to stand.

"Oh, Dad. I'm so sorry," London said, amazed that through his morphine-induced fog, his dad had actually heard some of the news on the TV in his room. London was sure that the medication prescribed after his dad's heart attack had prevented any disturbance to his rest.

"Dad," he continued. "It wasn't a dream, dad."

Together, the men began to cry as London shared what happened. London's mother entered the room and dropped a cup she had been holding. Coffee spilled down the front of her and coated the tile floor.

"Jesus Christ, Joseph. You're awake!" she exclaimed. Noticing the tears, she asked more sympathetically of her husband, "Are you in a lot of pain?"

She rushed to the bedside and took his hand. "Where's the nurse?" she asked London with worried eyes.

"Anna calm down," Joseph said to his wife. "I just woke up, dear. Getting caught up on what I missed," he said tenderly.

London's mother stood vigilant. "Why the tears, Joe? What's a matter?"

The man pushed through a hoarse voice and weak demeanor. "Nothing is forever, Anna. Shit falls down." He lifted an arm and pointed one finger toward the window. "As big as they are, as tough as we build them, as strong as the walls are...they all fall down."

"Joey, honey, what the hell are you talking about?" London's mother petitioned, not linking the recent world events.

London's cheeks were stained with tears. He couldn't help but wonder if his father was talking about the towers or his own failing health. Like the sturdy towers, his father now lay as a pile of rubble from a force much stronger than he. The heart attack had been destructive; parts of his heart no longer pumped any of his life force. Like the Trade Center, this mass of a man was helpless;

his death inevitable.

Beep! Beep!

The cars that were stopped at the light now caught up to London, who was still parked in the center lane.

"Move it, asshole!" one driver shouted as he swerved around.

London waved his hand in surrender and took his foot off the brake. "Fuck!" he said out loud, and turned the radio up louder to create a distraction.

Forty minutes later, he pulled into the parking lot of Reflections on the Bay. He glanced at the clock: 7:45. He paused to check his reflection in the rearview mirror and pulled into the valet parking.

"Good evening, sir," said the boy waiting to park his car.

"Hey, man," London replied, slipping the valet a $20 bill and flashing a smile. "Take good care of my girl."

He opened the double doors to the restaurant and entered, expecting that he'd find an eager reporter waiting for him at the bar. He was greeted by a hostess.

"Good evening, sir. Welcome to Reflections," she said, smiling at him.

"Hi..." he hesitated, reading a gold embossed name tag, "Renna."

"Do you have a reservation tonight?" she asked.

"I do," he replied, glancing around the corner into the bar. He noted that only two couples and an elderly gentleman, whom he guessed was not a SPIN reporter, were seated there. "But it appears the rest of my party if not here yet," he said, displeased.

"Would you like to be seated now, sir?" Renna asked.

"No," he replied. "I will be at the bar."

"Of course, sir," Renna replied, marking a note in her reservation book. She looked back up at him and stared. He looked familiar, but she wasn't sure why.

"Something wrong?" he asked her.

"Oh...no...," she replied, smiling.

London moved into the bar and was soon grateful for the time to have a drink and loosen up before the reporter arrived. The memory from the car had rattled him and he decided that the time to clear his head was a good thing. He didn't want any of that to come up in the interview. This was not about his personal life. It was about music and the record. He rarely spoke of personal memories; he saw no good in it.

"Dirty martini," he said to the brunette behind the bar, whose full lips were stained with a deep crimson lipstick. "Extra dirty, please," he said, flirtatiously. "Gin and three olives."

"You got it," she replied and turned to retrieve the bottle of Bombay. She had to reach a little higher than eye level and when she did, her short black skirt got even shorter. She had strong legs. He guessed she took a step or spinning class on a regular basis. He could see the outline of a tattoo on the top of her thigh. It looked like a Clef note.

"Nice tattoo," he commented, when she put the drink in front of him. Again, he smiled.

"Yeah...thanks," she replied, not returning the flirtation.

"What made you get a music note on your thigh?" he pushed.

"Oh, long story," she answered.

"Tell me the short version," he petitioned. "I got some time to kill."

The older man at the end of the bar gestured for a refill.

"Be back," she said to London. "Duty calls."

He sipped his martini slowly at first, but the smoothness of the gin and the coolness of the glass soon got the best of him and he swallowed more quickly. By the time the tattooed girl returned to share her story, his glass was almost empty.

"Wow. That was quick," she commented. "Another?"

"It's your fault for making it so perfectly," he answered. "So sure, I'll have another."

She smiled. This time, the gin bottle was on lower shelf. She had left it there, almost in anticipation that he'd be having more than one.

"Thank you," he said, as she placed the second glass.

"You're welcome," she replied, lingering in front of him.

"So, about that story....you gonna tell me or what?" he asked.

"It's not really that exciting," she replied. "Classic tale. Girl meets boy with guitar. Boy writes song. Girl falls in love and gets tattoo. Boy doesn't. The end."

"Tragic!" he exclaimed, a little too loudly; the alcohol was now dulling his senses.

"Shhhhh...." she whispered. "It's fine. Really. Fine."

"No," he replied. "Not your story!"

She paused, confused and looking for explanation.

"There are only two olives in my martini!" he joked, diverting her emotions from the story she had just shared. "I know I asked for three!"

"So you did," she replied. She reached across the bar to scoop a handful of olives from their pool of juice. With careless plops, she dropped them one at a time into his drink.

"Funny," he replied, taking a sip. "Funny...and delicious." He noticed her name tag: J. Savoca. "So what's the 'J' stand for?" he asked playfully.

"If I wanted people to know that, I would have put it on the tag," she replied, in equal jest. My friends call me Savoca, so why don't you just use that?"

"Well, it's nice to meet you, Savoca," he replied playfully. He had forgotten that the whole reason he was in the bar was for the SPIN interview. "Like the martini story, you, too, are funny. And I bet you are delicious as well."

The girl's face turned pink, but her eyes lit up with a fire he had seen many times before. His cell phone rang. "Excuse me," he said, retrieving the phone from his pocket.

He glanced at the caller ID and saw that it was Nathan, a reminder of why he was out. He also noticed the time: 8:15. The reporter was now late.

"I'm glad you bugged me about being on time, man," he barked at Nathan. "I'm still sitting here waiting."

Savoca turned her attention to other customers.

"Hey, London," Nathan answered. "I just talked to a woman at SPIN. Their reporter got lost or some shit like that, but she's on her way. Hang tight, OK? She should be there within the next 20 minutes."

"Yeah, fine," London replied. "I'll try to keep myself occupied."

Nathan knew what London meant. "Don't get shitfaced, London," he commanded in a stern tone.

"OK, Dad," London replied sarcastically. "I'll try and hold it together. Scout's honor."

"You're no fucking Boy Scout, London," Nathan said. "Jesus. I knew I should have gone with you."

"Nathan, I'm fine," London reassured him. "I'm just sitting here talking to Ms. Savoca and we're doing OK." He winked across the bar at the woman, who was now holding the bottle of gin and pointing to his again empty glass. "I'm mint, man. Like you said, I'll nail the interview and it'll be great. I'm just celebrating in advance."

Nathan breathed heavily into the phone.

"Please stop worrying, Nate," London begged. "Really, I'm fine. I'm relaxed and I'm in a good mood."

"OK," Nathan said with reservation. "Call me when you're done with the interview."

THIRTY-THREE

If she hadn't forgotten her recorder on the kitchen counter of Lucy's apartment, Katorah Alexander would have been perfectly punctual – even early – for her interview with London Drake. Instead, she had already made her way through New York and was almost on the ramp to the Lincoln Tunnel when she realized her omission.

"Shit!" she exclaimed, making an illegal U-turn. She fumbled in her purse to retrieve her cell phone.

"You can't be there already," exclaimed her sister on the other end of the call.

"No, not there, not even close," said Katorah. "I forgot my freaking recorder. Can you look to see if it's on your kitchen counter?"

"Hold...on...lemme see. Yep, here it is," said Lucy.

"Shit!" Katorah repeated. "I'm coming back to get it."

"Coming back?" Lucy questioned. "Won't that make you terribly late? Is it worth it?"

"It's a feature interview, Lucy. I'll do much better if I have it," Katorah said. "Besides, these rock star kinds of guys are never on time."

The recorder retrieval added 30 minutes to Katorah's commute time. Although Lucy met her downstairs so that she barely had to stop the car, she did have to circle back 15 minutes.

"Thanks, sis," she said to Lucy through the open passenger's side window.

"No problem, Kat," said her sister. "Be careful. Knock 'em dead."

As she pulled into the restaurant's parking lot, Katorah picked the closest spot she could find and quickly jerked the keys out of the ignition.

He fingers slipped from the key ring and the keys dropped to the floor. She reached around, unable to see because her interior light had blown out just two days before. The red Mitsubishi Eclipse was fancy to her when she'd bought it new in 2003 – her first new car purchase – but now was showing signs of needing replacement. She hoped the SPIN magazine job would lead to the kinds of promotions and salary that would afford her something new.

Katorah retrieved her keys and stood upright next to her car. She tugged on her black skirt so that it was once again positioned right above her knee. She walked up the cut flagstone path and into Reflections on the Bay.

"Good evening," said Renna, the hostess who had greeted London 40 minutes earlier.

"Hello," said Katorah, as she glanced around the lobby and into the bar. "I'm meeting someone here...," she told the greeter. Her eyes darted from side to side. "A man...dark hair...."

"Ah, yes," Renna said. "I believe he is in the bar area," she said, turning her attention to the ringing telephone behind her.

Katorah peeked into the space. It was more crowded now than when London first arrived. She paused, waiting for the hostess to be available again. "Dumb question, I know, but can you be more specific? I've never met him in person before."

Renna peered again into the bar area. "He's at the end of the bar. Black jacket and jeans," she told Katorah. "The man talking to the bartender."

"Great. Thanks," Katorah said.

When she turned the corner into the bar, Katorah saw the man Renna had described. He indeed was seated at the bar and was engaged in a conversation she felt uncomfortable interrupting. The two looked to be having quite a good time. She hoped he hadn't even realized her tardiness. "Excuse me, Mr. Drake?" she quietly questioned. "Mr. Drake?" she said louder, tapping him on the shoulder.

London's eyes moved to the mirror on the wall opposite him so that he could see Katorah's reflection behind him.

Renna moved to the opposite end of the bar.

He turned on his stool to face the reporter. "Hello, sweetheart," he said, mistaking her for a fan.

"Mr. Drake," Katorah began and then paused as his eyes met hers. She recognized him. He was the man from the elevator...the one who helped pick up her belongings when she dropped her purse to the floor. She was embarrassed.

"Can I help you?" London asked charmingly, mistaking her light blush with the glow of excitement.

She stood speechless. *He doesn't remember me*, she thought to herself. *Oh thank God.*

"Mr. Drake, I'm Katorah Alexander from SPIN magazine."

"Oh!" London exclaimed. "Glad you made it in one piece."

Shit, she thought. *He noticed that I was late.*

"Let me just cash out here and we'll get our table," London said to her. "I'm starving."

"I apologize for my lateness," she said. "I came in from the city and there was an accident near the tunnel."

"An accident?" London questioned, calling her bluff. "Lucky me. I came that way too. Must have just missed it," he said and cocked his lips into a crooked smile.

While he intended to reprimand the reporter's lateness, London found himself drawn to Katorah's striking chocolate eyes and warm, olive skin. Her dark hair was pulled back into a loose bun, a single hair stick seemingly holding it in place. There was something familiar about her that he just couldn't place. He had no desire to be mean to her, or even arrogant.

"Can I cash out, please?" he called to Savoca, sliding an American Express Platinum card across the bar. When he took his receipt, he noticed that the bartender had written her phone number at the bottom, with a note that said "Call me sometime." She also drew a little smiley face.

"OK, let's get started, shall we?" he asked Katorah and then moved quickly to the hostess station. "My date and I are ready to be seated," he told the hostess.

Date? Katorah thought, not sure why he would say such a thing.

As they were escorted to their table, Katorah did not miss any of the restaurant's beauty. The rich mahogany woodwork was offset perfectly by the crisp antique white table linens. A wall of windows revealed a view of the bay, lit up with trees and walkways that seemed to call one to venture outside. It certainly was a different setting than the ones in which most interviews took place. She wasn't sure SPIN would appreciate the charge a place like this would impose on her credit card. But, knowing they approved it in advance, Katorah decided to enjoy the ambiance. It wasn't often she dined in places like this.

The table reserved for them was in the far corner of the restaurant in front of a bay side window. The sun had just set on the Northeast Inlet and the horizon was still lit in hues of pink and orange. Katorah paused and took in the beauty.

"Lovely view, isn't it?" London asked.

"It is," she answered, and then quickly remembered why she was there.

"So, Mr. Drake, I'd like to record our conversation if that's OK with you," Katorah said, retrieving her forgotten recorder from a small black bag.

"Only OK if you call me London," he replied. "No need to be so formal."

Katorah again noted the slight slur in his voice. "You're not drunk, are you?" she asked.

"Drunk?" London replied. "Hell, no. Just a little lubricated," he replied flirtatiously. "You should have a drink and catch up," he said, smiling coyly.

"Mr. Drake..." she began.

He interrupted. "London. Call me London."

"OK...London..., as you know this interview is for a feature story in SPIN magazine. If you think it would be better to reschedule, we can do that," Katorah said in a firm tone.

London picked up his napkin, unfolded it, and placed it intentionally in his lap. "Ms. Alexander, I have already spent an hour driving out here, and at least 30 minutes waiting for you. I think we should do the work we both came here to do. And its fine for you to record our conversation...if that will make your job easier."

Katorah paused, turning her face to again look out on the water.

The twinge of familiarity London felt when the reporter first greeted him grew stronger. There was something about her mouth and the way her lips quivered when she spoke...like she could laugh or cry at any minute... that made London believe they had met in some other venue. He couldn't place it. "Are you familiar with my music?" he asked her. "Have we ever met backstage before a concert?"

Katorah ignored the first part of the question, hesitant to admit that she had only first listened to his CD a few days before the interview. "Backstage?" Katorah asked. "No. I haven't yet had the pleasure of seeing you perform," she said smiling.

"Because you look..." London began.

The short conversation was quickly interrupted by a waiter who greeted them. "Welcome to Reflections on the Bay," the waiter said. "My name is Benjamin and I will be your server for this evening. May I start you with a drink?"

London deferred to Katorah.

"A glass of Sauvignon Blanc, please," she said.

"Oh, we have a wonderful 2008 Sauvignon Blanc from Wairau Valley Vineyards in Marlborough, New Zealand," Benjamin offered. "Many of our wine customers love the crisp, elegant, and fresh taste of this particular vineyard."

Katorah smiled, almost giggling at the waiter's enthusiasm. "Well then, how could I refuse such a recommendation?" she asked. "Sounds wonderful to me, Benjamin."

Benjamin nodded and turned to London. "And for the gentleman?" he asked.

"The gentleman will be having the unsweetened iced tea, please," London answered.

"Very well," Benjamin replied and disappeared to retrieve the drinks.

"I thought I'd give you some time to catch up," London joked. "I'm sorry if it seemed I had a few too many before you got here. I got lost in conversation at the bar. I really am very excited to be interviewing with you and SPIN magazine."

London could hear Nathan's voice in his head. "Play nice," Nathan would say. London figured this was what he meant.

"Well, then," Katorah replied, "shall we get started?"

"Of course," London answered, thinking that he'd much rather this be a social event than work.

"And if you're good, maybe you can graduate to wine with dinner," Katorah said, trying to return the kindness London had just displayed. She smiled warmly at London for the first time. Raising the glass that Benjamin had placed on the table in front of her, Katorah toasted. "Che notte questa è bella," she said.

"I agree," said London. "This is a very beautiful night."

Katorah smiled again, surprised that he had understood her Italian.

"Wow! I didn't figure you for Italian," London remarked. "Your name is very unique...didn't really know what to make of it," he joked.

"Actually, my mom is Italian, and my dad is Greek," Katorah replied. "Put them together in a blender, add a little sarcasm, throw in a zest for writing, and here I am," she said, laughing.

Katorah pressed the button on her recorder, motioning that she was ready to work.

Had she not, London would have said what was on his mind: *Your Mom is Italian and your Dad is Greek. Put them together and you get... breathtaking.*

THIRTY-FOUR

"So, London, let me start by saying that I really did enjoy the tracks off the new record. How did you come up with the name of the album?"

Silence.

"London?" Katorah questioned. "Are you still with me?"

"So sorry," he replied, motioning toward the view. "I got lost in the ocean out there." He stared at the reporter, thinking that any view would be beautiful with her in it. Something familiar about her nagged at him. He just could not place it. He refocused and answered her question. "Longing for Monday is a line from a track on the record."

"Of course," Katorah replied, as if she remembered.

"That song is about my first great one," he chuckled.

"I'm sorry. You're first great one?"

"Yeah," he replied. "Like in *A Bronx Tale.* Have you seen it?" Without letting her answer, he continued. "You get three great women in your life. She was my first."

Katorah nodded, her full attention on London.

"I remember going to bed late the night before," he told her. "We had made love for hours...love making that was filled with a sense of urgency," he said. "In all reality, we were making love for the last time. The next morning I woke up and she was gone."

Katorah interjected, "Let me guess...that was a Tuesday?"

He smirked and quoted a line from a hit song on his record. "Now I long for Monday, because Tuesday means you're gone."

Katorah was filled with questions. "Did you go after her? Did you hear from her again? Has she ever shown up at a concert?"

His blood pressure rose. Light beads of sweat formed on his brow. She sounded like a giddy school girl gossiping with her girlfriends. Her hunger for so much information all at once was uncomfortable for him.

"Simmer down there, lady," he pleaded. "One question at a time."

He looked for Benjamin to bring him a drink. These questions were personal; they'd make him revisit feelings he had buried years ago. He looked around the room and finally drew the waiter's attention. He ordered his fourth martini of the evening.

"I thought you were going to slow down on the drinking?" Katorah asked, as Benjamin walked away from the table.

Not happy with the accusatory tone of the question, he snapped back at her. "If the interview is going to continue like this, the drinks will need to keep coming," he quipped.

"Continue like what?" Katorah asked. "My questions are appropriately based around your music."

"Yeah, how about asking me how long I have been singing? Or who my influences are? Or shit like that," he beckoned.

"Mr. Drake," Katorah began.

He interjected. "Don't call me that. Please," he said, "Call me London."

Benjamin interrupted just long enough to place the martini glass on the table. Without hesitation, London lifted the full glass to his lips and gulped. In no time, his glass was more than two-thirds empty.

"London," Katorah continued, "the questions you want me to ask have been asked a thousand times. Don't you want your fans to see a deeper side of London Drake?"

He sat with his head down. He was motionless. Then, lifting his eyes to meet hers, he answered calmly. "I love my fans, Ms. Alexander. I am thankful for them every day. But trust me. They don't want the truth. Fiction is what they want...the life of a rock star...the glamour, the larger than life experiences. All of that makes them want to love me. That story is an easier pill to swallow than the truth. If they knew the things that really make me tick...the things that make me a man, just a regular human being trying to figure out who the hell he is...they'd be bored, or terrified, or outraged. People don't want real life. They're looking for drama and bullshit."

"I happen to think you're wrong, Mister...London," Katorah replied.

Her comments caused a boiling in his stomach. He wasn't even sure where the rage was coming from. He guessed that it was a combination of his own insecurities and the alcohol, but it launched out of him. "You do, do you?" he asked. "Trust me. My fans wouldn't understand the shit. Hell, I don't even understand it. I can't ask them to love me if I don't give them what they need. And I sure as hell don't want them feeling sorry for me."

Katorah sat confused. She hadn't read anything about London Drake in her research to prepare her for such darkness in his spirit.

"You know what?" he finally said. "Fuck this. Fuck this interview. You can't come here, acting like you want to know me and then pushing for the intimate details. You want to write a story? Write it about the music. Write it about the concerts. Write it about any bullshit thing. But don't expect me to just open up a dark closet to you and invite you to have a dress up. It doesn't work that way."

"London, I don't appreciate your tone," Katorah replied. "I am a good reporter. I do my research. And I work hard to tell a story. It's not about bullshit for me."

"Really? You do your research?" he asked. "Do you think my real name is London? Who the hell is born with a name like that?"

He was being mean and disrespectful. Katorah was fighting back tears. She had wanted this to go so well. Determined not to cry she answered. "You are a dichotomy...mister-whatever-the-hell-your-name-is. You say you don't want me to pry, but then you expect me to know the intimate details. Make up your mind, Mr. Drake."

Suddenly, he realized that their two voices had drawn the attention of the other diners. He lowered his voice to a more reasonable level. "Excuse me, Miss Alexander. This interview is over."

He rose from the table, calmly placed his napkin on the chair, and moved toward the rest room.

THIRTY-FIVE

Inside the men's room, London stared at his reflection in the mirror. What had just happened? Why did he get so upset? He bent over the sink and splashed cool water on his face. He definitely had drunk too much. His head was spinning.

When the frustration inside of him subsided, he was overcome with feelings of embarrassment and regret. Why had he been so abrasive with such a beautiful woman...a woman who had only been trying to do her job? He decided that an apology was in order.

Exiting the rest room, he made his way back through the bar toward the dining room. He could see that Katorah was still seated at the table. He was relieved.

"Katorah," he said, standing over her at the table. "I am very sorry for the way I reacted to your questions. I obviously had too much to drink this evening, and I really don't even know what to say."

She stared up at him, her black eyes sparking in the candlelight.

God, she is beautiful, he thought. "I hope you will accept my apology," he said, retrieving his wallet from a back pocket and signaling for the waiter.

Benjamin approached the table. "Can I help you sir?" he asked. London handed him a roll of cash; more than the bill even warranted. "Keep the change," he said to the waiter. Then he turned toward Katorah. "Again, I apologize, Ms. Alexander," London said.

Katorah didn't know what to say. She sat silent at the table, sipping her glass of wine; the same glass she ordered when she was first seated.

Turning to leave, he smiled coyly at her. "Thank you for an interesting evening," he said and then vanished toward the front door.

Katorah reached across the table and with shaky hands clicked the stop button on her recorder. She could not believe the conversation she had just captured on tape.

THIRTY-SIX

Katorah sat quietly at the table and sipped one more glass of wine. Her nerves were a wreck. She felt disappointed and sad, wondering how she might have conducted the interview differently. As it was, she had no story. The topic would certainly be assigned to a different reporter and she wondered what that would mean for her new career in the city. When she could no longer stand the insecurities eating away at her, she retrieved her coat and made her way out to the car.

A turn of the ignition blasted the voice of London Drake at her. The CD she had been listening to in preparation for her meeting was still in the player. *My reality runs faster than I do*...she heard him sing.

"Fantastic," she said out loud, pushing the eject button in frustration. "My reality sucks pretty badly at the moment too."

When the disc was in her fingertips, she paused to wonder about the man she had just met. Holding the CD up so that it caught the light from the parking lot, she wondered if London Drake was really as complex as he seemed. Or, was his character really just as thin as the CD she held?

Twenty miles away, London was regretting that he had not gotten a driver for his trip to the restaurant. His head throbbed. He struggled to understand why he had grown so intolerant of the reporter and her questions. Why did she seem so familiar to him? Why couldn't he place it? He was sure they had met before. Did his inability to make that connection make him unable to trust her? He acknowledged that she had really done nothing wrong. Besides being late, she was professional. But she did not respond to his charm tactics the way other women usually did. Was that what bothered him? Had he grown so upset because he knew she would see through the bullshit lines he usually fed? Whatever it was, he could not stop thinking about Katorah Alexander.

He spun his car recklessly around one curve after another. His cell phone rang, adding to his frustration. It was Nathan. Deciding to avoid the predicted reaction, he ignored the call and let it go to voicemail. He hoped the passage of the night would calm emotions. Of course, he also knew that ignoring problems never made them go away; that was a real and persistent message in his life.

When morning did come, Katorah was on the phone with her editor first thing. She listened to the Muzak play on the line as she waited for Colleen Louis to pick up her call. It was only 8:30 a.m., but Katorah hoped the editor had already had at least one cup of coffee.

"Hi, Kat. You're calling early. Whatcha got for me?" were the first words she heard.

"Good morning, Colleen," Katorah replied, more optimistically than she felt. "Colleen, I'm sorry, but things didn't go quite the way I had expected last night. I think Mr. Drake was not having the best of days."

A hush came over the line.

"Katorah, did we get the interview or not?" Colleen asked in her no-nonsense kind of way.

"I didn't get what I need to write a story," Katorah replied. "I'm sorry."

"What the hell does that mean?" Colleen asked, now annoyed that she had to fish for information.

"I don't know, Colleen," said Katorah. "The interview just didn't flow right. I was late and..."

Katorah paused. Why was she taking the blame for what had happened? Why didn't she just let Colleen listen to the recording?

"Jesus, Katorah. We're holding space for this story."

Katorah sighed into the phone. She didn't know what else to say.

"Get your ass in here, Katorah," Colleen finally said. "And bring what you got. We'll call his agent and figure it out."

Before Katorah could respond, Colleen hung up.

THIRTY-SEVEN

When Lucy emerged from her bedroom, Katorah was already dressed and gulping a cup of coffee.

"Wow, you wanna take a breath between swallows there, Champ?" Lucy cautioned.

Katorah lowered the mug from her face. "Gotta get moving," she told her sister. "I just talked to my editor about last night. My ass is on the line."

"Yeah..."Lucy started hesitantly. "I heard you come in last night. You were much earlier than I thought you'd be. Was Mr. Drake a shallow excuse for a rock star?" Lucy chuckled at herself. Katorah's deep exhale prompted her to think the amusement was not shared. "What happened?" she questioned.

"Well, I'm pretty sure I blew it with the London Drake story," Katorah replied. "Let's just say that if I get fired today, I won't be surprised."

"Fired?!" Lucy exclaimed. "For what?"

"Last night was a disaster," Katorah replied. "At the very least – and I mean the very least – it will be ages before I'm offered a feature story again."

Knowing that her sister was a talented writer, Lucy grew confused. Before she could ask any more questions, Katorah began spilling her anxiety all over the kitchen table.

"I'm not even sure what happened, Lucy," Katorah said. "He was half in the bag when I got there, sitting at the bar flirting with some bartender."

"And?" Lucy asked tenderly.

"And we got a table." Katorah hesitated, remembering an odd detail. "But he started the whole thing off in a really weird way, Lucy," she said. "He told the maître d' that I was his date."

"Date?" Lucy asked. "Why would he do that?"

"I don't know. I found it odd. Almost like he was nervous about being at an interview from the start." Katorah stood quiet, reflecting.

"Then what?" Lucy asked.

"We sat at a table – a really nice table," Katorah told her, a slight smile on her lips. "He was charming...apologized for the drinks he had...made some small talk. I ordered a glass of wine. We toasted...he speaks some Italian."

Again Katorah paused. She hadn't realized the night before how London had danced around the start of the interview. Now, in retrospect, she wondered why he had been so slow to attend to the business of the evening. If she hadn't been so focused, Katorah wondered if the evening would have turned into more of a social outing than an interview.

"And?" Lucy pushed again.

"And then I pulled out my recorder and asked if we could get started."

"Well, all that sounds just fine to me," Lucy protested. "Can't see why you'd get fired for having a glass of wine, for Christ's sake."

"Oh, it's not about the wine, Lucy," Katorah rebutted. "I did fine up to that point."

"OK?" Lucy pushed.

"I don't know what to tell you," Katorah said with frustration. "I started to talk about the title track of the album...to ask him some questions. He seemed OK at first. But then, all of a sudden, it was like I asked him to give me a kidney or something. He totally clammed up and got defensive. I can't identify what I might have said to trigger his response."

"His response?" Lucy asked, trying to understand.

"Yeah," Katorah continued. "He got really upset with me. Started yelling at me..."

"Yelling at you?" Lucy asked, now annoyed that her sister had been treated that way.

"Well, more acting like I had pried about something very personal," Katorah said. "But we were talking about the album and the lyrics. He seemed open to the conversation. I mean, I'm writing a story about where his inspiration comes from, right?" Katorah asked, looking for affirmation that she had acted appropriately.

"I wasn't there, Kat," Lucy replied. "But it doesn't sound to me like you did anything wrong."

Katorah was getting visibly upset. "I know, Lucy. I just don't get it. He went off on this rampage about how I should have been asking him about his musical influences and when he first picked up a guitar. That's not feature story information, right? I mean, I do things outside the norm."

"You're the one with the writing experience, Kat," Lucy replied, hoping that would ease her sister's mind. "I think you know what makes for a good story. Personally, I think a story about what makes someone tick is a hell of a lot more interesting than knowing that they got laid the first time to Iron Maiden or some shit like that."

"That's what I thought, too," Katorah replied. "I even tried explaining that to him. But then he went off about how if his fans really knew who he was they probably wouldn't even like him anymore...that they'd feel sorry for him."

"Oh, give me a fucking break," Lucy replied, a touch of anger now in her voice. She felt protective of her sister all of a sudden. "Doesn't he think people are smart enough to know that the glossy photo on the magazine cover is all airbrushed? We all have our faults, Kat. If you lose a job over some arrogant asshole who thinks he's better than everybody else, then fuck it."

Katorah paused. With melancholy in her voice she replied to her sister. "But that's just it, Lucy. I don't think he thinks he's better than anyone. In fact, it almost seemed to me that he's in over his head pretending to be somebody he's not. That must be a very lonely place to be."

"Really?" Lucy asked. "Now you're defending him?"

"No," Katorah said hesitantly, remembering the warmth of London's smile.

"Then what?" Lucy questioned.

"I don't know. You'd have to listen to him," Katorah answered, trying to sort the ideas in her head.

"Listen to him?" Lucy asked. "Did you get all this on tape?"

Katorah stared at her sister; the answer evident. "I gotta get outta here to see my editor," she said before Lucy could ask to listen to the previous night's exchange. "She's pissed and I need this job."

Lucy moved toward her sister to hug her. "Be firm with your boss, Kat," she coached. "You were doing your job. You can't control a loose cannon. Play her the recording."

THIRTY-EIGHT

Within 30 minutes, Katorah was in the SPIN building. She scurried toward the elevator, pressed the button for the 7th floor, and began planning her own defense.

When the elevator doors opened, she proceeded through the double glass doors to greet the receptionist. "Hey Lisa, how's it going?" she asked.

"I'm glad I'm not you today," the girl responded. "Colleen's got a period with your name all over it."

The butterflies in Katorah's stomach moved from a light flutter to full blown rumba dancing. She exhaled deeply and moved down the hall to the editor's office.

Colleen was on the phone; her door was open.

Katorah stood just outside the threshold and waited to be acknowledged.

Colleen waved her in and motioned for her to take a seat while she finished a phone call. "I'll be in touch," she finally said to her caller and hung up without saying goodbye.

"Col..." Katorah began.

"No, no, no, Katorah," Colleen interrupted, raising her hand to Katorah's face. "I don't wanna hear it. I've heard enough this morning to last me all day."

"But Colleen, I don't know what I did wrong," Katorah interjected.

"You? What you did wrong?" Colleen asked, laughing under her breath.

"I know this was a big chance for me," Katorah continued. "I know it didn't go as well as we both would have liked."

"You're damn right it didn't go the way we planned," Colleen answered. "But Jesus, Katorah, Mr. Drake sounds like quite the handful."

For the first time that morning, Katorah relaxed. "You know what happened?" she asked her boss.

"Well, not exactly, but I think I have a good idea. Based on what I've heard so far, the picture is getting pretty clear."

Katorah sat silent; confused.

"It seems Mr. Drake not only has a temper and a drinking problem, but he also has a conscience," Colleen said.

"I don't understand," Katorah replied.

Colleen again picked up the phone receiver and held up one finger on the other hand to Katorah. This time, she enabled the speaker and Katorah could hear her dialing into voicemail. Proceeding through a series of prompts, Colleen finally reached the message she wanted to share.

Katorah immediately recognized the voice of London Drake.

"Good Morning, Ms. Louis. This is London Drake. I'm calling with an apology to your magazine...(pause)...and more specifically to Ms. Alexander. I fear that I was out of line during last night's interview... (pause)...I probably drank too much.... (pause)...and I got angry for no good reason...(pause)...and I might have compromised Ms. Alexander's ability to do her job."

Katorah's mouth dropped open. She sat quiet, listening to his voice.

On the recording, London chuckled with what Katorah interpreted as embarrassment. "I am honored that SPIN wants to feature me and hope that we can reschedule the interview at a time convenient for you in the near future," he continued. "Please do share my apology with Ms. Alexander... (pause)...I look forward to hearing from you."

Click.

Silence filled the room.

Katorah watched Colleen intently, unable to believe the apology she'd just heard. She carefully tucked her own recorder back into the bag at her feet.

"Isn't that something?" Colleen asked.

"Something," Katorah replied, still surprised.

"Of course, I immediately called Drake's agent. He was just as apologetic."

Katorah sat staring, trying not to let her mouth drop open in disbelief.

"I'm going to assign Peter to the story, Katorah. Maybe Mr. Drake needs the influence of a man across the table. And we really can't waste any more time getting this story."

Colleen lowered her eyes to some papers on her desk.

"Peter?" Katorah objected. "This is my story, Colleen."

"Katorah, I appreciate your initiative on wanting to finish this article and I hope you know that I have a lot of faith in you as a writer. But the truth is that you are new here, and these entertainers always like to take advantage of the new writers. Let Peter handle Mr. Drake."

Katorah stood from her chair in protest. "Believe me, Colleen, I will handle London Drake!"

Colleen motioned for to Katorah to sit back down. "Your story, huh?" she replied, impressed by Katorah's gumption.

"Yes, Colleen," Katorah replied, remembering Lucy's advice to be firm.

"Well then I guess you better go get it. Deadline is still Friday," Colleen declared.

Katorah stood and turned to leave her editor's office. Just as she got to the doorway, Colleen reinforced her earlier statement. "I want that article on my desk first thing Friday morning." Then, almost waving her hand in the air, she said, "Go. Handle it."

THIRTY-NINE

London was startled to alertness by the incessant banging on his front door. His intercom had been going off minutes earlier to announce a guest, but when London failed to answer, the visitor had obviously proceeded upstairs on their own.

Bang...Bang...Bang...Bang!

"Alright," London hollered from the bedroom.

Bang...Bang...

"I'm coming," he hollered again, wrapping a robe around his naked body.

London stumbled to the front door and turned the dead bolt counter clockwise. Nathan burst in just as the door opened, not waiting for an invitation.

Oh, shit," said London half under his breath.

"Oh, shit! Oh, shit? That's all you have to say to me? I called you twice last night and half a dozen times this morning," Nathan exclaimed. "I get you an interview – a big deal, grown-up kind of interview – and you screw it up. You know I hate being blindsided, London. I think you need to muster more than an 'oh shit.' You have got to be kidding me, kid."

London stood silent. What could he say? "She was late, man—," he began.

Nathan interrupted. "Shut up, London. I think you said enough last night."

London began to wonder exactly what he heard.

"I just got off the phone with the SPIN editor, man. She called me, trying to make sense of the message you left for her....you know, the one about you getting drunk and angry. What do you think all that looked like to the reporter?"

London raised his hand like a child at school waiting for his turn to speak.

"Really?" Nathan asked. "You really wanna say something to me now? I don't want you to say a fuckin' word, London. Jesus Christ."

London stood silent.

Nathan paced back and forth in front of the living room windows.

A few minutes passed and Nathan exhaled, hard and deep, as if he were expelling a fly from his lungs.

"I'm sorry, man," London finally said. "I know I fucked it up. And I did call and apologize...I said I was sorry. What else can I do? I guess there isn't really anything else to say."

Nathan turned. His face had softened from the chiseled anger it held when he first arrived. "Oh, you have plenty to say, London," he said. "And you're gonna say it. The world is gonna read every word you have to say, you hear me?"

London looked confused.

"Believe it or not, they still want to do the interview. I don't know why, but for the grace of God, they do."

London started to protest, then quickly grew quiet.

Nathan continued. "So, you're gonna do that interview and you're gonna do it right this time. You will answer every god damned question they throw at you and you'll be gracious and cooperative."

"Nate, don't you think you could be a little easier on me?" London asked.

"This is easy, London," Nathan said. "I don't know why, but SPIN is interested in giving you a second chance. We don't get many of them. Don't blow it."

London sat on the edge of the leather sofa and lifted his hands to his head. He bowed his face in surrender.

"I just have to say one more thing to you, kid, and then I'm leaving," Nathan said. "When I walked into that club all those years ago and saw you and Jon playing, I knew you had it in you to be star. I have put myself on the line for you and your temper time and time again and I just can't do it anymore. I don't have the strength to fight your demons. You have to do that. Let them go, London....before they destroy you."

Nathan paused. He moved toward London as if he were going to offer a hug, but then walked toward the door. He turned back to London once again. "I can't continue to watch you fall down, London. I believe in you and your talent. I'd like to think that part of my mission on this earth is to help you touch the world with your music. And I think I have always treated you like you were my own kid. But damn it, London, I'm struggling at the moment to like you."

London looked at him, a pain across his face.

"Don't get me wrong, kid. I love you...I always will. But like you? Not so much at the moment."

"What can I do, Nate?" London asked. "I'm really, really sorry."

"Make this right, London. Do what you need to do." Nathan buttoned his coat and left London alone in the apartment.

In the silence, London broke down in tears, his heart broken for having disappointed someone who had always gone the distance for him.

FORTY

Katorah set a coffee cup on the table and clicked a button to pause the recorder she had been using to capture their conversation. Her eyes were fixed on London's in a noticeable moment of silence.

Unlike their first meeting, London was polite and helpful. He answered all of her questions...some more vaguely than Katorah liked, but she didn't push too hard. She focused on the messages in London's music and avoided questions about past relationships. That seemed to work. The two also met over coffee in the middle of the afternoon. *Why mix in alcohol?* Katorah figured.

"I think I have all I need to write a really great article about you," Katorah said after a 45-minute interview. She smiled and London held her gaze, returning it with a smile of his own.

Two weeks later, London's face was inside SPIN magazine. London himself paused at a curb side magazine stand at the corner of Broadway and 33rd to read a tagline on the magazine cover: HAVE YOU MET LONDON DRAKE? BE WARNED. HE'S NOT THE SIMPLE BOY NEXT DOOR.

Thumbing through the magazine, London found the four pages dedicated to him. He first noticed the photos which had been taken by a SPIN photographer after his interview with Katorah. Some were printed in black and white. The feature photo was full page, full color.

London's eyes shifted to the opening paragraph:

"If you haven't yet heard of London Drake, his new CD is not something you should miss. An unabashed ode to his own life experiences – both good and bad – the listener walks away with not only an appreciation of Drake's

musical talent, but also feeling like they just spent 45 minutes engaged in an intimate conversation with Drake himself. His messages are poignant and applicable to the life we all live."

London smiled and continued to read. He read the entire article once and then went back to read the closing paragraph again:

"Seemingly a person who gets everything he wants, Drake is more just the boy next door whose song writing offers something for every kind of music lover. His life experience gives him dimension that is so often missing in modern music and so tangibly connects him with the listener."

London was pleased. Katorah's story captured everything he would want the reader to know about him...his influences, his inspirations, and his hopes for the record.

When London turned to pay the clerk for the magazine, he noticed that while he had been busy reading, a woman next to him had been busy checking out something else: him. Wearing a skirt too short to begin covering her long legs, the woman playfully lowered her face away from London's eyes and used one long finger to push the glasses she wore further up on her face. Her eyes darted back up at London and she smiled.

London's eyes moved away from her for just a moment to notice the flower cart on the street just behind her. He returned her stare and smiled at her.

Twenty minutes later and fifteen blocks away, Katorah stood on the 7th floor talking to Colleen and waiting for an elevator. Just as the elevator chimed its arrival, Katorah's phone rang.

Colleen quickly used the interruption as segue to her next meeting. "Go ahead and take that," she told Katorah. "Have a good weekend...Don't forget the article due Monday," she reminded and disappeared behind a mahogany office door.

The elevator doors opened just as Katorah answered the call.

"Katorah Alex..."

Inside a now moving elevator, the call dropped. It had not been a number she recognized, but figured if it was important the person would call back.

When the elevator door opened in the lobby, Katorah pushed by a flurry of people eager to occupy the space from which she was trying to escape.

When she was finally free of the crowd and able to focus on moving ahead, she stopped in a startle. Before her, in the middle of the elevator bank, was London. He held the most beautiful sunflowers she had ever seen.

"Do you make it a point to hang up on every guy who brings you flowers?" he asked teasingly.

"London," she replied in surprise. "What are you doing here?"

"I came to see you, Ms. Alexander. I wondered if you were free."

"Now?" Katorah asked in a tone she didn't mean.

"Right now," London replied firmly, nodding his head once in affirmation and then smiling. "How about you and I go for a walk and maybe have some dinner...no recorders allowed?"

"Now?" Katorah repeated, almost unable to believe that he stood there with flowers, asking her out on what appeared to be a date.

London chuckled. "Well, unless you have somewhere else you need to be."

Katorah smiled back. Her eyes darted from one side of the lobby to the other and then back to London. She tried not to reveal that she had been thinking about him since they last saw each other. She wondered what he had thought of the article, what he had really thought of her.

"Somewhere else?" she asked out loud, but mostly to herself. "No, London," she finally said. "I don't have anywhere else to be right now. I would love to walk with you."

"Perfect!" London replied and exchanged the flowers he was holding with the heavy attaché case Katorah had slung over her shoulder.

"Why, Mr. Drake," she commented, "I see chivalry is alive and well."

"Sometimes, Ms. Alexander, all you have to do is give a man a chance to be a gentleman," he said with a wink.

Katorah followed London's direction on the street, never even questioning his route. The two walked at a stroll's pace, with no expressed rush to reach whatever destination – if any – he had in mind. Wandering down 3rd street, they approached the Village, deep in conversation.

"So, London, what made you move to New York?" Katorah asked him. "Why not California or even Nashville?"

"Well," London replied, "While there are lots of musical connections in Nashville, I think it's a little too rural for me. And California just seems too superficial, if that makes sense."

Katorah shook her head.

"I don't think I'd be inspired in a place like L.A.," London continued. "I prefer my streets paved in a little more struggle, a little more personality."

Stepping off the curb to cross Bleeker Street, Katorah took the opportunity to entwine her arm around London's. She paused in their walk to ask a question. "Are ya getting hungry yet?" Katorah asked, in a tone London found adorable. "'Cause I don't know about you, but I'm starving."

"Sure. Let's get something. Feel like anything in particular?" London asked in reply.

"Actually, I know a perfect little place....right....near here," Katorah said, turning her head to look down the street. She bent at the waist to peer past London and get her bearing. "Come with me!"

For the first time on their walk, London followed Katorah. She held his hand and walked at a faster pace than before. She seemed almost giddy and London panted lightly to keep up with her. When she finally stopped, they stood under a tattered turquoise awning that read "Peanut Butter & Co."

"Here?" London asked in surprise. "Really?"

"Definitely here!" she told him.

"You're kidding?" London asked again.

"No, I'm not!" Katorah told him. "Really. For real."

"Damn!" London exclaimed jokingly. "You're a cheap date!"

The two paused to laugh for a moment.

"Come on, handsome," Katorah finally said to London. "Take me to Elvis!"

'Elvis?" London questioned. "OK. Now I'm confused. I thought you wanted something to eat."

"Oh, silly," Katorah replied. "That IS something to eat. Just come on!" she said, already opening the glass door. "You'll see!"

London followed without further question. The tiny restaurant was crowded and Katorah suggested that he get them a seat while she got in line.

"I got this," she told him, handing him the sunflowers. "Trust me."

London didn't object. Instead, he waited for a young mother to clean her toddler's peanut butter sandwich remnants off a table in the back of the small dining room. He smiled at her as she gathered her trash and moved away from the table.

"Thanks," he said to her politely and claimed the now open seat.

London watched Katorah take her place in line, curious about what she would bring back. Then, a couple seated next to him attracted his attention.

Although the couple was obviously in their late 60s, London surmised from their conversation that they were on a first date. Given the size of the restaurant, he couldn't help but overhear them. They talked about their interests. She shared a story about a dance class she had attended; he talked about the morning's New York Times crossword puzzle. Their interest in each other sparked London to wonder if he would ever connect with another person like that.

His thoughts turned to his own grandparents. He remembered the love they showed for each other; how on Sunday afternoons, they would gather the family around the table for dinner and share stories. He remembered the feelings of security and how his definitions of love and belonging were first formed. But just as his thoughts began to shift to more somber memories of his family, Katorah again stood before him, dropping a paper plate on the table.

"Jeez!" he exclaimed, in response to the size of the sandwich in front of him. "That's one crazy looking peanut butter sandwich!"

"London, meet Elvis. Elvis, meet London," Katorah joked and took a seat.

He sat staring at the sandwich, already cut in half. Katorah reached across the table to claim her piece. He watched as she opened her mouth and chomped down into the gooeyness. A smear of peanut butter remained on her cheek.

He laughed and scooted his chair closer to Katorah to wipe her cheek with his napkin.

"You better hurry up and taste this before I eat it all," Katorah warned. She smiled as she chewed and swallowed hard.

"You see this couple over here?" he asked, nodding his head in their direction. Katorah shifted her eyes to look.

He picked up his half of the sandwich. Peanut butter oozed from between the layers of soft bread.

"I think they are on a first date," he said, leaning in to finally bite the sandwich. The tastes of honey and bacon were surprisingly delicious with the peanut butter.

"You were eavesdropping?" Katorah asked innocently.

He found himself unable to answer, from the stickiness in his mouth.

Katorah sat quietly, watching him chew and finally swallow. She pushed a tall glass of cold milk toward him.

"OK," he replied. "Two things. One: this sandwich is delicious."

Katorah smiled.

"And two: how could I not hear them?" he whispered. "We are practically sitting WITH them."

"OK." Katorah conceded. "Good point. Although there was no judgment in my question," she reassured him. "I love to people watch."

"I find it kind of amazing," he replied.

"That I like to people watch?" Katorah asked.

"Um ...no...I like that," he replied. "Amazing that they are on a date."

"Why?" Katorah asked. "I think it's adorable. "

"Imagine the kinds of heartbreak these two have already seen in their lifetime," he told Katorah. "And yet, here they are, sitting together and willing to jump into something new. That's kind of ballsy, don't ya think?" he asked.

"Well," Katorah replied almost immediately. "I guess you could look at it like that. But what if you imagine all the love they have seen in their lifetime? Doesn't that make you think that they'd want to experience even more?"

He quietly chewed his sandwich and pondered her question.

"I think it comes down to how we see love," Katorah added. "You know...as a risk or a reward?"

"Hmmm," he replied, still considering.

"What's your definition of love, London?" Katorah asked.

"Love is many different things to me," he replied. "I think it should be simple and something that grows easily over time. I guess I think it should be what gets us through when the chips are down, if you know what I mean."

"Tell me more," Katorah petitioned.

"Well," he continued, "Let's say you and I are in a relationship." He paused to take a sip of milk, not noting that Katorah appeared slightly embarrassed. "To me, it should be as simple as you and me and nothing else," he offered as clarification. "Whatever stuff we accumulate along the way...houses, cars, money...they should all be extras. They aren't the things that define a relationship, define love."

He could tell from her eyes that Katorah was carefully considering his response. He wasn't sure if she agreed or if she was preparing an opposing response. His answer came when she leaned into him and gently placed her mouth on his. The salty sweet taste of the peanut butter sandwich was obvious on her lips.

"I've been looking forward to that. I'm glad the waiting game is over, Kat," he said to her when they parted. As he leaned in again, his chair was bumped.

"Excuse me, young man."

He turned to look. The man who had been sitting at the table next to him stood behind.

"I'm sorry to interrupt," the man said. "It's tight in here," he chuckled. "But the peanut butter is just irresistible, don't ya think?"

"That it is," London replied, gazing into Katorah's eyes for a moment. Then he rose to clear a path for the man.

"You kids on a first date?" the man asked, unafraid to pry.

London laughed. "I was gonna ask you the same thing!" he said and laughed.

Soon the older woman was standing, too. Her still blonde hair was tied in a loose bun on the nape of her neck. She smiled warmly at London and Katorah.

"First date this week!" she interjected, her blue-gray eyes almost sparkling. "We had our first date 40 years ago!"

The man now extended his hand to London. "Name's Marino," he said to London, who was now offering his hand in return. "And this is my wife, Katherine."

"Well it's nice to meet you Mr. and Mrs. Marino," London replied. "Have you really been together for 40 years? Wow. You just seemed so interested in one another...I assumed..."

"Well, we are interested in each other!" Katherine interrupted. "There's nothing better than spending time together." Reaching for her husband's hand, she shifted her eyes toward Katorah.

"40 years flies by in an instant when you're with the man who likes to share an Elvis with you."

"I think I might be in trouble," Katorah replied, smiling first at the woman and then fixing her gaze on London.

FORTY-ONE

"So, tell me about this apartment," Lucy asked of her sister over coffee.

"It's small," Katorah replied, still dressed in a robe and slippers, and wiping sleep from her eyes. Her dark hair was pulled into a loose ponytail on the very top of her head. She wrapped both of her hands around a large mug and took careful sips of the hot coffee. "But I think it's time I got out of your hair."

"You know you are welcome to stay as long as you'd like," Lucy interrupted. "If you feel like you could save some money and get a bigger place, then stay."

"It's New York, Lucy," Katorah reminded her sister. "Everything is expensive. I might as well start out small and see what happens. Besides, it's very homey. Maybe one day this week you can head over with me to check it out. It's only about a 10-minute walk from here."

Lucy rose from the kitchen table and turned toward the refrigerator. "Hungry?" she asked and turned back, holding a pint of blueberries. "I was thinking about pancakes all night. If you eat some, I won't feel as guilty. And we'll put fruit in them to make them healthy," she laughed.

Katorah glanced at the clock to note the time. She wasn't meeting London for lunch for another couple of hours.

"Sure. Why not?" she answered and took a seat at the table.

"Excellent!" Lucy exclaimed.

As Katorah watched Lucy mix the batter with a long wire whisk, her thoughts soon turned to London and their dinner the night before. She couldn't help but smile.

Almost as if she had eyes in the back of her head, Lucy interrupted Katorah's thoughts with a comment. "So you came in late last night," she observed. "And the sunflowers are lovely."

Katorah had filled a large, clear vase with water the night before and placed the sunflowers on a counter in the living room where the morning sun would greet them. She expected to be asked about them.

"They are lovely, aren't they?" she replied to her sister, who had yet to really ask a question.

Lucy turned and stared at Katorah who sat quietly sipping her coffee. "Oh come on, Kat," Lucy finally demanded. "Spill it."

"Spill what?" Katorah replied in an attempt to sound innocent. "There's nothing to spill."

"Well then, where did you get the flowers?" Lucy finally asked.

Katorah noticed a line of smoke from the now hot griddle. Her coffee mug still up to her lips, she extended one finger toward the stove and widened her eyes as a sign for Lucy to pay attention.

Lucy turned for only a moment to move the griddle to a cooler burner and then turned back again to face her sister.

"What?" Katorah asked playfully, now unable to hold in a laugh.

"Come on, Kat," Lucy pleaded. "Must we always play this game?"

Katorah laughed harder and then finally answered her sister's question. "Someone surprised me at work last night."

"Oh, I love getting flowers at work!" Lucy exclaimed.

"No...not really AT work," Katorah clarified. "It was more after work."

Lucy looked confused. Realizing that she was talking in riddles, Katorah finally succumbed to her sister's curiosity. "Do you remember that story I was working on...the one about London Drake?" she asked.

"How could I forget that story?" Lucy asked. "That guy was such a jackass."

Katorah paused and stared at Lucy.

"Oh no, Kat, not HIM?" Lucy asked. "Really?"

"Come on, Lucy," Katorah begged of her sister. "I told you how nice he was the second time...about how he called the magazine and apologized."

"Yeah, yeah," Lucy replied. When she turned back to the griddle, Katorah guessed that she didn't want to hear any more of the story. Her sister's disappointment poked through the bubble of her enthusiasm like a sharp pin. And while she knew her sister was just being a protective mother bird, Lucy's response made Katorah angry.

"That's not really fair, Lucy," Katorah said to her sister after a few seconds passed. "Not everyone makes a great first impression. Sometimes people need a little time, ya know? Sometimes you just have to give them a chance."

Lucy flipped two pancakes on a plate and turned to put them down in front of her sister. Katorah raised her eyes to meet her sister's.

"I'm sorry," Lucy said and turned again to get her own plate. When she was seated at the table again, she asked a more positive question. "How did he know you like sunflowers?" she asked and passed Katorah the syrup.

"Isn't that funny?" Katorah responded with a renewed giddiness. "I have no idea. But they are just beautiful, aren't they?"

"They are," Lucy replied and smiled.

When the two finished their breakfast, Katorah loaded the sticky dishes in the sink, emptied the remaining cup of coffee into her mug, and disappeared into the bathroom to shower.

Noting her sister's enthusiasm about London Drake, Lucy pulled the latest issue of SPIN from under the pile of mail on the counter and sat on the couch to read her sister's article.

FORTY-TWO

London walked down 77th Street, keenly aware of the city around him. He loved the tall buildings, the flash of the theater signs, the scream of the traffic, the hustle and bustle of the streets. New York's diversity suggested to him that there was a place for every person; always a way to identify with the city and with its people.

He turned down Broadway and pushed through the revolving doors into the ON THE AVE HOTEL. The grand lobby welcomed him with its charm and warmth. When he'd asked Katorah to meet him there for lunch, he figured she could pick from one of the restaurants and then they could stroll away the afternoon in Central Park. Away from mid-town, the pace could be a little slower.

The large clock on the lobby wall revealed that he was a little early for his date. Rather than venture into the bar, he moved toward the polished baby grand piano that sat in the lobby. Without a sign to indicate otherwise, he felt invited to take a seat. He rarely got to play on such an instrument. Although guitar was his more frequent accompaniment, the piano was always dear to him.

Without a specific melody in mind, he brushed his fingers over the smooth ivory keys. He ran his right hand up and down the sleek keyboard and soon landed on a sequence of notes for a song. Softly playing the introduction to the Commodore's hit "Easy," he closed his eyes to draw on a memory of the first concert he'd ever attended with his mom.

He recalled the echo of a Madison Square Garden crowd, the darkness of the stadium, and then the image of Lionel Richie spotlighted at a beautiful white piano. Still only tapping the keys lightly, he opened his eyes and smiled at a woman who walked through the lobby holding the hand of a small child. She returned his smile, but kept walking. His fingers still tickled the keys of the piano. Again, he closed his eyes. He could hear the crowd at the Garden; he remembered how he'd felt like Lionel Richie was singing a message just for him to hear. Now, his gentle tapping became a more even method. He was actually playing the song. He began to sing the opening verse. Then, he continued to sing the refrain and the second verse. As he did, his playing gained momentum and his voice gained volume. Soon, despite no intention to do so, he was performing for a small crowd that had gathered in the lobby to listen. When he finished the song and reopened his eyes, he smiled humbly for the crowd that was now clapping.

"Oh, thank you," he said sheepishly to the gatherers. Then, he saw Katorah just past the small circle of people. He smiled more widely at the sight of her and rose from the piano bench to greet her.

The smile she returned was full and genuine.

"That was beautiful," Katorah said as London reached her. "Really beautiful."

"Thank you," he replied. "Didn't really mean for it to become a performance. I sort of just lost myself in the piano."

"I could tell," Katorah replied. "It seemed really intimate...something special."

He explained his memory about the Madison Square Garden concert. "It's funny how one moment can stick with you like that," he told Katorah.

"You're lucky to have it," she replied. "I don't think you should ever let it go."

He leaned forward and kissed her lips. He backed away, smiled, and kissed her again. "So I thought we'd have some lunch and then maybe take a stroll around Central Park," he said. "How's that sound?"

"Sounds good to me," Katorah replied. "What are you hungry for?"

He chuckled, making her blush. Then, wanting to be a gentleman, he suggested sushi at one of the hotel's restaurants.

"We'll have one dancing dragon roll, two spicy scallop, a tuna avocado, and two shrimp tempura rolls," Katorah told their waiter, and smiled. "Oh, and two hot teas," she added.

He sat quietly and watched. When they were first seated, he handed his menu to Katorah and told her to pick whatever she liked. She hesitated at first, but he argued that the previous night's peanut butter sandwich was such a hit that he'd like to see if she could continue the streak.

Katorah laughed and agreed.

Once the waiter was away from the table, he clapped his hands quietly in agreement. "Well, you seem to have quite good taste," he joked. "Present company excluded, of course."

"Oh I don't know about that," Katorah rebutted. "So far, the company has been just as wonderful..." Katorah paused and then continued, "Well, almost as wonderful...as the food!" Again, she laughed.

He noticed the dimples around her mouth when she smiled and the way her dark eyes became small slits of their normal size. When she laughed, he swore that a light came out of her. *She's beautiful*, he thought. "So tell me about you," he petitioned. "I feel at a slight disadvantage given that you know more about me than I do about you."

"Benefit of my job, I guess," Katorah joked. "Besides, I bet I've only scratched the surface of all there is to know about you."

"Nope," he chided. "This is all there is. Really. I'm paper thin." He laughed out loud at his own sarcasm. Then he fumbled with a chopstick, swirled a dragon roll in soy sauce, and pushed the roll in his mouth. The next few words were a jumbled mumble that pushed Katorah to be the speaker.

"Hmmm. Well, where do I begin?" she asked rhetorically. "You already know I'm a writer. I went to Monmouth University. I studied journalism, but I minored in psychology."

His eyes widened as he continued to chew. He nodded as a gesture for her to continue.

"I have one sister. Her name is Lucy and she's older than me. She acts more like a mom than a sister sometimes, but I know that she loves me and she's just always looking out for me. I've actually been living with her since I came to the city to work...although I just recently found a potential place of my own."

"Oh, yeah?" he asked, encouraging Katorah to keep talking. He meant that he wanted to know more about the apartment, but Katorah continued in another direction.

"And I'm a Pisces who likes to take long walks on the beach," Katorah said with all seriousness. Then, when she couldn't hold in her laugh anymore, she blurted it out. "I'm sorry," she finally said, still laughing. "For a minute there I felt like I was writing a profile for Match.com."

He laughed too. "I know. Dating is hard, isn't it?" he asked.

"I'm the worst at it," Katorah replied.

"Wanna bet?" he answered, both trying to make her feel better and warning her at the same time.

FORTY-THREE

The afternoon proved to be a delightful time for a walk around Central Park. London held Katorah's hand as they strolled. Some moments were filled with conversation; others were perfectly quiet. But he found every moment completely wonderful. There was something about Katorah that made it easy to be around her, he had decided. She had a casual playfulness about her that made London want to breathe more slowly, to relax. When she spoke, he wanted to listen. And when he spoke, she seemed to cling on every word as if it were the most important thing she could be doing.

About an hour into their walk, Katorah asked him if he'd like to sit on a bench. "I like to people watch," she told him. "Mind if we just sit for a while?"

"Oh, sure," he replied. For someone who always felt like his own life was in the spotlight, he welcomed the opportunity to turn the focus on others. "So how does this work?" he asked Katorah after they were seated.

"Work?" she asked in reply and then clarified. "Well, there certainly aren't any rules," she told him. "But I like to sit and watch people. It makes me wonder about their lives. Maybe it's the writer in me. I'm not sure. But I wonder why they are in the park, who the person is that they are with, or where they are headed. I wonder what kind of lives they have, if they are happy in their career, what's important to them. Basically, I wonder about every person's story, if that makes sense."

"Hmmm," he replied. He had a story. He wondered if Katorah would still be sitting with him if she knew it. He tried to push away the doubt and asked her a question. "And do you like to talk to these strangers?" he asked.

Katorah turned her gaze from the bevy of strangers and looked at him.

"And what do you think?" she asked.

He laughed.

"I talk to everyone," Katorah answered. "I get that from my dad. We talk to people in line at the market; we make conversation with strangers on the train. And just put us in a waiting room!"

"Wow," he replied. "That's annoying!" he joked. He actually liked the confidence Katorah's personality displayed.

"I mean, I talked to you," she told him. "Probably more than you would have liked that night."

"Well, of course you talked to me," he replied. "If we hadn't talked, how would you have written your article?"

"Um. No," Katorah clarified. "That's not when I meant."

Just then, a young boy on roller skates went speeding past their bench. He stumbled on a stone, but then regained his composure and spun in a circle on his skates. His friend quickly followed behind on a bicycle. "Nice recovery, dude," the rider called to his friend. "You almost ate the road," he chided.

"Shut the fuck up," the skater responded. "I didn't actually fall, did I?" he asked.

"Wow," London muttered with disapproval. "How old is that kid? Eight or 10 maybe? With that mouth?" Then he rephrased. "Wow, how old am I?" he laughed. "I sound like a grandpa."

Katorah laughed too. She extended her arm and placed her hand on his knee. "Kids grow up so fast these days," she said. "There's so much pressure to be perfect. There's hardly a chance to just be a kid."

London knew far too well about needing to grow up too soon. Pangs of melancholy filled him. Before it could ruin his mood, he changed the subject. "How about some ice cream?" he asked and rose enthusiastically from the bench.

Two scoops later, Katorah patted her belly and wiped her face with a napkin. "So, London," she asked. "How come there's no one special in your life?"

"You mean because I'm such a catch?" he joked.

"You must meet a lot of people...women..." Katorah continued.

He could sense a hesitation in her that he hadn't seen before. He tried to ease her worry. "Musicians get a bad rap for being with lots of women," he offered. "I mean, some of the hype is true. There are guys like that. But

I think there are guys like that in every profession. Not all of us are in it for the one night stand," he lied, knowing that more often than not in recent history he had been.

"Uh huh," Katorah answered, not quite convinced.

"It's actually really hard to meet people in this life," he told her. "City after city is hard. And you never know if a girl likes you for you or for the fame they think you bring. It can actually be pretty lonely never knowing who you can trust."

Katorah stopped walking and turned toward him. Sincerity filled her eyes and she stared squarely at him. "Just for the record, I'm pretty trustworthy," she said. "I'd share an ice cream with you even if you weren't London Drake." She raised her hand and placed it on his cheek. "I think there's something special about you and I can't wait to learn a little more."

He leaned in and kissed her...a deep kiss that took her breath away.

When he pulled back, Katorah stood motionless, her eyes still closed.

"You OK?" he whispered, running his hands down her arms.

"I'm fine," she answered. "More than fine," she clarified and opened eyes that he could see a future in.

FORTY-FOUR

"Do you really think she'd understand all this?" the man asked London. "I mean, come on. The only reason she's with you now is because she sees the promise of fame and fortune in the future. She doesn't really know who you are...who WE are. Isn't that right, son?"

"No that's not true," he told his father. "She's special, dad. She's good."

And what do you know about good, my boy?" his dad asked. "How many times do I have to tell you, son? People are selfish and judgmental. They will love you in the good times and then stab you in the back when times get tough. Didn't you learn that lesson yet? Don't you remember what it looks like?

"No, dad. Don't say that. Don't drag them into this. They have nothing to do with this...with her."

"Don't be so sure, London. What do you think...that she wants to love someone as fucked up as you? Do you really think she's signing on to carry your luggage around her whole life? I mean, come on, London. Get real."

"You're wrong," he told his father. "I am ready for this. I can do this. I deserve this."

"Deserve?" his father asked, laughing. "You really think people get what they deserve? Did your grandmother get what she deserved? Fuck no. She loved someone and look where it got her. It'll get you to same place, my boy. Stabbed in the fucking back."

London shot up in the dark and paced back and forth in his bedroom. *Don't do this*, he told himself. *Don't self-sabotage.* Still, the nightmare was vivid. It had shaken him.

"Patricia, it's London," he said to a voicemail box. "It's 5 a.m. and no, I didn't expect you to answer. But I need to make that appointment for next week." He paused. "Actually, next week is too far away. Any chance you can get me in later today or tomorrow? Something's happened....I'm OK....well, not really OK...I mean, I'm not gonna jump off a bridge or anything...at least not tonight..." he rambled. "Please call me when you're in the office. I'd like to make that appointment." He hung up the phone and clicked on the TV.

Three minutes later, his cell chimed a text message. *Hey handsome*, the message said. *Just woke up with you on my mind. I'll leave it up to you to figure out the exact details.*

He couldn't help but smile. His first instinct was to text back or to even call and wish Katorah a good day, but the memory of his nightmare lingered. Were his father's words worthy of his attention? Maybe he was right not to trust, to keep an arm's length away. He turned off the cell phone and shifted his attention back to the TV.

A relentless banging on the front door woke him from sleep. After Katorah's text message, he had taken a Klonopin and fell asleep on the sofa. At first, he thought he was dreaming the bang, but when it continued, he was forced to open his eyes.

"Yeah?" he called from the couch. "What is it? This better be good. Is the building on fire?"

Again, the knocking. He rose from the couch and moved toward the door. He peered through the peephole to see a building security guard on the other side. He opened the door. "Is the building really on fire?" he asked with some alarm.

"Mr. Drake," the guard said, "I'm sorry to disturb you, but I was asked to come up and make sure everything is..." he paused, glancing inside the apartment, "OK."

London opened the door wider and invited the guard in. "OK? Was there a call about a disturbance or something?" he asked. "I was fast asleep on the sofa. But maybe the TV is up too loud?"

"No, sir," the guard clarified. "We got a call downstairs...from a Dr. Leonard. She asked us to come up and check on you. Said she's been trying to reach you all afternoon."

"Afternoon?" London asked, pushing his hands through his hair. "What the hell time is it?"

"It's 3 p.m." the guard replied.

"Jesus!" London exclaimed, remembering that his cell was turned off and the message he had left for Patricia earlier that morning. "Well...you can see that I'm fine," London said, now motioning the guard back to the front door. "I will call Dr. Leonard. No need for worry."

"Thank you, Mr. Drake," the guard replied. "Are you sure you don't need anything before I go?"

"Nope. I'm fine. Thanks for your concern. Sorry for the... misunderstanding."

Jesus, London thought to himself. *Now I'm on suicide watch? What the fuck?*

He picked up his cell and dialed Patricia. "Good...afternoon," London said to the annoyingly cheerful receptionist who answered the call. "This is London Drake calling to make an appointment with Dr. Leonard."

"Mr. Drake," the receptionist said, almost as if she'd been waiting for his call. "Can I please put you on hold for a moment?"

Before he could answer, music was playing in his ear. After a few minutes, the call was again picked up on the other end.

"London?" a voice he recognized as Patricia's asked. "London, are you OK?" The level of concern in her voice annoyed London a little. "What's happening? Where are you?"

"Hi, Patricia," he said calmly. "I'm at home and I'm fine. I'm sorry if I alarmed you. I turned my phone off after I called you and I fell asleep. I'm OK."

Patricia exhaled into the phone. He guessed she was releasing her worry. "I got your message, London. You sounded worried and burdened. And then you said something about jumping off a bridge...and then you didn't answer your phone. I was concerned."

"I'm sorry," he replied. "But I think I said I wouldn't jump off today," London said trying to make a joke.

"For future reference, therapists don't find humor in bridge jokes," Patricia chided back. "I have an open appointment time at 2 tomorrow. Should I put you in?"

London agreed. "See you tomorrow," he said.

FORTY-FIVE

"London, I'm happy to see you," Patricia said.

"You, too," he replied and smiled.

"I have to admit that I was beginning to wonder if you were coming back," Patricia told him. "It's been how long now? Five weeks?"

"Six," he corrected. He had cancelled two appointments since their last meeting.

"Hmmm," the therapist said. "Time flies. Come in and take a seat. Sounds like you have a lot going on."

"Life's been busy," he explained, without being prompted.

"Oh, yeah?" Patricia asked in reply. "Well, I'm glad you were able to make it in today," she said, paging through her notes. "In your message this morning, you sounded very anxious. The last time you were in we began some visualization, right?" she asked rhetorically.

"Yeah," he replied. "I was supposed to begin picturing myself happy... and deserving of an intimate relationship."

Patricia lowered the pages of notes and removed her reading glasses. "And move beyond self-victimization," she said, completing London's thought.

He fidgeted nervously in his seat.

"But I get the sense that you're having some trouble with all of that." She paused. "What's going on? How have things been since your last visit?"

He chuckled. A question about how things had been in his life was never one that had a simple answer. "Did you see the latest issue of SPIN?" he asked, already guessing the answer. The recycled magazines in the waiting room – the ones with the address labels peeled off of them – were most certainly ones Patricia had brought from home. Old issues of Time, some Better Homes and Gardens, and the occasional People were offered to those who waited to see Patricia. But he had never seen a SPIN on the table.

"No," she replied. "I'm sorry I haven't."

He reached into a laptop bag and retrieved a copy. "I brought you a copy," he said. "I guessed you might not have seen it,"

"Oh?" Patricia asked, puzzled. She repositioned the reading glasses again on her nose and peered down at the cover. Before she could spot the tagline herself, he was standing next to her, pointing to his name. "And I take it you are pleased with this article?" she asked, thumbing her way through the pages.

"I am," he told her. "But there's more to this story."

Patricia closed the magazine and placed it on the table next to her.

London retook his seat, but sat only on the edge, his right knee shaking up and down with nervous enthusiasm. In ten minutes, he told the Cliff's notes version of the initial interview, how he called to apologize, and how the magazine agreed to a second meeting.

Patricia listened intently until London finally paused, took a deep breath, and shifted back in his seat. "Were you surprised that you had such a visceral reaction to the reporter's questions that first night?" she asked him. "More specifically, do you have a clear understanding of what prompted that reaction?"

"What?" he asked. Instead of the therapist applauding his efforts to apologize and revisit the interview, she'd gone right to what he had done wrong. "It took a lot for me to call and apologize like I did," he told her. "Don't you think it's good that I did that?"

"Well, of course I do," Patricia said reassuringly. "I think you demonstrated a maturity and commitment to your career that is noteworthy. But the initial interaction concerns me. It demonstrates a pattern of defensiveness that we've been working together to resolve. If we don't talk about what prompted it, how can we be sure that you understand it and – therefore – avoid a similar response in the future?"

He pouted. He knew that Patricia's intentions were good, but he was eager to move ahead with the rest of the his story about Katorah...about how they had been out on two wonderful dates since then, about how he felt a connection with someone, about how he was not rushing to get her into bed because he saw the potential for something greater with her.

Hoping to pacify the therapist and move on, he answered Patricia's question. "That evening was a terrible mix of alcohol and self-defense," he told her. "I went into the interview thinking that it was going to be a disaster. So I made it a disaster. I know what I did," he said. "That's why I felt bad about it. That's why I called and apologized. That reporter was just doing her job. The way I handled it had nothing to do with her or her questions. It had everything to do with me and my own self sabotage."

Patricia sat back in her chair. She seemed impressed at his ability to own his actions; to move away from being a victim. It was exactly what they had talked about in their previous session.

"But I did call and apologize and we were able to move forward," he told her.

"And from the looks of it, the article turned out great!" Patricia now responded with enthusiasm.

"That's not all that's great," he continued, happy to be moving on to the rest of his story. "When the article came out, I even said 'thank you' to that reporter."

"That's great, London," Patricia said. "I'm glad you were able to acknowledge work that you thought was good, especially when it was so personal about you and your music."

"It's funny," he continued. "There was just something about this girl... something that prompted me to want to know more."

Patricia looked confused.

To clarify, he described how he went to the SPIN building to surprise Katorah and how a simple thank you turned into a spontaneous date. He found himself rambling on about all of the qualities he found so endearing in Katorah.

"I think it's wonderful that you are feeling a connection with someone, London," Patricia told him.

"But you know what's messed up?" he asked his therapist. "Mixed in with all these good feelings is this nagging sense that it just won't work out. It's almost like I already know that someday she will leave me...because she's so perfect...and I am....just so flawed. I had a terrible nightmare last night, Patricia," he said, dropping his head. "It's what prompted me to call you so early this morning."

He continued to tell Patricia about the nightmare.

She listened intently, scratching notes on her pad. When he finished, she spoke. "London, you need to give yourself credit for the effort you've made to date," she reminded him. "Given what you've been through, it makes sense that you have fears about the future...a feeling like the rug will be pulled out from under you. But you are moving in a positive direction. Let's keep that momentum going."

He nodded.

"I think you might be putting the cart before the horse," Patricia told him. "This is certainly too new of a relationship – if you'd even call it that already – to be worrying about the future. Let's focus on positive thoughts while we continue to resolve the feelings associated with your past. How does that sound?"

"It sounds good," he said, with a deep exhale. He noted the time and rose from his chair.

Patricia followed him to the door. "Continue to put positive energy into yourself, London," she told him. "Live with the enthusiasm you demonstrate when you talk about this new lady." Patricia opened the office door for London. "See you next week?" she questioned.

He nodded in agreement.

FORTY-SIX

Before Katorah knew it, five weeks had flown by and the warmer days of early fall had transitioned into a cooler, crisper time of year. Life for her was busy. She was still working frantically to establish her credibility at SPIN and had finally decided on a place of her own in the city.

London's schedule was similarly busy. He was writing regularly for his second album and Nate continued to push him to allow interviews. He spent more time on the radio talking about the new record than he thought they spent actually playing his music. But he was energized around the sophomore album and optimistic that it would do well.

In between their own personal commitments, he and Kat spent as much time as they could together. Sometimes it was a quick cup of coffee; sometimes lunch; and more rarely, they got to spend more than just an hour or two together. In between quick meet-ups, they texted constantly.

He was amazed at her ability to make him think.

She was impressed with his ability to make her laugh, even on the roughest of days.

"So who's the girl getting all your attention these days?" Alex asked London over lunch. It had been a couple of weeks – longer than the usual amount of time – since Alex had actually seen London. She just guessed it was because he was spending his free time with someone new.

"What makes you say that?" he asked, unable to hide a grin that took any innocence away from his question.

"Oh, London, give it up," Alex chided. "When I don't hear from you in a couple of weeks, it's for one of two reasons. You're either in a really shitty place mentally, or there's a new girl. And since you look almost giddy, I'm guessing it's the second of the two reasons."

He swallowed his spoonful of French onion soup and looked his friend dead in the eyes. "I'm in trouble, Lex," he said.

"I figured as much," Alex replied, ready to gossip.

"But before we talk about me, what's going on with you? Have you started making wedding plans? I think I might have a date!" he joked.

"Thinking that long term, huh?" Alex replied.

"Well, not that long," he answered quickly. "I mean a wedding is what? 6 months away maybe?" He laughed.

"Eh," Alex answered. "We're not in any rush. To tell you the truth, the whole wedding planning thing isn't really my thing. We'll get to it sooner or later. But I'd be happy to just fly to some island, say 'I do' and have a frozen drink on the beach. My mother, on the other hand, wants the whole big deal. So...we'll see. No plans yet. And no plans to make plans."

"You're OK with that?" he asked.

"Yep. Totally fine. George has been great since we got engaged. That's all that ever really mattered to me. We'll get around to a wedding eventually." She took a big bite of her turkey sandwich and washed it down with a gulp of iced tea. Then she revisited her earlier line of questioning. "So this girl...do I know her from someplace?"

"No. You don't technically know her," he replied.

"Huh?" Alex asked, confused by the last statement. "What's that mean? Wait...did you meet her at a gig when I was there and I don't remember? How old is she, London? Jesus, she's not 21 is she?"

"Wait....hold on," he said, raising his one hand to motion Alex to stop talking. "No, she's not 21. She's actually almost 30! Her name is Katorah..."

"Ka...what?" Alex asked.

"Katorah," he answered. "It's Greek."

"No, no. I heard you about her first name, "Alex said. "What's her last name and why does that name seem familiar to me. Wasn't that the reporter's name who interviewed you for ..." She paused.

He grinned. He knew that Alex had read the SPIN article, but forgot that she would be the one to pay attention to the writer's name.

"No wonder it was such a great article!" Alex joked. "Apparently she knows more about the mysterious London Drake than most people know!"

"No, no," he stopped her. "It wasn't like that. She actually wrote the article before she liked me!"

"Hmmm. I'm pretty sure she liked you well enough when she wrote it," Alex said, smiling and pushing for details.

"Well, I hope so," he said. "But we actually didn't go out until after the article came out. I wasn't even sure that she'd go out with me."

"You can be pretty persuasive when you want something, London."

"That's the thing, though, Lex. I don't have to work hard at this. It just feels right...and easy. I don't know..."

"Does she live in the city?" Alex asked.

"She actually lives in my building," he told her. "She's new to the city though...living with her sister. It's actually a funny story...how we met, I mean."

"I thought you said she is the SPIN reporter," Alex asked confused.

"Oh yeah, she is," he clarified. "But I actually met her for the first time weeks before the interview. She was in the elevator...apparently coming home from a date that didn't go very well...she was all flustered...dropped her purse all over the elevator floor...mumbled some crazy girl shit...and then got out on the 12th floor. I was in a lousy mood that night...didn't want to be bothered...but I remember thinking that there was something beautiful about her that night. Since then, I've learned that my initial impression was right."

"But wait...that same girl is the SPIN reporter?" Alex asked, trying to follow his story.

"Yeah. Crazy, huh? Funny thing is that when she showed up for the interview, she looked familiar, but I couldn't place her. Her hair was different or something. She was wearing less makeup. I don't know. It wasn't until a couple of dates in that she mentioned that night in the elevator to me." He chuckled. "Honestly, it kind of freaked me out a little. It's almost like we are supposed to be together or something."

"Oh no," Alex replied. "You ARE in trouble."

"What?" he asked innocently.

"When you start talking about fate and meaning, I know you're for real, London."

"I don't know what I am, Lex," he said. "But I think I might be happy."

Alex smiled. Those were words she didn't hear her friend say very often. "I'm happy for you, honey," Alex said and placed her hand on his forearm. "So when do I get to meet her?"

"Why? So you can size her up?" he asked, smiling.

"Um. Yeah. Pretty much," Alex answered. "I mean if another girl is going to take some of my time with you, I have to at least make sure she's a little funny. She's not funnier than me though, right?"

"Funnier than you?" he rebutted. "Impossible. But I think you'll like her. She's quirky, but really smart. And she likes KISS. What more is there?"

"Well, I guess we will see," Alex replied lightheartedly. "So set something up soon. I can't wait to meet her."

"You mean before I screw it up?" he asked, only half joking.

"I didn't say that, London," Alex quickly answered.

"No, you didn't," he replied. "I guess I just keep thinking I will. I carry a lot of baggage."

"Yes, you do," Alex responded matter-of-factly. "But maybe you'll open up some of that baggage this time and actually let a girl iron out some of the wrinkles with you. It's your wrinkles that make you interesting, honey."

"Yeah. And they also make me messy, Lex."

"Well, it's like I always say: If a girl isn't willing to get a little messy with you, then she's not worth your energy, right?"

"Yeah. I guess. I just have a hard time accepting it all myself. How can I ask anyone else to, ya know?"

"London, you don't have to share everything all at once. Start with the carry-on bag and work from there. But if you want someone to love you, that person has to know you. And to know you means knowing where you came from. Your family was full of love. Share that part," Alex reassured her friend.

"Thanks, Lex," he said sincerely. "I think you're right."

"Maybe you'll be walking down the aisle before I do!" Alex suggested.

Before he could swallow his iced tea, he was laughing, and then coughing liquid into his napkin. "See!" he said. "No one is funnier than you!"

FORTY-SEVEN

"I don't know how I lived with Lucy these couple of months without all this stuff!" Katorah joked with London as they stood on the sidewalk watching movers unpack a tractor trailer full of furniture that had been in storage.

Just then, one of the movers dropped a large box off the back of the truck. The box split open, spilling contents all over the street. Kat, too, dropped a large cup of coffee she had been holding and scrambled toward her belongings.

"Why is it that you're always scrambling to pick things up off the ground when I'm around," he joked, referencing the night in the elevator.

"Very funny," Katorah retorted. When she stood back up, she held a pair of white lace underwear in her right hand and a teal blue bra in her other. "I don't need all of New York looking at my skivvies, now do I?" she asked waving the undergarments over her head.

The man who dropped the box still stood on the truck ramp, staring down at Katorah. When she turned her head to look up at him, he shifted his eyes away from the lingerie she was holding. Then he disappeared into the back of the truck.

"At least it wasn't a box full of things that could actually break," Kat said, stuffing the contents of the broken box into a new empty box the mover had thrown down onto the street.

London just watched her. He wasn't sure if helping her would be appropriate. He hoped that the first time he touched Katorah's underwear that she would actually be wearing it. The very thought of that stirred him to excitement. It wasn't usual that he waited this long to have sex with a woman. But he didn't want to rush things with Kat. He moved slowly, cautiously.

Once Katorah had her box repacked, she moved toward the front door of her new apartment building. "Let's go upstairs," she said to him. "I can't wait to see where they've just dropped everything."

Once inside the tiny apartment, Katorah was surprised to see that the movers had actually followed directions. With the exception of one box labeled "bedroom" that was in the kitchen, everything else seemed to be in the right place. She'd have to rearrange the furniture to better fit the space, but having it in the right room was a good start.

"So?" she asked him. "What do you think?"

He glanced around the small space. It was less than half the size of his apartment. But he tried to see the potential and remembered that he hadn't always lived in such a big apartment.

"I think you'll make it great," he said and smiled.

"I know it's small," Kat said, almost apologetically. "But it's what I can afford for now. And at least we won't always have to go to your place."

He paused. She was making decisions that involved him.

"Really, Kat, I think it will be great," he reinforced. "It's close to work; it's a nice neighborhood."

"Thanks, babe," she replied and leaned toward his face for a kiss. "It will take me a while to get all these boxes unpacked, but I think you're right."

"Ms. Alexander," a man interrupted, knocking at the door. He held a clip board and was looking for her signature. "That's everything. Truck is empty."

Katorah reached for the clipboard, made one last look around the apartment, and then signed off on the move. She fumbled in her purse and handed the man a fifty dollar bill. "Thank you," she said and walked him toward the door. When she turned back to London, he was seated on a box top, one leg crossed over the other.

He perused the boxes, stacked from floor to ceiling around him.

"I know," Kat said as if she could read his mind. "Not tonight. I'm staying at Lucy's for a couple more days until I can make sense of this mess."

"Can't say I blame you," he replied. "But you've got to be hungry by now. How about we go to my place for dinner? I have some steaks in the fridge. How's that sound?"

"Don't tell me you're going to cook for me?" Kat asked, almost surprised.

"I happen to be a pretty good cook," he defended. "I think I even have some ice cream in the freezer for dessert. Then, if you want, you can hop the elevator to Lucy's...or you can stay with me tonight," he coyly suggested.

Thirty minutes later, the two pulled up in front of London's apartment building. "I'm just going to stop in at Lucy's for a minute," Katorah told him when the elevator stopped on the 12th floor. "Why don't you get dinner started and I'll see you in a few minutes?"

"Sounds good," he told her. "Follow the delicious aroma to find me," he hollered down the hall once she exited the elevator.

Katorah stood in front of her small closet at Lucy's for 10 minutes, trying to decide what to pack for her overnight stay at London's. While she hadn't told him that she'd accepted his offer to spend the night, she had been playing the evening through in her mind the whole ride home. So many times she had fantasized about how his hands would feel on her body. Up until now, they had only kissed. His hands had wandered up and down her arms, over her back, and had cupped her breasts, but never had he pushed past that. The truth was that she ached to lay with London; to be naked with him, and to feel the weight of him on top of her.

Her nervous feeling surprised her. *Really, Kat*, she said to herself in the elevator. *It's only sex. You've done this before.* But for some reason, the anticipation of being with London unnerved her. She felt almost giddy.

Floors above her, London too struggled with what was to happen. He lit candles, deliberated over music, and carefully set the table. He opened a bottle of red wine and allowed it to sit uncorked on the table to breathe while he marinated two rib eyes from the fridge. By the time Katorah joined him, the steaks were sizzling on the grill, filling the apartment with a delicious aroma.

"That smells amazing," she said as she turned the corner into the kitchen. "Of course, I could just be really hungry," she joked.

"Trust me, Kat," he told her. "I really am a pretty good cook. Wine?"

"Would love some," she replied.

"Medium rare, right?" he asked her and turned back toward the kitchen. The two had dined together enough times already that he knew how she would like her steak.

"Yes...please," Kat answered.

"Why don't you have a seat at the table?" he suggested. "I got this. Almost ready."

Katorah took his suggestion and before she knew it, London emerged with a Caesar salad and two perfectly cooked steaks on a platter. "Looks great!" she said.

He sat and watched Katorah take the first bite. Her eyes met his as she placed the tender piece of steak in her mouth. He waited while she chewed and then smiled when she did. "See!" he exclaimed. "Good looking and a good cook. What a lucky girl you are!" he teased.

Conversation flowed easily over dinner, as it always did when the two were together. Katorah told him about a new assignment that would take her to Las Vegas for a few days.

He actually knew the artist Katorah was scheduled to interview. "Want me to call ahead and tell him not to be a jerk?" he asked, only half kidding.

"No need," Katorah responded. "I actually have some experience in that department. So I think I can handle it," she chided back.

Once the dishes were cleared, he invited Katorah to move into the living room. "I have a couple of movies, if you're interested," he told her.

Katorah countered his offer with one of her own. "Actually, I don't think I'm up for a movie," she said, making him think she might just call it a night. "How about if we spend some time with each other?" she asked.

He grew stiff at the suggestion. He moved toward her as she unbuttoned her blouse. When he reached her, he pushed his hands inside the open blouse and slid it off her shoulders onto the floor. Then, his mouth met hers, gently at first with a tender kiss. When she nibbled at his bottom lip, he knew what she wanted. He lifted her and carried her to his bed.

FORTY-EIGHT

When Katorah woke, the room was dark and she was alone in the bed. She could still smell London there with her, his scent on the pillows and on her body. She lay for a moment, remembering the sensation of the night before. It gave her tiny goose bumps and made her skin tingle even then as a memory. He had been so gentle with her, so in tune with her body. The way they moved together was like the rhythm of an old love song, sweet and romantic. And yet, he filled her with a passion that was hot and unquenchable. She blushed a little thinking about how he'd satisfied her again and again and how she'd so selfishly let him.

Alone now, in the bed they shared only a few hours earlier, Katorah rolled to the edge and rose from her resting spot, wrapping the cotton sheet around her bare shoulders. She moved into the hallway, careful not to stub her toe or trip in the dark. In the living room, she found London. He was seated with the guitar, lightly strumming the strings and producing a soft melody. The only light was from what was left of the taper that burned on the dining room table.

When her eyes adjusted to the darkness, Katorah moved closer to him and cleared her throat softly to prevent a startle. He turned to see her.

"Well, hello," he said, smiling.

"Hello, yourself," she said. Her eyes sparkled in the candlelight.

"I'm sorry. I didn't mean to wake you. I just...I just had a song in my head that I wanted to play around with. Wanted to get it out to see how it sounded. Was I too loud?"

"You didn't wake me," she replied.

"Oh?" he asked, puzzled at what might have stirred her to alertness.

"No. It wasn't your rumble that woke me," she said. "I'm afraid it was more the rumble in my own tummy," she said playfully.

"Ahh...the tummy rumble! It'll get you every time." He rose from the bench to move toward her. He was struck by how lovely she looked with her hair tousled and wearing nothing but his bed sheet. "Perhaps we should try and remedy that?" he said. "After all, I can see how you might have worked up an appetite."

Katorah blushed again. He was now directly in front of her, his arms wrapped low around her waist. "Funny," she said as his mouth met hers mid-sentence.

She tasted sweet to him, her mouth wet and warm. He moved from her lips to nuzzle his face in the nape of her neck. He pulled away from her to break his embrace and turned toward the kitchen. "What'll it be?" he asked her. "Not that I have many gourmet options available."

"Come on now, London. Dinner last night was delicious. So now I know better. But I'm a simple girl," she said coyly.

"Simple?" he replied, disappearing into the kitchen. "Oh, Miss Alexander, there is very little that is simple about you."

"Really?" she replied. "I'm not the one with the alter ego and manufactured first name."

He was quiet. She wondered if she misspoke and waited for a reply.

He popped back around the corner, holding a spatula and a carton of eggs. "How do you like 'em?" he asked completely avoiding her last comment.

"What?"

"Your eggs...how do you like 'em?"

"Oh..." she answered, "Can you fry them and flip them without breaking the yolk?"

He smiled wider. "Can I ever!" he replied. "You still underestimate me."

She moved toward him, taking the spatula from his hand and placing it on the counter. She wrapped her fingers around his now empty hand and moved it to her mouth. She kissed the back of his palm, softly, sweetly, and looked into his eyes. "Actually, I don't, London. I'm pretty sure that you can do just about anything you set your mind to doing."

"Well, you may be right, Kat," he said with a hint of sarcasm. "I just may be the most brilliant egg flipper you'll ever know. Now get out of my way and let me work!"

Katorah disappeared into the bedroom just long enough to borrow a pair of sweatpants and a t-shirt she had seen hanging on the back of the door. When she returned to the kitchen, London had the toast made, the coffee brewed, and two eggs perfectly fried and flipped on a warm plate.

"Well look at you," he said as she took a seat at the table.

"Yeah, well I thought I'd better put on some more appropriate dining attire," she replied. "I hope you don't mind?" she asked innocently.

"Well, it is pretty ballsy to put on a man's Kiss concert t-shirt," he said. "But you do make it look good."

"I actually remember this tour," she said. "My best friend at the time – Vicki French – was so in love with Gene Simmons. We tried to get tickets, but it sold out before we could. So I never got to go."

"That's a shame," he replied. "It was the first time since the late 70s when the entire original band played together. I saw them in Madison Square Garden. Will never forget it."

"Oh I can imagine!" Katorah said. "The 2004 Rock the Nation tour was amazing. It was one of the first concerts I covered as a reporter. I was so nervous!"

"Nervous?" he asked. "I can't imagine that a musician would ever make you nervous. Weren't you the one who said to me that we're all just people like everyone else?"

"Well, yes, I did, but come on. It was freakin' KISS, London. KISS. By the time they closed with Rock And Roll All Nite, I think everyone in the place was completely mesmerized."

"You make a good point," he replied. "I guess you are worthy of wearing the t-shirt. Just don't plan on taking it home with you," he cautioned playfully.

"Oh man, are you kidding? I wouldn't dream of it!" she said and swallowed a mouthful of egg.

He watched as she dipped the toast into the center of the egg and then and raised it to her mouth. He watched her sip the coffee. He watched her dab the corners of her mouth with the white cotton napkin.

This must be the most beautiful woman in the world, he thought to himself and then quickly wondered, *How the hell did I get her at my kitchen table?*

"So," she said interrupting his thoughts. "How did you pick it?"

"Pick what?" he asked, thinking she meant the silverware or the plates.

"Your name," she clarified. "How did you pick London?"

He sat quiet, almost surprised that she remembered what he had blurted out in anger at their first meeting.

"I mean, London is a pretty unique name," Katorah continued." Did you know someone with that name...maybe someone you admired?"

Her tone and curiosity were innocent, almost like that of a child who asks her parents "Where do babies come from?" They ask their question out of pure interest, not expecting the answer to be quite so complex.

"Well," he replied. "It's actually not like that at all. You're right in that it's not a common name, but that's only a small part of why I use it. It's actually a tribute to my grandfather."

Katorah stopped eating and focused her gaze on him. "Oh?" she said. "Well then, no need to talk about it if you don't want to. I was just curious."

"Why wouldn't I talk about it?" he asked.

"Well," Katorah replied," If you'd like to tell me, I'd love to know. But, if it's too personal ..."

He stopped her. "It is personal, Kat. It's about my life. But if you want to know..." He paused, looking for her to encourage him to continue.

"I'd like to know," she affirmed.

"OK then. What do you know about Audrey Hepburn and the movie 'My Fair Lady'?"

"Hmm. Well, not a lot, really," she replied. "I've heard the name of the movie. But I've never seen it. And, I'd recognize a picture of the actress, but I can't say I've ever seen her in anything."

"When I was little, my grandfather was in love with Audrey Hepburn," he replied. "He would watch 'My Fair Lady' over and over and over. We used to tease him that he must have had the entire movie memorized."

Katorah smiled.

His tone of voice softened as he talked about his grandfather. "One Sunday," he continued, "he was watching the movie yet again. And for some reason, I decided to join him. It must have been raining or something and I remember that I was really bored. So I ventured into the living room and sat down on the floor next to his chair. You don't know what the movie is about?"

"No," Katorah replied.

"The movie is set in England – it's actually a musical – and the lead male character is an arrogant professor of phonetics. He believes that the tone and inflection in a person's voice is what determines that person's opportunities in life. He also believes that he can take any woman and teach her to speak in such proper English that people would believe her to be a duchess."

"So he works on Audrey Hepburn's character?" Katorah asked.

"Yes. My grandfather was in love with her. He never took her eyes off the screen when she was on."

"I see," said Katorah.

"In the movie, she plays a young woman who sells flowers. She is from the slums but she very much wants to get a job working in a flower shop. So, she goes to the professor looking for help. Long story short, she goes through lots of training – some of it pretty harsh at times – and eventually adopts an accent that makes her seem like she is from the upper class."

"So was the professor's name London? Did you admire his character?" Katorah asked.

"Oh no, not at all," he replied. "There's really much more to the story, but the bottom line is that it is set in London. My grandfather hated the idea that people would be judged by the accent in their words, but the romanticism that Audrey Hepburn brought to her part – how she came from the common people and was able to pass herself off as something much greater – he just loved that."

"Why do you think that was so?" Katorah asked, now fully engrossed in his story.

"I don't know for sure," he replied. "But I think it was because he came from humble beginnings. He worked hard – like Hepburn's character did – and he wanted to be respected and admired."

"I see," said Katorah.

"He didn't say a thing to me, not a word, the entire time the movie played," he said. "But when it was over, he looked down at me and said, 'You know what, kid? No matter what hand you're dealt, there's always a way to improve it. Life really is romantic, especially in London.'"

"Wow, what a story," Katorah said.

"Yep. So...to answer your question, I picked the name 'London' because it reminds me of that movie. It reminds me of my grandfather. It reminds me to use my voice as a tool for getting what I want out of life. It lifts me out of what I came from and reminds me that romance is still very much alive in the world, despite the fact that most people aren't worth a shit. It motivates me."

Katorah wasn't sure what to say. Before she had a chance to mutter anything, or to even ask what his first name was originally, he was once again standing close to her.

"Guess your eggs were good?" he said, noticing the now clean plate.

"The eggs were fantastic," she replied. "No more tummy rumble."

"Great!" he said. "But now I seem to have a rumble of my own."

"You do, huh?" Katorah asked shyly.

"I do," he said. "Wanna help me get rid of it?"

Before she could respond, he had her off the chair and in his arms. He kissed her fiercely, transferring the intimacy of their conversation into a physical act. He ached to be inside of her again. And she was eager to have him.

With one swoop of his arm, he pushed the setting off the kitchen table, sending Katorah's plate crashing to the floor.

She positioned herself on the table top as he moved his hands down her body and slid his sweatpants off of her. She wrapped her thighs around his waist and encouraged him into her just as the sun began to break through the kitchen window.

FORTY-NINE

With her ear pressed against his bare chest, Katorah could hear the echo of London's heart beating. The rhythm of beats matched the pattern of her own breathing and almost tricked her into mistaking his heartbeat for her own. A tangle of sheets surrounded them in London's bed.

Katorah propped herself on one elbow and looked at him.

As she moved, London watched her dark hair fall over her bare shoulders.

She posed a question that broke the silence. "What are you thinking?" she asked him.

"Thinking?" he questioned. The truth was that he was simply enjoying the moment in a space with very little thought. He was just content.

"Yes," Katorah continued. "Are you thinking about us? I mean, where are we headed? You know...as a couple?"

The distinction gave him pause. He was never fond of labels.

Deflecting the question, he gently brushed the hair from Katorah's shoulder and placed a gentle kiss in the space just below her ear. "Well, I am headed to the shower," he jested. "Let's deal with the heavy stuff once I'm clean and fed."

Katorah chose not to push. Instead, she leaped over him and made a mad dash toward the bathroom. She slammed the door behind her and laughed out loud. "Ladies first!" she shouted. "You're a gentleman, remember?"

He laughed at her playfulness and remained on the bed waiting for his turn. Reclined on a stack of pillows, he relaxed. Usually, the intimacy of a woman in his shower somehow unnerved him. Today, however, he was comfortable – even more than comfortable.

When Katorah emerged from the bathroom, a billow of steam followed her.

"You really know how to steam things up," he flirtatiously joked.

"Oh yeah?" Katorah asked rhetorically, dropping her towel on the floor. "What do you mean?"

He rose from the bed and moved toward her, his excitement now physically obvious.

Katorah moved into him and grasped him in her warm hand. "Why don't you take that shower so I can work on getting you dirty again?" she suggested.

He recognized that her remarks were not a question but an expressed intention to please him. He moved into the bathroom and turned the spigot to start the rush of water. Unlike Katorah, he kept the door open.

"I don't have any clean clothes here," she called to him from the bedroom.

"I can't hear ya, babe," he shouted over the water. "What did ya say?"

This time, Katorah went into the bathroom to make her statement.

"Just help yourself to whatever you want," he told her. "T-shirts are in the dresser. Sweats are in the closet."

Katorah skipped into the bedroom and rummaged through the tall chest of drawers. She picked an Old Navy t-shirt and pulled it over her head. Then she moved to the walk-in closet in search of the promised sweat pants. Weighing her options, she picked a pair with a drawstring and pulled them up over her hips. She moved to the mirror to check her look.

Her own reflection caused her to take pause. Despite the fact that she was now dressed in clothes not her own and too big for her, she was pleased with what she saw. She looked happy, glowing. The flush on her cheeks was one indicator. She also wore a smile that she couldn't seem to erase.

Katorah's observations were interrupted by the sense that she was being watched. The feeling confused her, as she could still hear the shower running in the bathroom. And then it became clear. From the still open closet, she noticed two little eyes peering at her from the top shelf. Chloe was perched atop a stack of papers and folders and sat still, staring at Katorah.

"Ah, Chloe!" Katorah exclaimed, turning from the mirror to face the cat. The motion prompted Chloe to jump abruptly from the shelf, spilling the papers on which she sat all over the floor.

"Ugh. Messy cat," Katorah reprimanded. "You're gonna get me kicked out of here," she said, now laughing. She moved to the closet and crouched to begin restacking the papers.

As she gathered the spill into a pile, Katorah couldn't help but notice some of the content on the pages. She wondered why London would have gathered press clipping that seemed to date back more than 20 years. She was suddenly stopped dead in her tracks by a headline that she couldn't ignore.

Two Deaths in Jersey Suburb Called Murder-Suicide

Katorah read further.

Essex County N.J — An autopsy of a 65-year-old Essex County woman, allegedly killed by her husband, determined she died from multiple stab wounds.

Essex County Prosecutor Domenik Denucci said Ayda Drake's body was found in the bedroom of her duplex on Rosebud Lane. She shared the first floor of the home with her husband, Christopher, who was also found dead on the scene from what an autopsy revealed as suffocation by hanging. Drake's son and his family are the current residents of the second floor in the same residence.

Denucci said the 11-year-old grandson of Christopher and Ayda called police at 3:55 p.m. Monday afternoon, screaming that his grandparents were hurt. Police arrived at the scene to find Ayda's husband Christopher hanging from a rope in their kitchen. He was pronounced dead at 4:12 p.m. Ayda was later pronounced dead en route to Mercy Hospital.

A feeling of shock overcame her; she knew that she had stumbled upon something very personal to London. Her hand covered her open mouth as she stared at the photo of the elderly couple in the newspaper clipping. Below the photo was another photo of a man and woman, gripping a young boy in an embrace. Katorah recognized the people in the photo...they were younger versions of people whose pictures were framed in London's apartment: his parents. Tears welled in her eyes. She gasped out loud when a smaller piece of paper fell from the stack she held onto the floor. It was a note; a suicide note that began: *"Please know that I love you all...her the most."*

"Did you find what you were looking for?" she heard a visibly agitated London ask. He now stood behind her.

Katorah jumped in a startle. She hadn't heard the shower stop.

"London, I wasn't looking for anything," she quickly said in defense. "I wasn't snooping. Chloe was up on the shelf and I scared her and ....." She stopped speaking.

He was not listening. Instead, he was now down on one knee, scooping the fallen articles back into a folder. His face was stoic. She wasn't sure how to read his expression.

"Honey, that little boy in the article...was that you?" she asked.

Her question pushed him to respond. "Katorah, please drop it," he firmly pleaded.

"But London..." she pushed.

"Just fucking drop it!" he now demanded, at a level that prompted Chloe to seek refuge under the bed.

She stood motionless, petitioning him silently with sad eyes.

"Tell me, Katorah," he continued. "Exactly what do you want to know?"

Without waiting for an answer, he continued. "Do you really want to know that when I was eleven years old my grandfather murdered my grandmother? Do you want to know that he then killed himself? Or maybe the juicy part is how I found them both. Is that what you want to hear? No, No. Wait. Maybe you want to write a story about the nightmares that plague me every fucking night...gory visions of hanging, bleeding, and screaming?"

Tears ran down her flushed cheeks.

He continued, screaming. "Rock star has crazy past. How's that for a headline, Kat? Maybe you could include something about how I was ridiculed every day of my life after that in that fucking town. Don't forget to include how I changed my name so it wouldn't be the same as his. Oh no, no. I got it! Maybe you just want to save me from all of it. Is that it? Save poor little London from his little life of tragedy."

He paused and took a breath. He exhaled deeply and turned away from Katorah. When he turned back to face her, he was calmer, but his comments were no more kind. "I know, Kat," he offered and she moved toward him.

Before she could reach him, he continued. "Maybe you would like to hear how I want you to finish getting dressed in whatever the hell you need to wear to take your pretentious, information-seeking ass out of here?"

She was speechless. She knew there was no sense in argument. He was not in a place to hear it. But she also did not want to leave. Completely torn and defeated, she crumbled to her knees on the floor in front of him. Choking on her own tears she began to mumble. "I am so sorry you went through this, London, but it doesn't change my opinion about you. I care about you, London. I want to be here for you."

All expression left his face. He said two words and pointed: "The door."

"London," she pleaded. "Please don't do this. I want to be here with you."

"You say that now," he retorted, "but you will leave. Everyone I love leaves me."

Love? she thought. *He hasn't said that before.*

"That's a lesson I learned very early. But don't you worry," he continued. "Like some kind of asshole, I keep picking myself back up and piecing myself back together hoping that it will be different someday; that I might actually find someone I can trust. Just save us both the trouble of building something up only to watch it fall. Eventually, everything falls down. All of us...we all just fall down."

Without words, she moved out of the bedroom and through the living room toward the front door. She grabbed her handbag off the couch and fished keys from a deep pouch, never looking back at him. When her hand was finally on the door knob, she paused and turned to look at him. When he did not ask her to stay, she turned and let herself out.

Only when London could hear the slam of her car door did he allow himself to collapse. Like a dead weight, he fell like a heap on the loveseat and buried his head in his hands.

"Fuck!" he shouted in anger and frustration. "Fuck, fuck, fuck."

And then in defeat and desperation, he changed his expression. "Why, God? Why?" he muttered, summoning divine intervention.

Chloe, sensing his grief, emerged from her hiding place and curled up on his feet at the base of the sofa.

Part Four

ALIVE

FIFTY

"Woke up this morning to an empty frame
Felt you whisper in my ear 'things ain't the same'
Didn't want to believe it, felt like a bad dream
seems like one way or another you just want to be free."

Click!

A voice from the control room said, "London, I don't know what the hell is going on with you tonight, but I'm just not feelin' it man."

"Tyler, I don't know what you want from me," London replied. "I'm giving you the best I got in here."

"Well, we're all gonna have to do better," the voice replied. "This is mediocre at best."

London knew he was right.

"Let's just take a break and have a drink. Everyone take half an hour."

London walked into the control room, frustrated and angry. The voice he had heard in his ear was that of Tyler Schramm, the Grammy nominated producer who worked on London's first CD. "Sorry to snap at you like that, Tyler. I just feel like I'm second guessing myself in there," he said apologetically.

"Yep. That's exactly what it sounds like in here too," Tyler said. "It's what it's sounded like the past two times you've been in here, London," he said with a slight tone of impatience.

"People have high expectations of this record, man. It's a little overwhelming. I am a little overwhelmed," London said, hoping for some empathy.

"Listen to me London," Tyler replied. "I know the pressure. I know

204 J.A. Blake ~ Nick Moccia

the industry. A sophomore album imposes even higher expectations than a first album. But what this boils down to is your ability to communicate in a genuine way. That's what made your first album a success. It's what connected people to you during your tour. People have to believe you when you say something. Your voice has to make them believe that you're happy, or that your heart is breaking, or that you have no fuckin' clue what to do next. They need to be able to connect and relate to you," Tyler said. "Otherwise, we're wasting our time."

London thought about his first record. Recorded only 12 months earlier, "Longing for Monday" had sold 500,000 copies and earned gold status in America. That was impressive for a first album, in his opinion.

"You're a Sinatra fan, right?" Tyler asked.

London nodded.

"Many would argue that Sinatra wasn't the best singer in the world," he said. "But most would agree that he was a great communicator. People love him because they can relate to him."

Again, London nodded.

"Just remember, kid, there is a distinct difference between singing the words and feeling them. That difference is what got you to the dance in the first place. Whether or not you keep jivin' is up to you."

London took a deep breath. "Thanks, man," he said. "I appreciate the advice. I do. How about we break for dinner and try again in about an hour. That OK with you?"

"OK with me," Tyler replied. "Just remember, time is money. If you're gonna waste time being phony, you might as well stay the hell home. Only bring genuine here. You'll be OK."

"Got it," London replied, as he swung open the control room door and made his way to the receptionist desk.

"Hello, Mr. Drake," said the young red haired girl behind the desk. "Something I can help you with?"

His first instinct was to say something inappropriately flirtatious, but he recalled Tyler's advice and swallowed the childish remarks. Instead, he asked for a menu. She handed him the latest offering from the deli on the corner.

"Good night for a Caesar salad, I think," he said to her as she picked up the phone to place his order. "I'll be in the lounge when it comes."

Inside the lounge, he was alone. He was grateful for two things: the quiet and the mini bar. He weighed his choices carefully and opted for wine. Splashing the Cabernet Sauvignon into a crystal glass, he moved to the row of windows that stretched from floor to ceiling on the East side of the building. He took a slow, deep sip of the wine and admired how the lights on Broadway lit up the sky and the street below. It was 10 p.m. and yet the street was almost as bright as daylight. The view from the 18th floor made the figures below so small. Cars moved like pieces on a board game. He wondered if his view was like God's as he looked down on Earth.

He must be so disappointed in us, he thought.

With another sip of wine, he noticed something on the corner that looked like an empty cardboard refrigerator box. What caught his attention was the movement from inside the box. He wondered if a dog had maybe taken temporary residence. What he eventually saw, however, was the figure of a man tossing and turning to shelter himself inside the cardboard. Every time the man would manage to get his body covered, the cool autumn wind would blow like a cruel jokester, ripping the paper back off his body. London's eyes welled with tears at the sight of the man's struggle; melancholy filled his heart.

"That's so wrong," he said out loud, just as the receptionist entered the room with his salad.

"Excuse me," she asked. "This isn't what you wanted?"

He turned and looked at her. "What?" he said.

"The salad, Mr. Drake. Is it not what you wanted?"

"The salad's fine," he replied. His sadness turned to an angry frustration. "It's the world that's fucked up. Why do we have to struggle so god damned much?"

The receptionist said nothing.

He looked at her and realized that she must have been all of about twenty-one. Certainly, she was too young for his cynicism; too inexperienced. "The salad is fine. Really," he said. "Thank you."

But his irritation grew. He was angry at himself for not appreciating where he was. He was angry for knowing he should feel more grateful. And he was frustrated with his inability to write something meaningful and to deliver something with which people could connect. His heart ached knowing that his own frustration and fear destroyed the potential for a meaningful relationship. He missed Kat.

Was it really that long ago that I knew what it felt like to want something, to need something? he asked of himself.

He thought more about Katorah. He had wanted her. And yet his own inability to move beyond the past blocked him from that happiness. Fire swelled in his core. A recording was just not going to happen; not tonight.

He pulled his cell phone from his pocket and called for a car. A familiar driver was working the service. "Brandon, I need to get home," he told the driver whose voice he recognized.

"Yes, sir. I'll be downstairs in 10 minutes, Mr. Drake."

"Brandon, for the eightieth time, please just call me London. I'm a person, just like you."

"Sorry," the driver said. "I'll be right there, Mr. Drake."

On his way out, London walked down a hallway where some of the studio's albums hung. His own Gold album hung there, a reminder of past success. But he no longer found happiness there. Rather, he felt a pressure that he wasn't sure he could handle. It was asking him to be better than even he believed he could ever be.

FIFTY-ONE

"Jesus, London, what's with the mood?" Alex asked.

"What mood?" London asked in reply. "I'm fine."

Alex glanced down at the turkey sandwich that he had barely eaten. Instead, he had broken little pieces of the bread apart until there were crumbs piled on the edge of the plate. "Your sandwich doesn't think you're fine," Alex retorted.

He gripped what was left of the sandwich with one hand and pushed it into his mouth. "See?" he said with his mouth full. "Fine."

"Oh Jesus, London," Alex answered. "Knock it the hell off and just tell me what's up. It's not just the turkey sandwich. You've been in a funk for a month now. I don't see as how bottling it all up is doing you any good." She suddenly realized she was being stern and remembered that the "bad cop" approach never really worked well with London. She softened her tone. "I'm worried, honey. Please talk to me."

He dropped remnants of the sandwich on his plate. "I don't know what to say."

"Why don't you just start talking," Alex suggested. She clearly wanted to do something to make the problem plaguing him a little better.

"I'm just an asshole," he said. "Like usual, I fucked something up and this time I can't fix it."

Alex sat quiet and waited for him to continue.

"The fucking ghosts of my past have once again surfaced to make my present a real fun place to be," he said.

"Your grandparents?" Alex asked. "What happened?"

He told Alex about his fight with Katorah. He paused in between parts of the story, trying to reflect on how it must have looked from Katorah's side. "I just don't know why it all makes me so angry, Alex," he said. "It's been decades, for Christ's sake. And I just can't let it go. I still – after all these years – carry it with me all the time. I'm tired of it."

"She'll come around, honey," Alex said, trying to reassure him. "Have you called her?"

He laughed a sarcastic laugh. "Yeah...about 10 times. I left a couple of messages for her to call me back, but she hasn't. I think I scared her, Lex. I was mean." He dropped his head.

"Come on, London," Alex said trying to ease his self-loathing. "She knows you, right? She'll come around. You're not a monster. She knows that."

"But Lex, I was a monster. I was mean and angry...so angry. And she didn't deserve it. You should have seen her. And it wasn't the first time she saw my temper," he shared, in reference to his first meeting with Katorah. "She's seen the monster before. And now she knows that I come from a family full of monsters. I'd be scared as hell if I were her. I'd be running, too."

"London," Alex reassured, "your grandfather wasn't a monster...you know that...and neither are you. Give her time, hun. Maybe she just needs some space."

"I love this girl," he told Alex. "It's killing me that I hurt her. It's killing me that she won't answer my calls. And it's killing me that after all these fucking years, I just can't let go of the past and be happy." His voice had risen in anger to a level that drew attention from the other Panera customers.

Alex looked surprised to hear the word love from him in reference to a woman. She reached across the table and placed her hand on his arm. "Let's get out of here, OK?" she asked.

In the car on the way back to London's apartment, Alex didn't push the conversation. She knew better than to ask for more than he was ready to offer. Once at home, she hoped he would talk more about Katorah and he did. He told Alex about their dates together, talked about Lucy, and said that he had plans with Katorah for the upcoming holidays.

"Now it's all shit," he said. "Like always, my fucking defensive attitude put walls between us that I thought had just fallen down. I'm in love with her, Alex," he said. "And now I don't know what to do."

"I'm sorry, honey," she said, trying to calm her friend. There was really nothing more she could say.

"Yeah. Me, too," he replied. "Me, too."

"Have you talked to Patricia about all this?" she asked. Again, London offered his sarcastic laugh. "Patricia will be permanently in business trying to help me," he replied. "Some days, I think I'm just hopeless."

"Not hopeless, London," she retorted. "Just complicated. It makes you interesting," she said, trying to lighten the tone.

"I'd like to be boring for a while," he answered. "Just to see what 'normal' feels like."

"Hmmm. Me too," she replied. Then, after a moment of silence added, "Oh come, London. You know we don't want to be boring." The two laughed. "Maybe a little less psychotic, but normal? Nahhhh."

She rose from the couch. "Gimme a hug before I go," she demanded. With her arms wrapped around him, she kissed London's neck and whispered in his ear. "I love you. Everything will work out." She knew that hearing her say it would make London feel better, for at least that moment.

"I hope you're right, babe," he said. "I love you, too. Text me when you get home so I know you're safe." He always said that when she left.

Once alone, London tried to distract himself from his thoughts and from the ache he felt deep in his chest. He watched TV, tried finishing a song, sorted his laundry, and then finally picked up his phone to call Katorah. When the call went to voicemail, he closed his eyes and listened to her voice. He ached so much to hold her again. But without leaving a message, he hung up.

FIFTY-TWO

"London, I'm glad to see you," Patricia said, as London took his usual seat.

He wondered how true her statement really was. He could hardly stand himself these days; he couldn't imagine that anyone would actually enjoy his company. "Let's see how glad you are in 20 minutes," he said, quite seriously.

Patricia joined him at the other side of the coffee table, opened her notes, and with one finger, pushed a pair of purple reading glasses higher up on her nose. "So tell me what's been happening since our last appointment," she said.

He exhaled. He wasn't sure he even wanted to say it all out loud. Instead he tugged at the t-shirt that all of a sudden felt tight.

"Take your time, London," Patricia said, to soothe him. "Take a deep breath."

"It's time to fix this," he simply said. "I'm ready to do what I need to do to close my past. I need to start building a future."

Patricia placed her tablet on the table in front of her and slid the glasses off her face.

"Remember the hypnosis thing you told me about a while ago?" he asked, referencing a method Patricia had offered London in past sessions. "I know I was skeptical, but I've reconsidered. I'm ready to do whatever the hell I need to do to heal, Patricia."

"Tell me what happened," Patricia said. "What is the trigger for this decision? What's brought you around to it?"

He knew there was no escaping the story of what had happened with Katorah. He recalled it for Patricia, including details of the time they spent together before their fight. He spoke tenderly of Katorah, melancholy in his heart. "I'm letting people who are dead ruin my life...my living," he said to Patricia. "I need to let that go and move forward."

"I'm encouraged by your determination, London," Patricia said.

She always offered something positive to the conversation. He wished he could find the positive for himself.

She continued. "I think you've done some great work up to this point. You are able to reflect more clearly on your own actions and I think you more clearly understand the triggers that upset you or make you anxious. Would you say that's true?"

He nodded. "I guess. It's hard for me to give myself any credit... especially now. But I know that my family is at the root of all of it. And I'm ready to resolve that."

Assured that London was in fact ready for the work, Patricia sat forward in her chair to again explain the therapy. "As I've already explained to you, what we are going to use is a form of psychotherapy called EMDR. Basically, when someone has experienced a negative life event – like rape or military combat, for example – the experience may overwhelm usual cognitive and neurological coping mechanisms. The memories of that event may be inadequately processed and are stored in an isolated memory network. The point of EMDR is to help the person process these distressing memories so that they are not recalled with such intensity and no longer make such an influence on a person's life."

He listened intently, but his face showed that Patricia's language was making it hard for him to really follow along.

"This won't be a quick fix, London," she told him. "But EMDR has been proven to help people build positive statements about themselves. Those positive ideas replace the negative feelings or beliefs that you continue to hold on to. Does that make sense?"

"It does," he said, with some disbelief in the process.

"Throughout the process, you will also learn how to feel in control, London. I know that's important to you," Patricia said reassuringly. "You'll experience that feeling of control while you are here and then you will continue to feel it outside this office. Your journal will become more important than ever, and I will teach you some techniques that you can use on your own to feel calm."

"Calm would be good," he replied. "I'm pretty scattered."

Patricia explained that people who engage in EMDR often learn techniques to improve their relationships, break through emotional barriers, or overcome limitations that have prevented them from living truly fulfilling lives. "I'm not trying to sell you on it," she said. "Every person is different. But I think it's worth a try, London."

"And how long do you think it will take to work?" he asked. "How many sessions?"

The question prompted Patricia to make a point even clearer than she previously had. "This isn't a magic bullet, London," she said gently. "There's no way for me to predict how many sessions it will take for you to see or feel results. I can't even guarantee that it will work at all for you. Like I said, every person is different."

He squirmed in his seat. He was obviously anxious for some kind of resolution.

"What I can tell you is that we've already done some of the work without you even knowing it," Patricia said.

He looked intrigued.

Patricia explained. "One of the earliest phases of EMDR is centered on building trust between the patient and therapist." She paused.

He sensed that she didn't want to just assume that he trusted her. "I hope it's clear that I trust you, Patricia," he offered. "If I haven't made that obvious, I'm telling you now. If I didn't trust you, I wouldn't keep coming back."

Patricia smiled and continued. "We've also done some of the assessment work we needed to do to move forward. I already understand the target event we'll work to resolve...the death of your grandparents. But we will need to identify a little more clearly some of the negative statements you associate with that event...in other words, how that event makes you think negative things about yourself."

He exhaled deeply and pushed his hands through his hair. "How does that play into all this?" he asked.

"We've spent a lot of time talking about your grandparents and their deaths," Patricia explained. "But we'll need to focus on processing those events. And processing doesn't mean talking about it...it's much deeper than that."

"OK," he said. "How does it work?"

"Well, I'm going to guide you through a process where we identify a statement that expresses a negative self-belief you hold related to your grandparents' deaths. In place of that negative belief, we will work on instilling positive feelings...something that applies to the present, instead of letting you carry something around from the past."

He knew that Patricia was simplifying everything for him as best she could. He also knew that he would indeed have to trust her to move forward.

"I'm on board," he said to her. "Let's get started. The sooner we start, the sooner we know if it's gonna help, right?" he asked, trying to sound optimistic.

"Well that's true," Patricia responded in appreciation of his effort. "But London, the issues with Katorah will still remain. Unfortunately, this won't resolve those. Those will be for you to make right, you know?" she asked soothingly. "We can talk more about your feelings associated with that argument if you'd like."

"No," he replied. "First things first. I can't make things right with anyone else until I'm OK with me," he said, very matter-of-factly.

"Fair enough," Patricia responded. "Shall we get started?"

FIFTY-THREE

Light music – a soothing mixture of tones – played in the background and Patricia sat close to London, her fingertips tapping bilaterally on his knees. He was nestled in the soft black sofa with his eyes closed; tribal rhythms and the flow of a keyboard lulled him.

Tap on his right knee.

Tap on his left knee.

Back and forth in pulse with the drum lightly thumping.

Tap...tap...tap...tap.

For many minutes, there was no sound except the music and the exhale of deep breaths. Finally, Patricia's voice softly entered the pattern. "We are going to begin. Please tell me about your earliest childhood memory," she said.

"I am in New York City...Madison Square Garden...Barnum and Bailey Circus," he replied. "I am with my parents. This is one of my favorite memories."

"And how old are you?" Patricia asked.

"Not sure...maybe five," he said. The memory grew deeper as he recalled his own tiny hand inside his father's large claw. "I'm little," he simplified. "My mom is so happy...seems mesmerized by my fascination with the pink all around us...pink cotton candy, pink bubble gum water ice, pink spinning lights. Just pink."

"Lights?" Patricia asked, looking for London to clarify the memory further.

"Like glow sticks, except on a string that you could twirl around. There are hundreds....no, thousands...I can see them shining across the whole arena," he said. "There are elephants, clowns on bikes, lions, and pink lights spinning constantly."

"How do you feel?" Patricia asked.

"I feel loved...safe," he answered. "I don't know if I ever felt safer than in this moment. It's wonderful."

"What makes you feel safe?" Patricia asked.

"I'm not sure," he replied. "My Dad made me feel safe...he was so big. And my mom's joy...her smile...it makes me feel happy. So strange..." His voice trailed off.

"Tell me...what's strange?" Patricia inquired.

"My mom and dad loved me so much," he answered, with a building confusion on his face. "But they didn't seem to know how to love each other. I think they did the best they could...I just wish...that things could have been different."

Patricia knew they were moving into a more difficult memory. She pushed gently. "Different how?" she asked.

"They spent years together after it was so obvious that they would have been happier apart. I wish they would have either worked out their differences, or just called it quits!" he explained.

"And why didn't they separate?" Patricia asked, knowing London would have an answer. But the answer did not come right away. Instead, a hush came over London.

Tap...tap...tap...tap.

Patricia sat patiently. It was important that London speak next.

Finally, he did. "My grandparents," he said.

"Can we talk about your grandparents?" Patricia asked tenderly.

"Yes," he replied, his right hand now gently quivering.

Patricia moved cautiously. "Can you tell me about that day?" she asked. Another pause.

"It started like any other day," he finally said. "I was walking home from school...it was chilly for September...and I walked alone because for a reason I didn't know, my grandmother was not there. She almost always met me after school."

He paused and took a breath. "I walked the path along Lincoln Avenue that ran parallel to a fenced-in golf course," he continued. "I remember running my fingers through the rusted metal fencing. I can almost still feel the grittiness of the steel on my fingertips, cold and rough."

"Was this your normal way home?" Patricia asked.

"Yes," he answered. "I stopped at the candy store to get some black licorice," he said. "But when I got home, I was surprised that my grandmother was not outside waiting. If she didn't meet me at school, she was always outside with Sandy," he said, referring to his childhood dog. "But not today..."

He paused, seeming to have lost his place in the story.

"Are you still with me?" Patricia asked. "How does this memory make you feel?"

He answered. "I remember feeling out of sorts as I reached the front door. I crouched down for the spare key. It was always under the mat. But it wasn't there."

His heart began to beat faster.

Tap...tap...tap...tap.

"I went to the neighbors' to use the phone, but they weren't home."

Tap...tap...tap...tap.

"So I went back to the candy store to use the pay phone."

"And what happened next?" Patricia asked with expressed interest.

"Hi, Momma! It's me."

"Hey baby, everything OK?"

"Yeah, Mom, but I think Grandmom and Grandpop are sleeping. No one is answering the door and the spare key ain't under the mat."

'Ain't isn't a word, baby."

He interrupted his own story with a laugh about his mother's grammar correction. Then he continued. "What happened next was a lot of waiting. I'm sure it was a matter of minutes, but I waited for what felt like hours to get into my house..." He paused, swallowed, and then continued. "If only I had my key...maybe I could have stopped him," he said angrily.

Patricia sensed his irritation and replied, "I know it hurts. But you had nothing to with what he did or did not do. This was not your fault." She paused and then repeated, "This was not your fault."

Tap...tap...tap...tap.

"Are we OK to move forward?" she asked.

After a moment, he responded. "Yes," he said. "The next thing I remember is my Dad pulling up in his Oldsmobile...black, with leather interior, white-walled tires and chrome spoked wheels. He really loved that car..." he said, his heartbeat slowing again. "On Sunday afternoons, we'd take a drive...him and me and my mother...and every time we'd drive by a building that reflected the car, he would slow down to marvel at his baby... that car was his baby."

"What a wonderful memory," Patricia said. "But let's not get sidetracked. Please take me back to where you were...standing outside the house waiting to open the door."

"I'm sorry," he replied.

"No reason to say you're sorry," Patricia said to reassure him. "This is your safe place. There is no need for apologies here."

He resumed the memory.

> *"Hey, dad, do you think they're sleeping?"*
> *"We have to make sure you carry your key, kid."*
> *"I know, dad. Sorry."*

He recalled that once the front door was open, he saw his dog tied to the railing in the hallway. The memory made him angry.

"Why does this make you angry?" Patricia asked him.

"She could hardly move," he told her. "She just looked so sad, tied to that railing."

"A railing?" Patricia asked, pushing London to more clearly describe the scene.

"Yes," he said. "We lived in a duplex with my grandparents. They lived downstairs and we lived above them. Poor Sandy was tied to the entryway railing just outside their front door. She was just pawing and scratching trying to get inside."

"And what happened next?" Patricia asked to guide the conversation.

"Pop? Ma?" KNOCK. KNOCK. KNOCK.

"I tried knocking, Dad....they're not answering. Maybe they went out?" BANG. BANG. BANG.

> *"Pop? Ma?"*
> *"Dad, why aren't they answering?"*
> *"Pop. Ma. Open the god damned door."*
> *"The dog was now barking uncontrollably... so loud...so chaotic," he recalled.*
> *"Come here, kid. You gotta help me."*
> *"What are you gonna do, Dad?"*
> *"We're gonna break down the door. On the count of three, I want you to push your whole weight into it. I'm gonna do the*

same thing. Ready? One...two...three..."

BAM.

"Again, kid. Harder this time. One...two...three..."

BAM. BAM. CRASH.

His breaths grew shorter.

Tap...tap...tap...tap.

"Tell me about this memory," Patricia said to London.

"It was so loud," he told her. "The impact of our bodies hitting the wood made the frame split at the hinges...like thunder. And once it was down, I started to move inside, but my dad yelled."

"Wait! Let me go first."

"Did you follow him?" Patricia asked.

"Yes," he answered. "It was so dark inside...not so much black...more like black and gray washed over in blue. All the drapes were fastened tightly over the windows blocking any sunlight. Once my eyes adjusted, I could see that things had been moved."

"Moved?" Patricia asked, looking for clarification. "Is the fact that things were moved disturbing to you?"

"Yes," he replied. "I got a sense in my gut that something was not right. The dining room table was pushed across the room against the far wall. A couple dozen checks lay neatly on top of their corresponding bills with due dates circled. There was a note."

"Dad, look at this."

"What is it?"

"Dad..."

"Take your time," Patricia soothed as London moved forward with his memory. "Are you OK?"

"And then I turned around," he recalled. "That's when I saw him."

"Oh fuck. Oh no. Oh, Jesus, oh Christ!"

Tap...tap...tap...tap. "What did you do next?" Patricia asked.

"I could not believe what I was seeing in front of my eyes," he said. "I shut my eyes as tight as I could...squeezed them shut...and then reopened them....closed again...then opened. I fell to my knees praying to anyone who would listen.

"No! This can't be real...make me wake up...this is a nightmare...this isn't real. Please, please, please...make this not be happening."

"I know that must have been a terrible experience for you," Patricia said.

His breath was now labored and beads of sweat formed on his brow. "But every time I opened my eyes, he was there...five feet in front of me levitating...feet not touching the ground. I kept blinking my wet eyes to refocus. And then...a noose...tied tightly around his neck...the black handle of a butcher knife jutting from his abdomen...his white t-shirt blood-soaked to the color of crimson. His side was split open like a piñata."

He bit his lip and tears welled up over his eyelids and ran down his cheeks.

"Do you remember what you were feeling in that moment?" Patricia asked.

"I felt helpless," he replied. "I felt out of control."

"Take a breath," she petitioned. "Try to relax. You are safe here," she said.

"It was such an overwhelming shock to see my grandfather swinging lifeless in front of me," he shared. "I didn't know whether to look...what to do. I was so scared. And then, when I diverted my eyes, it got even worse."

"How so?" Patricia asked.

"All I saw were her feet," he recalled. "And then my father's reaction... it was so horrible...so violent..."

"How did you feel about your place in that moment?" Patricia asked.

"My father grabbed me by the back of the neck and tossed me back out into the front hall. I remember feeling like a puppy that was being shooed out of the room. I just ran upstairs to our apartment, but I could hear my father screaming – almost howling in horror downstairs, 'Oh my fucking God. Someone murdered them.' He screamed it over and over and over again. I started back down the stairs to him...but then...POW! His huge fist right through the wall. And then he crumbled...just fell to pieces sobbing on the floor. I needed my mother."

"What was it about that event that made you need your mother?"

"I just needed to feel safe. I needed to feel like I mattered."

"Did you feel anything else?" Patricia asked.

"Yes. I felt like my family had been destroyed. And you know what? It had been. I learned later that it wasn't a stranger that had murdered them. He did it. My grandfather stabbed my grandmother...and then he killed himself. My mother told me later that my father actually pulled the bloody knife out of my grandfather's lifeless body. His own father...just hanging there."

"And what emotions or beliefs did that prompt inside of you" Patricia asked.

"I remember feeling confused and hurt. I remember believing that I didn't have anything to offer that would make people love me enough to stick around. And that feeling of being alone...it was safer than trusting other people who might hurt me again."

He cried hard. The flood of emotion was too much for him to control. It was the first time since his childhood that he had talked all the way through the story...allowed himself to feel all of it at once.

Patricia offered him a box of tissues and allowed him time to settle. She rose from her seat to click off the music. "You're doing good work," she said reassuringly. "I'm proud of you."

He exhaled and sat silent for a moment. He wiped his wet eyes and blinked furiously. "Whew," he said. "That was a lot. I'm exhausted."

"That's very normal. Your brain was doing some really hard stuff," Patricia replied. "But you did an excellent job, London," she said reassuringly. "Next time, we will focus on redirecting your feelings in a more positive way...the feelings about yourself, I mean."

"That will be good," he said. "Really good."

"So I will see you next week?" Patricia asked, confirming their next appointment.

He nodded.

"In the meantime," she said, "I want you to use your journal. Some of the feelings you experienced today may resurface. Write down if there's a prompt and then spend some time reflecting."

He rose from the couch and motioned toward the door. He really was physically exhausted. The experience had been painful, but in a way cleansing. He almost felt as if he should hug Patricia for leading him to it. Instead, he forced a smile and thanked her.

FIFTY-FOUR

Five days after his session with Patricia, London got a burst of new energy. Recalling the complete story for Patricia had been difficult. It was something he was previously unwilling to do, but now, a part of him felt liberated. The emotions he had smothered for so long were now out in the world, expressed to another person. And his journal was now full of reflections.

Since the therapy session, he had slept very little. Instead, at night when everything was still, he would write. There were very few complete sentences, but a lot of words on paper. If he felt an emotion, he wrote it down. Words like fear, loneliness, frustration, and anger appeared over and over again. But he also kept writing the words love and safety. Most of the time, he wrote these words together and followed them with a question mark, wondering if the two things could actually exist in unison.

When he returned to Patricia's office the following week, he had an agenda. He usually showed up for his appointment and followed Patricia's lead, but this time he was specific in what he wanted to discuss.

"I'm just so fucking angry," he told Patricia.

"Let's talk about that," Patricia replied in her usual way. "Can you be specific?"

"Since I was here last time, I've been writing...and writing a lot," he told her and fanned open the pages of his journal as evidence.

Patricia looked at the lined pages covered in black ink; some of the pages even had drawings on them that looked like fits of scribble.

"I'm exhausted because I'm not sleeping, but I'm also energized with this anxiety," he explained. "It's like I have this fire burning in my chest and if I don't figure out how to control it, it might just consume me."

Patricia sat forward in her chair. "And what is the cause of this fire, London?" she asked. "What is the fuel?"

"Last week did something to me, Patricia," he explained. "I don't know what, but before I came in here, I was at a standstill ... blocked ... emotionally and creatively. I couldn't write a song to save my life, couldn't describe how I was feeling, couldn't tell you if I was happy or sad. I was numb."

"And now?" Patricia asked.

"And now I can't fucking stop," he exclaimed and rose from his seat. He paced nervously back and forth in the small space between the couch and the coffee table and dropped his journal in front of Patricia. "Pages and pages of it, Patricia, and none of it really makes any sense to me. But I can't stop it from pouring out of me. It's like I keep writing down these words and emotions hoping that they will form some kind of equation...like a math problem. But one and one never equal two and I am never relieved of this...this...this anger."

Patricia sat back in her seat and said nothing.

He continued pacing, pushing his hands through his hair.

She waited until he finally sat back down, his right knee now bouncing up and down. "So we need to address your anger then," Patricia said. "It's a good place to start. Tell me what's making you angry, London."

He exhaled and lowered his head. When he raised his eyes to again meet hers, he simply said, "My grandfather, Patricia. My grandfather makes me angry."

Patricia waited.

"He was so fucking selfish, Patricia," he continued. "He just gave into his pain and his frustrations and he took the fucking easy way out." He stood again. "And he took her with him. He made the choice for both of them and it pisses me off. It was a bunch of macho bullshit. Did he even think about how it would affect the rest of us who were left behind? Did he think about the newspaper headlines, and how my father would have to face our neighbors? Did he think about my poor mother who was left to hold a family together who had been torn to shreds? I mean, come on."

Patricia encouraged London to retake his seat. She had counseled other clients who were dealing with the emotional baggage of suicide in their families, but London had never been willing to address the issue so directly in the past. She knew this conversation was a monumental step forward for him. He had moved past the denial stage of grief to anger.

"London," she said calmly. "Do you think your grandfather was able to think about all that at the time? Do you think he would intentionally hurt all of you?"

"Intentional or not, he did," he said. "He was clearly able to think rationally about lots of things," he replied, citing the payment due notices his grandfather had lined on the dining room table. "So why shouldn't I think that he was able to be rational?"

"I can't speak to your grandfather's state of mind, London," Patricia said.

"I just keep thinking that if I had gotten home a little sooner, maybe I could have stopped him," he said, in a calmer tone. "Maybe he was rational. Maybe I could have reasoned with him. Or maybe he would have killed me, too."

Patricia counseled London, moving cautiously forward. "London, people who commit suicide do so for many reasons. Sometimes they are sad or frustrated. Sometimes they are weary of physical pain or mental anguish. There are lots and lots of reasons. So while I can't give you a definitive reason for what your grandfather did, I can tell you with all certainty that you are not to blame. You were a child, London. There was nothing you could have done."

He began to sob. The emotions of 20 years poured out of him in tears that stained the journal pages he now held in his lap. "I'm just tired, Patricia," he said. "I'm tired of carrying this anger and frustration around with me. I want to let it go. I want to be happy."

"London," Patricia said and then redirected the conversation. "Tell me about a happy memory. Pick one where your whole family is together and describe for me how you felt."

He collapsed back into the couch and dropped his head back on the cushion. He closed his eyes. "There were so many happy times," he said, not opening his eyes.

"Pick one and tell me about it," Patricia said. He sat quiet for only a few moments and then began to share a memory. He told Patricia that as a child he would wait every day on the corner of Main and Eastwick – just right outside his school – for his grandmother. Since their house was only a few blocks away from the school, she would meet him there every afternoon at 3:40 p.m. and they would walk home together. If it was raining, she'd have an umbrella big enough for the two of them to share. If it was cool, she'd bring him an extra sweater.

He shared that sometimes he and his grandmother would stop in a diner that was just about half way between school and home. He was always sworn to secrecy about their afternoon stop; his grandmother feared that if his mother found out, he would be the one to suffer the consequence. His eyes lit up as he shared the experience with Patricia. "She would always say there was nothing wrong with having dessert before dinner every once in a while," he said with a smile. He recalled how they would always sit at the counter and enjoy a piece of pie. "I always figured that she was the one who made dinner," he said. "If she didn't mind ruining my appetite, who was I to object?"

"And how did this time with your grandmother make you feel, London?" Patricia asked.

"I still really like pie!" he joked in reply. "But I loved that little bit of extra time with her...just the two of us alone at that counter."

His eyes trailed off into the distance. Patricia could tell that he was not only remembering the event, but also the feelings associated with it. She let him reminisce a while longer. He broke the silence with a quiet laugh. "She always began the conversation the same way," he continued. "Now baby, tell me about your day," he said, mimicking his grandmother. "Her eyes were always so full of anticipation."

He told Patricia that he rarely had an exciting story to share. He was not a fan of school; he maneuvered through his day routinely avoiding any activity that would draw attention to him. "But rather than disappoint her," he told Patricia, "I would just make up stories...stories about things I'd seen happen to other kids...or I'd use my imagination to make the things that actually did happen a little more dramatic or funny than they really were."

Patricia laughed with him. "And how did that go?" she asked.

"It seemed to work!" he replied. "She listened intently, never interrupting. And she never questioned the details. She just nodded and smiled. So even if she knew I was making it all up, she never let on!"

"Your time with her sounds wonderful," Patricia said.

He nodded. "It was," he said. "But the best was what she said when we got home."

"She always said the same thing?" Patricia questioned.

"Yep. Every time," he answered. "We would get to the bottom of the steps at home and she would stop and turn toward me. I can remember how her hand felt cupping my chin so that she could direct my eyes up to meet hers."

"And what did she say?" Patricia asked.

"Remember, baby," he said, again in a voice not exactly his own, "this is our secret. Nothing wrong with sharing a piece of pie...and a piece of yourself...with someone you love."

Wrapping up the memory, he told Patricia that he was happy to keep the secret. He even went out of his way on nights when the two had stopped for their afternoon treat to ask for seconds at dinner, just so his mother wouldn't suspect that he'd eaten something after school. "I must have looked like the Cheshire Cat," he recalled for Patricia. "I would smile as wide as I could, lift my plate, and politely ask for more." He was now laughing, recalling how their secret was always safe.

"And how does this memory make you feel about your family, London?" Patricia asked.

"Safe...like we all belonged there," he said. "When we all sat together around that table...my grandparents, my mom, my dad, and me..." His voice trailed off. "It wasn't just my belly that was full," he finally said. "I remember feeling like my heart felt full, too."

FIFTY-FIVE

London was excited to be meeting his mother for lunch. Since she had remarried and moved to Florida right after he was signed by the record label, he missed seeing her more often. He looked forward to sharing details about his recent therapy sessions with her in person. He could read her better when she was seated across the table. He could judge her body language and interpret her reactions. When she'd told him that she would be up for the weekend to attend a baby shower, he made sure to schedule the time with her right away.

"Look at you all nice and tan!" he exclaimed when his mother turned to greet him in the restaurant. "Florida agrees with you, Momma!"

"Hey, baby," she said, extending her arms to hug him. She pulled back and looked more closely into his eyes and then pushed herself into him again to continue the embrace.

"I'm so happy to see you," he told her. "I missed you, Momma."

A young hostess escorted him and his mother to a table in the back corner of the restaurant. Once they were seated, she dropped two menus on the table and told them that their server would be with them shortly. When Emily did come to take their order, London ordered two unsweetened iced teas and a large sausage and spinach pizza for them to share. It was their "regular" order.

"So how was your trip?" he asked his mother.

She described a two hour delay in Orlando caused by some unexpected rain, but said that the flight itself was uneventful. "I sat next to the nicest lady," she told him. "She was traveling home from a baby shower. Isn't that a coincidence?" his mother asked.

He tried to sound interested through the small talk, but was eager to jump into a heavier conversation with his mother. He waited until she had finished her first slice of pizza before he brought up his therapy.

"So, Mom," he finally said, "I've been making some really great progress in therapy." He paused. "I feel like I'm really making some great movement forward."

"That's good, honey," his mother replied. "I'm glad you're feeling good about it. What in particular has you feeling so positive?"

"We've been working a lot on what happened to Grandma and Grandpop," he said, without looking up from his plate. "You know...trying to resolve my feelings about it all."

His mother lowered the slice of pizza she was holding and took a sip of her iced tea.

He interpreted the look on her face as frustration. He knew she never really understood why his grandparents' deaths were so hard for him to process and move past. He was surprised when she asked a follow up question.

"And how exactly are you feeling, honey?" she asked, in a softer tone than he expected.

"It's funny," he smirked. "For a long time, I didn't really know how I felt about it all. But recently, what I've uncovered is a lot of anger and a lot of resentment."

"London, you need to let that go," his mother said, in a more familiar tone.

"Mom, you know it's just not that easy for me. Quite frankly, I don't know how it was so easy for you," he said, in a more sarcastic way than he intended.

"Easy?" his mother asked. "Easy?" she repeated. "Oh, none of it was ever easy. When all that happened, it changed a lot of things. But what I realized is that it wasn't me...and it wasn't you...that died that day. I had to move on. I had you...I had your father...to care for. What you saw was me trying to survive. And just because I've moved on and found happiness doesn't mean I will ever forget that day or the things that happened after that day. I just refuse to be defined by them. I wish you could say the same."

He could feel his chest tighten. He had never heard his mother acknowledge the struggle before. It was refreshing to hear. But it also made him sad. "Mom," he said, "I'm working really hard to move past it all. I really am. And Patricia is great with me."

He told his mother about the EMDR. "It was the first time – in my whole life, I think, that I actually recounted that day so completely to anyone," he said. "It was...," he paused, "liberating."

Emily reappeared at the table and interrupted the conversation. "Can I get you anything else?" she asked, glancing at the unfinished pizza on the table.

London asked for a box and ordered coffee. His mother ordered the same. When the server left the table, he continued the conversation.

"How come you didn't put me in therapy right after it all happened?" he asked his mother. "I mean, don't you think that was a big deal for an 11-year-old?"

"Well of course it was," his mother rebutted. "And we did talk to your school and to the guidance counselor. But therapy didn't exist...wasn't recommended...like it is today. We worried about you, honey. I still worry about you."

He nodded. He had not known about the conversations with the guidance counselor. "They encouraged us to keep an eye on you," his mother continued, "and to watch to make sure you were pursuing your interests. You were doing fine in school. And you got so interested in music. We assumed you were OK."

His mother lowered her eyes to the table. He could tell she was upset. He reached across the table and took her hand. "I know you did your best," he said to her. "And now I'm doing my best, too. I have to get beyond the past to define my own future. I'm really trying hard to do that."

By the time Emily returned with coffee, he decided that he wanted dessert. He knew his mother loved a good piece of cake so he ordered a slice to share with her. Two forkfuls of the dense, moist chocolate dessert helped to lighten the mood at the table again.

"Alex said to say hello to you," he said. "She was going to join us, but she had another commitment."

"She's a wonderful girl, London," his mother said, hinting as she always did that maybe something more than friendship was possible.

"I know, Mom," he returned. "She's the best. I told you she is engaged now, right?"

His mother rolled her eyes. "Yeah," she replied. "You told me. I just hope he's a nice guy."

He withheld his comments about George. Instead he simply replied that

Alex seemed happy. He pushed the last bite of cake toward his mother's side of the plate and smiled.

"So what else are you up to?" she asked. "How's the new record coming?"

He exhaled. "It's going OK, I guess. I've been having a hard time in the studio," he told her. He didn't want to explain the situation with Katorah to his mother. She would only be disappointed that the potential relationship wasn't realized. "I think I'm just a little short on inspiration," he said instead.

His mother responded, surprised and confused. "You?" she asked, "Short on inspiration? I find that hard to believe. You have always been full of ideas. I swear you were born with lyrics and a melody inside of you."

"You were always my biggest fan," he replied, in appreciation. "It's just a lot of pressure."

"Do you still love it?" she asked. "Does it still get you excited?"

He was taken aback by the questions. He paused to think about them for a moment. "You know," he finally said, "it's been so long since I thought about what I do like that. Between the record label's expectations and the pressure of the studio, it's become more of a business than a passion," he told his mother. "At this point, it's hard for me to even remember how I ended up here...as a musician, I mean."

"Forget?" his mother exclaimed. "I will never forget! Music is inside of you, baby. Think back to elementary school. It was there even then. Don't you remember? Whatever else was happening in our lives...no matter what direction we were going...music was always your anchor."

He listened intently to his mother's advice. She was such a good reminder for him of who he was. Good or bad, she knew his soul.

FIFTY-SIX

The first door London tried on the elementary school was locked. It was 4:30 p.m. and he suspected that the building would be practically empty, except for the kids who had been caught chewing gum or without homework and were forced into detention. The last bus used to leave the street by 3:50 p.m. and from what he could tell that was still the case. But he also remembered that the custodians worked late into the night, scraping the gum off the underside of desks and polishing the floors with a wax that left the hallways shiny and smelling of a weird antiseptic.

Maybe the front entrance, he thought.

The glass double doors at the main entrance of the school were also locked. "Damn it," he said out loud, tugging one more time. As he turned in defeat, he heard a voice, faint, from inside.

"Just a minute," a man said, as he moved hurriedly toward the glass doors.

The man was middle-aged and tall. His dark suit was offset by a brightly colored tie that featured Cookie Monster counting cookies. London guessed that he was the principal.

"May I help you?" the man asked, moving his hand inside a pocket and then out again to reveal a key. "Are you from the book company? I expected you at 3, but you're more than welcome to bring them in now."

He pushed the door open toward London, who hesitated.

"Uh, no," London replied. "I'm not a...delivery guy. My name is London. London Drake." He paused for a moment, waiting for the man to recognize him.

The man stood silent, just looking at London and waiting for more information.

"I went to this school. I was in the neighborhood," London continued and grinned.

The man grew a little impatient with London's unintended lack of clarity. "And how can I help you?" he asked.

Finally, London revealed his purpose. "I'd like to talk to the principal about maybe setting up a tour." He hesitated. "Is that...you?"

"Yes," the man replied, extending his hand. "I'm Tim Cook. Why don't you come in for a minute?"

"Thank you," London replied and followed the principal into the building.

"Give me just a minute," Mr. Cook said, as he escorted London down the hall and into an office on the right. "Have a seat and I'll be right back. I just want to ask our custodian to be on the lookout for that book delivery."

London took a seat in a deep leather chair and glanced around the office. The orange striped wallpaper of the 70s had been replaced with fresh paint in a neutral sand color. Rich oak cabinets now replaced the metal filers that used to mark the office, but it was still recognizably a principal's office. On the edge of the desk sat an apple-shaped business card holder that held cards: MR. TIM COOK, PRINCIPAL.

He felt a degree of anxiety starting to rise within his chest. He'd never been called into this office as a boy for any good reason. He'd never been a Student of the Month, or a prized spelling bee champ. Rather, his presence in the office had usually been the result of some altercation in the cafeteria where he was the victim of teasing or horseplay. As an overweight child, the cafeteria was the perfect place for the other kids to point out his weight. One particular incident involved a girl – Julie– whom London thought for sure would be the love of his life. For a moment, he was lost in reverie:

On a Tuesday morning in February, he'd finally gotten the nerve to write Julie a note in homeroom. He had liked her since September of their 5th grade year and after five months of pining, he'd gathered the inner resolve he needed to actually tell her. He had noticed her, every day, in the cafeteria line. Some days she wore her silky blond hair up in a ponytail; other days, she let her hair fall loose. Some days she wore skirts and tiny sweaters; other days she wore plaid pants and a polo shirt. But two things were always the same. She was always smiling. And, every day at lunch, she bought an apple. He noticed how she always ate the apple first, before any of the other lunch options on her tray. He surmised that she must really like apples.

With brave determination, he finally decided that he would tell Julie about his feelings. After all, she had always been nice, smiling in the hall, or asking to copy his homework. He was reasonably certain that his affection might be mutual.

"Dear Julie," he scribbled on a piece of yellow lined tablet paper. *"You are sweet like an apple. Do you want to go to the movies with me?"*

He signed the printed note in cursive and made sure he was in school early that day to leave it on Julie's desk. With it, he left a shiny red apple – one that he'd bought from the local market with part of his allowance. It had taken him 10 minutes to pick it out. Around the stem, he'd tied a white ribbon, like the one she often wore in her hair. It was a perfect bow.

When Julie came into school that day, he was already in his seat, two rows over and three chairs back from where she sat. Her first response was that of confusion. He translated her expression as one of intrigue. Soon discovering the note, Julie read it and then glanced around the room. With a coy smile, she glanced back at him and then quickly tucked the apple in her book bag.

He waited all morning to hear back from Julie. They had homeroom. She said nothing. When the bell rang, she scurried out of her seat and into the hallway, swallowed by the other students. He would not see her again until lunch.

In the cafeteria, he went through the line and took his seat at his usual table. He waited. When lunchtime was half over and Julie had not yet shown up in the cafeteria, he began to worry. Had something happened to her?

"Hey asshole," a voice said from behind him.

He turned on the bench to see Stan, the class bully, standing behind him. He turned back toward the table, hoping that Stan was not talking to him.

"I said, hey you, fat boy," Stan repeated. "I'm talking to you."

London turned again, swallowed hard, and felt his heart begin to beat faster. "Hey Stan," he mumbled. "Need something?"

"I gotta message for you," Stan replied.

"A message?" London asked.

"Yeah, that's what I said. You hard of hearing or something?"

By now, the other kids in the cafeteria had turned to look.

London could feel small beads of sweat forming on his brow. "Uh no, I heard you," he mumbled.

"Well good, I'm glad you can hear," Stan said. "Wasn't sure your thick head would let any sound in."

Kids began to laugh.

"I gotta message for you from Julie," Stan said.

London was sure his heart stopped beating.

Stan reached into his own book bag and pulled out the shiny red apple. The bow, once tied so meticulously, was now hanging loose from a broken stem. With grubby fingers, Stan lifted the apple to his own mouth and wrapped his lips almost all the way around the fruit.

London couldn't ever remember seeing a mouth so big and so mean.

Ripping some flesh off the core, Stan tossed the apple at London. It bounced off his chest and rolled to his feet. "Oh, here's the message," Stan said and followed his initial toss with a crumpled piece of paper.

London reached out to grab the paper, his face now redder than even the apple had been. He stood silent.

Kids began to chant, "Read it, read it, read it."

London stood still, silent. He was fighting tears.

"Well, go ahead, read it," Stan ordered.

London did not.

"I said, read it, you stupid, fat shit."

Again, London stood silent, unmoving.

Stan grew impatient and lunged forward, pushing London to the floor. Finally, three teachers swooped in, like vultures after a kill, and pulled Stan off of him.

London's sweaty palm gripped the crumpled paper tight.

Later, as he sat in the principal's office waiting to tell his side of the story, he flattened out the note and read it.

"If you lose 500 pounds, I'll go out with you. Julie."

London rose from his seat and began to wander around the office. As he moved to the windows, he noticed that the sill was adorned with framed photos...images of two small boys with gap toothed grins; a photo of the field from inside Cowboys Stadium; and a snapshot of two older people that London guessed were Mr. Cook's parents. London immediately felt like he knew Mr. Cook a little better and then caught himself in that moment. *Funny*, he thought, *to be making assumptions about someone's life based on a line of framed photos on a windowsill. But isn't that how we make our assumptions? By what we can see?* London wondered what assumptions people made about his life when they saw him on stage, under the bright lights, looking like a rock star.

Mr. Cook soon reentered the office. "Sorry about that," he said. "Now how can I help you?"

"I was actually hoping to see the auditorium," London said.

"The auditorium?" Mr. Cook asked and then moved ahead to other questions. "I think I'm just a little confused. Are you a parent now? Do you have children you'd like to send here?"

"Children?" asked London, unable to even imagine himself as a father.

"Mr. Drake, what is it exactly that you're here for?"

Recognizing that his unscheduled appearance at the school was likely to be the subject of some question, London was quick to resolve some of Mr. Cook's confusion.

"It's quite simple, really," he said. "I went to elementary school here and it has been a number of years since I've been in this neighborhood. I was curious about how the school might have changed. And – honestly – my best memories of that time in my life were made in the auditorium. I am a singer and a songwriter," he told the principal. "That career path began here, in this school."

"I see," he said.

"So really, all I want is to just take a look," London explained. "If that would be OK."

"I think it would be just fine," said Mr. Cook. "Let me walk you down."

When the two entered the auditorium, it was dark, except for the emergency lighting. "Wouldn't want you to trip," said Mr. Cook. "Just wait here a moment and I'll get on some of the lights." When he disappeared behind the long black curtain, London took a seat in the back row. It was quiet, dark. And then, a few popping sounds. Light. Mr. Cook came from behind the curtain.

"I hope the stage lights will do," he said. "The PTO just donated this lighting system and I can't quite figure out more than that." He held a hand up over his head, eyes squinting to see into the darkness for London. His voice in response filled the black space.

"The stage lights are perfect. So much nicer than the ones I remember,"

London replied, trying to sound impressed. In reality, the lights he had grown accustomed to were far brighter than the ones in the auditorium, but he could sense Mr. Cook's pride and didn't want to undermine that in any way. He rose from his seat and made his way toward the stage.

"Any questions?" Mr. Cook asked. "Anything I can tell you about our school play, our concerts? Anything?"

"No," London answered. "Oh, wait," he retracted. "There is one thing. Does Miss Wynne still work here?" He didn't know why he bothered with his question. It had been almost 25 years since Miss Wynne was his teacher. It seemed most likely to him that she was no longer there.

"Rose Wynne?" the principal asked. "Why yes, she's still here. In fact, we just honored her at our spring concert. She is retiring this year."

London was happily surprised.

"If you'd like to leave her a note, stop back in the office on your way out. I can put one in her mailbox for you."

London did not reply. He stood silent on the stage, gazing out into the empty seats.

"OK, Mr. Drake, you have about 10 minutes and then I'm going to have to get ready to lock up again." Mr. Cook told him. "Take a moment. I'll be back in my office if you need something."

"Thank you, thank you so much," he replied.

Alone in the auditorium, London noticed how different the space felt to him now. It once seemed so huge to him, the ceilings so high, the seating enough for masses of people. Now, he noticed how he had to duck in certain areas so as not to hit his head on the second floor balcony, and how there was probably only enough seats to accommodate only an eighth of the fans he now drew. And yet, he suddenly felt at home.

He closed his eyes. He could feel the heat of the lights on his face. Tipping his head back, he stretched both arms out to his sides. He stood, absorbing the flood of memory that overtook him.

You can do this honey, he heard in his head. It was a soft, encouraging voice; the voice of Miss Wynne, his music teacher. *Just sing from your heart.*

He could hear the music begin; a song by Styx. In a low voice, eyes still closed, he began to sing:

I'm sailing away
Set an open course for the Virgin Sea

'Cause I've got to be free
Free to face the life that's ahead of me

The melody swirled in his head. His heart began to pound. He was again a boy of 10, standing on a stage in an auditorium full of people. His voice quivered as he continued, but grew louder:

On board I'm the captain
So climb aboard
We'll search for tomorrow on every shore
And I'll try, oh Lord ...

His voice cracked. A tear flowed down over his cheek. Eyes still closed, louder still, he continued:

And I'll try, oh Lord I'll try to carry on.

He dropped his head and opened his eyes, now wet with tears. The ballad was now playing at full volume in his head. The bombastic, guitar-heavy second half of the song vibrated his ear drums.

He moved across the stage, this time looking out into the lights and imagining his grandmother. Although an illusion, he could see her clearly, as if she were really there. He pictured his mother, Miss Wynne, parents of other kids, and some of his classmates. All of them, without exception, had eyes fixed upon him. He remembered all of them anxious to hear more.

He sang out, in full voice:
They said, "Come sail away, come sail away, come sail away with
*   me lads*
Come sail away, come sail away, come sail away with me
Come sail away, come sail away, come sail away with me baby
Come sail away, come sail away, come sail away with me"
And even louder:
Come sail away, come sail away, come sail away with me
Come sail away, come sail away, come sail away with me
Come sail away, come sail away, come sail away with me
Come sail away, come sail away, come sail away with me

When he finished singing, he turned his back to the seats and again closed his eyes. His head filled with the sound of applause. Squatting, he brought hands up to his head, cupping his forehead with both palms, sobbing. The memory was so crisp, so vibrant, as if he were reliving the moment.

With a deep breath, he struggled back to his feet.

"This was the moment," he said out loud, almost shouting. "This was the fucking moment!"

Laughter soon replaced the melancholy he felt. He laughed out loud, pure joy in his spirit, giggling like a child. He had forgotten that feeling, forgotten the one moment in his life when he'd felt utterly and completely alive. He had forgotten what led him to even pursue music and why that journey had become so important to him. But now he remembered. It was not this auditorium or this school that made him feel at home. Rather, it was the moment when his voice lifted people to their feet, when it made his mother cry, when it brought a light to his grandmother's face that he had never seen. It was in this moment that he, for the first time, had felt completely at home in his own skin.

He jumped down off the stage, almost a childlike enthusiasm alive in him, and rushed back to the office. Mr. Cook was now seated on the floor, sorting through a large box that London guessed was his book delivery.

"Ah, they came!" London exclaimed, catching the principal by surprise.

"Why yes, they did," he replied, noticing the change in London's tone. He rose from the floor and brushed wrinkles from his pants. "Was your visit worthwhile?"

"Yes, yes it was. Thank you so much for letting me in," London replied. "I'm sorry to just sort of barge in like I did. I really appreciate your help."

"Oh, not a problem," said Mr. Cook. "Besides, if you hadn't come, I might have left a little earlier and missed my delivery." He smiled and motioned London again toward the door.

"Well, I'll be on my way," London said. "But if I could, I'd like to leave that note for Miss Wynne."

"Oh, of course," said Mr. Cook. He reached across the counter and pushed a piece of paper toward London. Then, he reached into a cup and handed him a black ballpoint pen.

London paused. Then he wrote:

"Dear Miss Wynne, I don't expect you to remember me, but I was a student of yours. I just wanted you to know that your work and your caring

made a difference in my life. Today, I carry on. Thank you."

London signed the note, clicked the pen closed, and handed the neatly folded paper to Mr. Cook. "Again, thank you," he said.

Once out on the street, London breathed in deeply, the crisp air filling his lungs. He exhaled with conviction, almost purposely expelling some of the demons that had for so long filled his chest with a heaviness he couldn't explain.

FIFTY-SEVEN

Once the key was in the ignition, London knew that his day's journey was not over. There was one other place he needed to go; he had avoided it for too long. But now, with a refreshed sense of purpose – and because the cemetery was literally around the corner – he decided that it was time.

Inside the cemetery, he was surprised that he remembered exactly where he needed to go. He had only visited twice before, but somehow he felt called to the location of his father's grave. He stood over the tombstone, staring down at the carved letters that spelled his father's name. He ran his hand over the cool stone, feeling the impression of the carving under his palm.

"Hi, dad," he whispered and brushed tears from his cheeks. He squatted first and then sat cross-legged in the grass over the grave. "Ten years already," he said into the sky. "Time sure does fly." He sat for only a few minutes longer, but as he stood, he noticed the empty grave to the right of his father's. The plot had been purchased at the same time as his father's, intended some day for his mother. Now that she was remarried, he wondered if he wouldn't end up in the ground there someday. He shook the thought from his head. It wasn't yet time for thoughts like that.

A cool wind began to blow as he brushed the grass and dirt from his blue jeans. Tiny leaves from a tree not far from the grave scattered around him and drew his eyes closer to their source. Under the tree – only 10 feet away – were the headstones of his grandparents. He closed his eyes to feel the warmth of sun on his face for just a moment. It gave him the resolve to move forward toward the graves. When he stood above them, he noted the names of his grandparents and more poignantly the dates of their deaths. Same date. Same year. It chilled him to the bone. But rather than run from the past, he was determined to follow through on what he had come to do.

He knelt on one knee, first in front of his grandmother's grave. He leaned forward, almost hugging the cold stone. "I miss you," he whispered. Tears seeped out of his closed eyes. He tried to hear her voice, to remember the love in her eyes. "I love you," he said.

Then, opening his damp eyes, he shifted his attention and his focus toward his grandfather's headstone. He could feel a familiar anger welling in his chest. But, as Patricia had suggested, he forced his thoughts to remember a more positive feeling. He kept his eyes open, stared at the name on the stone: Drake.

"Drake," he whispered. "Your name, my father's name, my name," he muttered. "I wish our history could be different. I'm trying to understand what happened and why you did what you did. But I'm also trying to remember the man you were – and I need to focus on the man I need to be. I am such a work in progress. We are not perfect," he said. "I forgive you."

He stood, almost robotically and turned from the graves. As he made his way down the grassy hill toward the cemetery gates, he paused at the bottom of the church steps. One at a time, he climbed the cobblestone steps, thinking back to the memories the church held. This was the church in which his parents were married. It was where he was baptized. It was where his loved ones were eulogized. This church knew his family: it had celebrated their joy and it had mourned their sorrows. He needed to go inside.

He pulled open a heavy wood door and walked up the center aisle of the church. As he did, he saw a priest standing on the pulpit, flipping pages of a bible and leaving marks at certain pages. He guessed that he was preparing for Sunday's mass. The priest looked up and smiled at him.

"Am I disturbing you?" London asked, halfway up the aisle.

The priest closed the bible and left it at the post. He moved away from the altar and toward London. When he was closer, he replied to London's question. "No disturbance at all," he said. And then because he did not recognize London, the priest introduced himself. "I'm Father Jerome," he said. "I don't think we've met."

London flushed with embarrassment at his absence from church. "Is it too late for confession?" he asked.

"Too late?" the priest asked, almost confused by the question. "It is never too late for confession, son," he said. Since they were alone, he motioned for London to take a seat in the pew.

The priest sat silently waiting for London to begin.

"It has been so long," London finally said. "I don't even know where to start."

"Well," the priest reassured him. "There really isn't a wrong place. Start where it makes sense for you. God will fill in the gaps."

London turned and looked the priest in the eyes. Then he diverted his eyes to the large crucifix hanging over the altar and said, "Forgive me Father, for I know that I have sinned..."

FIFTY-EIGHT

"Forgive me girl for I know that I have sinned
Brought you to hell and back again
Forgive me love for I knew not what I do
I know you won't come back

I guess I should have told you
But, the words got in the way
That night I should have held you
Instead I watched you walk away"

"Sounds great, man!" London heard from the control room.

He gave Tyler the thumbs up and wrapped his headphones around a mic stand. "Jon's guitar sounds bad as shit on that track," he said. "I'm feeling good about this one."

"Real feeling comes out in your voice on this one, London," Tyler told him. "This is gonna be a really solid second record."

Just as Tyler delivered the compliment, Nathan walked into the control room. "It better be solid," he said, only half-joking. "Especially since it's gonna be part of a national tour."

Tyler got the hint and excused himself from the room.

London pretended like he didn't even hear the comment, assuming that Nathan was just being his normal "put the pressure on" self.

When London remained quiet for another 10 seconds, Nathan broke the silence. "I'm not kidding, you know?" he asked.

London turned to look at his agent.

"You know we've been shooting for that," Nathan explained. "I've been working my ass off to pull it together."

London was still skeptical. "Stop it, man," he said. "That's not funny."

"Who the hell is trying to be funny?" Nathan asked, adding credibility to his earlier remarks. "I hope you enjoy your Thanksgiving at home this year because you're booked in Radio City the second Saturday in December. And after that, you have 15 dates in cities from here to San Antonio."

London's eyes widened.

"Well, that's if you can handle it," Nathan joked. "You know...without ending up in the hospital or some shit like that."

London let the sting of Nathan's last comment roll off of him. He knew it wasn't meant to hurt him. Instead, he focused on the news Nathan had just delivered: a national tour. "You're serious?" he asked one more time just to be sure.

"More serious than ever," Nathan replied. "The record company likes the work you're doing with *Breakdown*. They think it will be a hit. And they want to be ready to announce a tour as soon as the song hits the radio. They're banking on you, London."

"Holy shit!" London exclaimed and had Nathan in a hug before he could protest. "That's awesome news, man! What great motivation to get this record done and out there."

"Tyler says you're close, right?" Nathan asked, to confirm. "We're still gonna make the target date?"

"I don't see why not," London said. "We were just putting the finishing touches on *Breakdown* and the rest of the songs are tight. Tyler's been doing an amazing job. Wait until you hear the finished version of *Remember Me*. I think there's a hit there, too."

"Awesome, man," Nathan said. "I'm excited. I have the papers on my desk back at the office...the proposed tour schedule, too. Why don't you swing by tomorrow and sign off? Bring Jon if you want. There's some stuff for him, too."

An hour later, London sat with Jon in a local sushi place. Jon could tell that something was causing London's state of excitement, but it wasn't until his Bento box was on the table in front of him did London share his news.

"I was in the studio this morning," London told his friend. "I gotta tell you, man, I am so amazed about how the songs are coming out. I'm so glad

244 J.A. Blake ~ Nick Moccia

you've been by my side for all of it, brother."

"It's great to see things coming along," Jon replied.

"They are more than coming along, Jon," London told him, and then shared the details of his conversation with Nathan. When Jon returned his enthusiasm, London grew even surer that things were moving in a positive direction.

"Everything is finally coming together," Jon said.

London couldn't help but think of Katorah. He so wished he could call and tell her about his day.

"Almost everything," he said to Jon. "It'd be perfect if I hadn't screwed everything up with Kat. I really fucked up with her. She was different then all the rest, Jon. She was the real deal."

"Maybe it's not too late to make it right," Jon offered optimistically.

"I've tried," London told him. "She won't talk to me. But you know what's fucked up?" he asked Jon. "I think she's still helping me. What I felt with her...what I feel now without her...it's all making this record really come alive...if that makes sense."

"It does," Jon replied. "Nothing like heartache to make a hit!"

London laughed. "I guess you're right, my friend," he said.

Lightening the mood, Jon lifted his cup of green tea. "To heartache," he toasted, holding the small porcelain cup over his head. "And to the hits it produces."

London lifted his cup to return the toast. As he lowered the cup to sip the tea, he wondered if Katorah had any idea what an impact she had truly made.

FIFTY-NINE

The sound of a Giants/49ers game bellowed from the living room of London's loft. He was bent over in the refrigerator looking for cranberry sauce. Alex was adorned in an apron, stirring a pot on London's stove.

As the clock winds down on this Thanksgiving edition of NFL Football, Eli Manning and his New York Football Giants will go into their bye week with a 7–4 record after a crushing defeat to the San Francisco 49ers.

"Sorry, babe," Alex said and kept stirring.

Across town, Nathan was watching the end of the same game. "Please Jimmy," he said to the bartender, "Turn this shit off and put me out of my misery."

"Sorry, Nate. You know I can't do that. It's not over 'til it's over!"

"Trust me, Jimmy, this one is over," Nathan said, with a disgusted laugh.

"OK, bud," the bartender said. "See you in two weeks for the Packers game? Happy Turkey Day."

Nathan stepped out of The Red Lion and onto the sidewalk. He pulled a half-smoked Cohiba from his left breast pocket and relit the tip. Woody smelling smoke billowed from every puff and left a trail that followed him down the street. After a few blocks, he hailed a cab and gave the driver London's address.

When he arrived, he chuckled at the paper turkey hanging on London's front door. The words, *Happy Thanksgiving*, were scribbled under the feathered tail. He knocked and waited for London to welcome him. When the door opened, he greeted London with two words: "Fuckin' Giants."

London laughed and hugged his friend. "Nate, you and I both know the Giants suck in November. They will wake up...they always do!" he said optimistically.

Alex emerged from the kitchen holding a turkey baster in one hand and glass of Merlot in the other.

"Hey, Alex," Nathan said to greet her. "Good to see you under better conditions," he said, referencing their last encounter at the hospital with London. He moved closer and wrapped Alex in a hug.

"I hope we can get past all this football disappointment to have a nice dinner," Alex joked, still hugging Nathan. "But I guess boys will be boys."

Free from the embrace, Nathan unzipped his coat and handed it to London. "Smells good in here," he said, noticing the table set for six. "Speaking of boys, is George in the kitchen?" he asked.

London opened his eyes wide and silently signaled as if to say, don't ask.

Nathan caught on quickly and followed with a different question. "Jon still coming?" he asked. He was unsure why, but his question seemed to lift the mood and prompted laughter from London and Alex.

"Jon is running a little late because he had to pick up his date," London said and handed Nathan a glass of wine.

"A date?" Nathan asked. "Oh, do tell," he petitioned. "I can't wait to hear this. What is it with the holidays? Everybody falls in love."

"Apparently not everybody," London said. "Only those who deserve it."

"Stop it, London," Alex interjected. She was never patient when he started to feel sorry for himself. "Every choice we make has consequences and you hurt her. If she didn't care, she wouldn't be hurt. So just give it some time."

"I'm sorry, London," Nathan said. "I guess you haven't heard from her?"

"It's like I never existed," London told his friend. "Just like that... poof...gone. I just wish she would take my call. I feel like I've been really working hard in my therapy sessions to understand my anger...and my fears. I'd like to move forward...with her. I know if she would just give me the chance, I could be the man she needs me to be."

Nathan listened, nodding his head.

"I'm such a work in progress," London continued. "But she makes me want to be a better version of myself, if that makes sense."

The doorbell interrupted what was turning into a very serious conversation. Alex welcomed the interruption. She wanted the holiday to be happy. "Let me get that!" she said. A few minutes later, she came back into the room where Nathan and London were now seated and watching TV. With her was London's cousin, Charlotte, who held a tray of green bean casserole.

As children, Charlotte and London had been close like siblings. They spent hours playing board games or hanging out upstairs while their parents played cards at the dining room table after Sunday family dinners. Many of the memories London cherished most included his cousin. When their grandparents died, however, the cousins' relationship suffered; two sides of a family pitted against each other. It was almost 15 years –at his father's funeral – before the cousins were reunited and promised to never again splinter apart.

"Cuz!" he exclaimed and rose to greet her.

"I can't believe I beat Grace here," Charlotte said. "I got stuck in all kinds of traffic and thought for sure I'd be last to arrive."

"Oh come on," he said to his cousin. "Gracey has never been on time for anything in her life and now that she's dating Jon, we have no chance of seeing her even close to schedule." He laughed. "Jon makes being late an art...he is the self-proclaimed King of Lateness."

"Good point," Charlotte said. "But the fact that they are even together still blows my mind. Talk about opposites attracting."

"Eh, who are we to judge?" he lightheartedly asked. "If she talks all the time – and she does – Jon can stay in his comfort zone."

"Kitchen?" Charlotte asked, lifting the casserole to eye level. London took the pan from her and moved in that direction. Charlotte followed, bending first to kiss Nathan on his cheek. "Don't get up," she joked.

Thirty minutes later Jon and Grace finally appeared. Their lateness did not go unnoticed or unmentioned. "We saved the best for last," Grace joked as everyone took their seat at the table.

London sat at the head of the table and encouraged everyone to join hands for a prayer. The circle of friends made him feel blessed. But he longed to have Katorah at the table with them. He guessed she was only a few miles downtown enjoying dinner with Lucy in her new apartment. He wondered if she was thinking of him.

Just as Charlotte pushed a knife through the pumpkin pie, London's phone rang. "Hey, Momma," he answered. "Happy Thanksgiving!"

It was just over a year since his mom had remarried and moved to Florida. It was still strange for him to couple her name with one different from his father's, but she was happy and that was all that really mattered to him.

Alex reached for the phone and quickly said hello. "Yes," she said into the receiver. "Everything was delicious. He is an excellent host," she said and handed the phone back to him. He talked for only a few more minutes, but it was long enough to lament the Giants' loss and to hear about his mother's dinner. "I love you. Talk soon," he said.

"I love you more," she replied and hung up. The two never said goodbye; it was too final. Instead, they looked forward to the next time they would speak.

"Who wants an after-dinner drink?" Nathan asked as he poured a generous shot of Bailey's Irish Cream into his coffee. Hands went up around the table. "Did you tell them all about the single?" Nathan asked London. Eyes fixed on their host.

"Funny you should mention it, Nate," he replied. "I was actually toying with the idea of playing it for all of you tonight...you know...before the radio debut tomorrow." He laughed. "But only if you're all interested..."

"Shut the fuck up, London!" Grace exclaimed. "Of course we want to hear it!"

He retrieved a disc from his briefcase and placed it in the CD player. Jon recognized the haunting opening of the guitar and smiled at his friend.

Forgive me girl for I know that I have sinned...Brought you to hell and back again...

Three minutes and fifty-two seconds later, the final lyric cried out from the speakers: *Please save my life before the breakdown.*

Alex knew immediately that the song was about Katorah. Before the others could respond, she bluntly addressed London. "So...are you gonna let her hear it?" she asked.

London rose from the table and retrieved the disc. He carefully placed it back in a paper envelope and laid it on the coffee table. "I'd love her to hear it, Lex. But given that she won't even talk to me, I don't know how that's gonna happen. It sucks. I'm afraid she will never know the truth."

"And what's that?" Charlotte asked, looking to catch up on London's love life.

"I am so in love with her," he said and turned his head. "And I'm just so, so sorry."

An obvious tension filled the room. "I'm so proud of you," Nathan said to again lighten the mood. "It really sounds amazing. And people out on the road are just gonna love it!"

"The road?" Alex questioned, a little put off that this was the first time she was hearing news of a tour.

London shot Nathan a look as if to say *Thanks a lot, big mouth.*

"It's true, Lex. It's a national tour. I leave in two weeks."

"And he debuts in New York!" Nathan blurted. "Radio City!"

Claps and cheers echoed around the table.

"Thanks, guys," London said, retaking his seat with the others. "That means a lot to me. It really does. I am so thankful for your support."

Five bottles of wine and two pots of coffee later, his guests had all left for the night. He sat quiet on the couch. Chloe cuddled on his lap and he drifted off to sleep. Alex was in her car driving home. *Breakdown* played from the CD she had earlier tucked in her bag and took without asking.

SIXTY

Alex stood shivering on Delancy Street and rooted through her oversized handbag. As the city bus rounded the corner, she found the final quarter for her fare. The brakes on the bus screeched and the doors opened before her. She boarded, dropped in her quarters, and moved to the back of the crowded bus. It was Black Friday and the 10 a.m. bus was packed with would-be shoppers and their screaming children. Alex settled on a standing position and raised her arm to grab a hanging strap.

"Miss?" she heard from over her left shoulder, just as the bus began to move. When she turned, she saw a handsome man with a dark beard who was wearing a Yankees cap. He extended his arm toward an empty seat; one he had occupied seconds before. "Would you like to sit?" he asked with a smile.

"A gentleman?" she questioned. "I wasn't even sure they existed anymore."

"Who says chivalry is dead?" the man quipped back and reached up to take the strap Alex had been holding. "Please, sit," he said.

She graciously accepted and took the open seat.

"So are you always giving girls a seat on the bus or should I feel special today?" she asked flirtatiously.

The man lifted the baseball cap off his head and pushed his thick fingers through dark curls. She caught herself staring. He pushed the hat back on his head, squashing the lovely curls she had admired.

"You look like you might be something special," the man said just as flirtatiously. Then he extended his hand for a more formal introduction. "My name is Avery," he said.

"Nice to meet you, Avery," she replied. "I'm Alex."

She shook Avery's hand and stared up at him. She knew that her best asset was her dark eyes. She used them to her advantage.

"So...Alex," Avery continued, "can I interest you in a cup of coffee?"

She paused before answering. Her thoughts diverted to George. Their relationship was never easy, but the last few months were particularly sorted; a kind of emotional rollercoaster she was getting tired of riding. Still, he held a piece of her heart. He always would. She delayed even longer in her response. Finally, she spoke playfully. "Avery?" she asked. "Are you hitting on me?"

"Only if you like it!" Avery retorted.

She reveled in the flirtation. She laughed out loud at Avery's response. It felt good to laugh with someone. She felt like a high school girl. As she crossed one leg over the other, her long coat fell open and revealed her leg.

Avery's eyes followed the length of her leg, from her now exposed knee down to her heeled foot.

She watched his eyes make their way back up to hers.

He smiled and blushed.

"Avery, I would love to have coffee with you," she finally replied. "But today is not the day."

Avery looked disappointed. "I know," he said, "it's Black Friday and you probably have a million stores to hit!"

She jumped back in quickly. "Oh, no," she said. "Today I am trying to help a friend who is – believe it or not – worse at relationships than I am!"

Avery raised a single eye brow.

Alex stood and looked out the bus window to assess their location. "It's a long story," she said again to Avery. "Maybe I can tell you about it over that coffee?" she asked and shuffled once again in her bag. As the bus came to a stop, she extended her hand. This time, it held a business card. "Why don't you call me and we'll share a story or two?"

Avery took the card and smiled.

As he tucked the card in his pocket, Alex extended her arm toward him again. This time, she reached up, snatched the baseball cap off his head, and moved toward the open bus door. She turned back to him and smiled. "I'm a Mets fan," she said, "but I think maybe I could learn to like the Yankees!" She winked and stepped off the bus before Avery could find any words to reply.

After a two block walk, she stood in front of the SPIN building. She paused to take a deep breath, pushed through the glass doors, and approached the security desk. She smiled as genuinely as she could, hoping it would encourage the security guard to be helpful. When he noticed her and smiled back, her confidence grew.

She noticed a name tag, pinned to his left breast pocket. "Good morning, Nick!" she said with enthusiasm. "Can you please tell me what floor the SPIN offices are on?" she asked.

"Do you have an appointment, Miss?" the guard asked. "I'll need to call ahead for you."

She now leaned forward, her elbow propped on the counter. "Oh," she said coyly. "Hmmm. An appointment?" she asked with wide eyes. "Do I need an appointment? I'm just dropping something off," she said innocently.

The guard, who she estimated was in his late 50s, began to reply. "You need—"

She interrupted. "I'll just be a minute or two. In fact, you won't even finish this muffin and I'll be back down," she said, pushing a cranberry chip muffin she had just bought at Starbucks toward the man.

"Muffin?" the guard asked noticing the gift being extended to him.

"Well, sure," she said. "I just stopped on my way and picked it up. In fact, I think it might still be warm," she said smiling. "Why don't you have it?"

The man shifted his eyes from one side of the open foyer to the other.

His hesitation prompted her to continue talking. "Really, I'll be quick," she said. "Please?"

The guard covered the muffin with his palm and directed her. "They're on the 7th floor. But if they ask, tell them you said you had an appointment. I can't be losing my job right before Christmas, for Christ's sake."

"Thank you, Nicky," she said. "And Merry Christmas!"

The elevator ride felt like an eternity. Once the doors closed and she stood inside, the reality of what she was about to do became clear. She had talked herself into being confident earlier that morning. Apparently her pep talk had worked. It got her this far and earned her a potential coffee date, but she worried that her charm would do nothing for her mission. She had to be successful...for London.

When the elevator doors opened, Alex saw a receptionist seated behind a mahogany desk.

"SPIN Magazine...please hold."

"SPIN Magazine...please hold."

"SPIN Magazine...please hold."

Without glancing up, the pretty young lady at the desk raised a finger asking Alex to wait.

"SPIN Magazine. This is Jennifer. How may I direct your call?" she asked of the caller. "No," she said. "He's not available. Would you like voicemail?"

Finally, Alex was acknowledged. "Sorry to keep you waiting," Jennifer said with a deep exhale. "This place is a mad house today. How can I help you?"

"Hello," Alex replied cheerfully. "I'm here to see Katorah Alexander."

"And what time is your appointment?" Jennifer asked, looking at an online calendar.

"I'm sorry," Alex said. "I don't have an appoint—"

"Ms. Alexander is not taking walk-in's today," the receptionist said. "Would you like to leave her a message?"

Alex knew that her charm would not get her in to see Katorah. The receptionist was just too busy for small talk. Instead, she reached into her bag to retrieve a CD jewel case. Tucked inside was London's recording of *Breakdown*, along with a Polaroid picture. She handed it to the receptionist with very clear directions.

"Please tell Ms. Alexander that a close friend of London Drake's was here and asked that she listen to this CD," Alex said. "And please don't lose the picture inside. It's important that she gets it."

"Is your contact information also included?" the receptionist asked.

"Ah, thank you," Alex said graciously. "Why don't I give you a card?" She positioned her business card over the CD case and stretched behind the desk to rip off a piece of tape. She pushed the CD toward the receptionist and paused. *This will be OK*, she thought. The receptionist went to take the CD, but Alex hesitated. *She will get it*, Alex told herself and lifted her hand. Once the receptionist took the CD and placed it in a large manila envelope, Alex finally turned to leave. "Thank you," she said with worry.

Once Alex was back in the elevator, the receptionist called down to Katorah's office. "There was an Alexandra Henny here for you," she told Katorah. "She said she is a friend of London Drake's and she left you a package. Want me to bring it down to you?"

SIXTY-ONE

Rinnnnnng .... Rinnnnnng...Rinnnnnng...

"Security, this is Nick."

"Nick, its Jennifer at SPIN. A woman is coming back down on the elevator...a Miss Henny. She came up only about five minutes ago. Do you know who I mean?"

Nick's face turned a shade of crimson. He thought he was about to be chastised for the muffin and lack of appointment. "Yes," he replied. "I'm sorry about that, but..."

"When she gets back down to the lobby, could you please send her back to our floor?" the receptionist asked, completely discounting the apology.

"Of course," Nick replied. "Everything OK?" he asked, but the caller hung up without an answer.

Several minutes later, Alex was riding the elevator again back up to the 7th floor. She was even more nervous than the first time. When the doors opened, a woman dressed in track pants and sneakers stood waiting for her. The woman's hair was pulled back in a simple ponytail and she wore little makeup, but she was pretty. The woman held Alex's CD case in her hand.

Before Alex could say anything, the woman blurted, "Please tell me he's OK!" Her face showed a genuine concern and she now held the CD up at eye level.

"OK?" Alex asked and then realized that she had caused alarm. "Oh God, yes. He's OK...relatively speaking. Are you Katorah? Can we talk in your office?"

Katorah's office was decorated with diplomas and family photos. Some writing awards were framed and hung on the walls. She and Alex made small talk until they were securely inside. Now, with the office door closed, Alex was eager to learn more about this woman who held her best friend's heart. She noticed a delicate frame on a bookshelf that held the photo of two women. A closer look revealed that one of the women was Katorah.

"That's me and my sister, Lucy," Katorah answered, still not sure of the reason behind Alex's visit. "It was taken two years ago in the Bahamas. Whenever one of us gets our heart broken, we just go on vacation!" Katorah laughed. "If you're gonna be miserable, it might as well be in paradise, right?"

The two women shared a laugh. "I will have to try that," Alex said, thinking that her own heartbreak was on the horizon. "Extra margaritas, please!"

When the laughing stopped, an awkward silence filled the room. Finally, Katorah spoke of London. "He's told me so much about you," she said to Alex. "I can easily see why he loves you."

Alex found an opportunity. "And I can see why he loves you so much," she said to Katorah.

Katorah spun in her chair and stared out the window. Alex waited. When Katorah turned back to face Alex, her eyes held tears. "Why are you here?" she finally asked.

"Tell me what happened," Alex asked gently. "Tell me your side."

Katorah exhaled. "I don't know what good that would do," she said. "I'm sure London told you what happened..."

"Katorah," Alex said with tenderness. "You and I know London. So we both know that his version of things is always colored in his perspective. But this time...this time, it feels different to me. He seems different to me."

Katorah shared the story of her last night with London. Her details of the evening were close to what London had recounted earlier for Alex. But what he didn't share was the intensity with which Katorah had pleaded for him to let her help. "It's not that I feel sorry for him," Katorah said. "But pain like that shouldn't be felt alone, you know? I really wanted to support him," she said. "I wasn't judging him or his family."

"London has been through a lot in his life," Alex said. "Sadly, what he witnessed at 11-years-old changed him forever. No adult...let alone a child...should ever have to discover something like that. He has scars, Katorah...and walls. In the last year alone, he ruined a tour, almost lost a record deal, and self-medicated with enough alcohol and pills that he ended up in the hospital," Alex continued. "But none of it made a dent. It all just made his insecurities worse."

Finally, Katorah interrupted. "Alex, I don't know that man. The man I fell in love with was warm and caring. He was thoughtful and romantic. I loved that man so much. But on our last night together, he was an entirely different person...so full of anger and hate. All I wanted to do was be supportive and he pushed me away. The man that I fell in love with was gone and I was faced with a man who wanted nothing to do with me."

"I know how scary that must have been for you," Alex said. "I've seen London's temper. And I'm not saying that you should just forget it. How could you? But what I am saying is that he is sorry. He knows with every fiber of his being that he was wrong. And ever since you left, he's been miserable. Miserable, Kat...and not starving-artist miserable...more terrified than I've ever seen him about anything."

"Terrified?" Kat asked.

"Yes. Like he's lost a part of himself that he's afraid he will never get back."

Again, Katorah sat silent.

"You matter to him, Kat," Alex said, "more than anything from his past. Since you left, he's been working harder than I've ever seen him work to get his shit together. It's almost like you gave him a new perspective; one he's needed for a very long time."

A phone on Katorah's desk buzzed and interrupted the gravity of the conversation. When it rang again, Katorah looked at the caller ID. "Excuse me," she said to Alex, noting that the caller was Lucy. When she answered, Alex worried that her conversation was not being persuasive at all.

"I will see you at seven," Katorah finally said, to close the phone conversation. "Yes, at Spiga."

Katorah hung up from the call and apologized to Alex. "My sister," she said. "I've spent more nights on her couch watching Bridget Jones than I care to admit lately." She chuckled.

"Oh, I understand that!" Alex said, her voice full of empathy.

After another moment of silence, Alex pushed the conversation again forward. "May I ask you something?" Not waiting for Katorah's approval, Alex threw her question out into the dead space between them. "You said you loved him, Kat. Do you still feel that way?"

258 J.A. Blake ~ Nick Moccia

Katorah rose from her chair and paced the room. "I fell in love with the London I described to you, Alex. I think about him every day. It's like he follows me everywhere I go. I see him in magazines, hear his voice on the damn radio, and when I go home at night, I feel like he's going to be there waiting for me. Everywhere I am, he is – that gentle, beautiful man that I would have done anything for."

Alex reached to retrieve London's CD, which now sat on Katorah's desk between them. She opened the case and pulled out the Polaroid she had tucked in earlier.

"This is my favorite picture of him. His mom gave it to me," Alex said and extended her hand for Katorah to take the picture. "Take it and turn it over."

Katorah took the photo and paused to look at a smiling boy. The child was dressed in white underwear, a pair of sunglasses, and shoes that looked to be his dad's. She laughed. "Look at that smile," she said. "He looks so happy...not a care in the world!"

"Turn it over," Alex instructed.

When Katorah flipped the Polaroid, she saw handwriting: *10 years old*. She looked up at Alex through teary eyes.

"Kat, one year after this photo was taken, that happy kid walked in on a tragedy and it changed him forever. But that happy kid is still in there. I see it every time he hits the stage."

Katorah sat again, but this time in the chair next to Alex.

"Since you left, he has been seeing his therapist twice a week," Alex told her. "When he talks, I hear an optimism and a hope I have never seen before, Kat. And one thing I know for sure, Kat, is that he loves you."

"I just don't know what to say," Katorah said. "I am so glad to finally meet you. And I'm so glad to hear that London is making some really positive steps in the right direction. But when it comes to our love for each other...it's not a simple black and white...it's filled with grey. And London made it that way."

Alex felt defeated. "I'm sorry I took up so much of your time," she said and rose from her chair.

Katorah embraced her as if they had been friends forever.

"Kat," Alex pleaded, "I can argue how much he loves you and plead for you to give him a second chance, but that's your decision. When you feel like you can handle it, please just listen to the CD I brought you. I think it will say things that I just can't."

For a second time, the two women embraced.

"I hope I see you again, Kat," Alex said with all sincerity and turned to leave. "Oh! I almost forgot," she said and turned back toward Katorah. She pulled an envelope from her bag and handed it to Katorah.

"More presents?" Katorah asked through teary eyes and a crooked grin.

"I promised myself the whole way here that I wasn't going to push too hard," Alex replied. "But his tour starts at Radio City Music Hall in two weeks. Maybe you could bring someone?"

Katorah took the envelope.

"I mean, don't bring a date or anything!" Alex clarified with a laugh and then let herself out.

Once she was again alone, Katorah slipped the disc from its case and popped it into her computer. She kept the office door closed and turned up the speakers. With her head pushed against the cold glass, she sobbed at the sound of London's voice.

When she arrived at the restaurant to meet Lucy, her sister was already seated and sipping a lemon martini. Katorah shimmied out of her coat, took a seat across the table, and stared at her sister.

"Hey there," Lucy said enthusiastically. "What's new?"

Without a word, Katorah dropped the two concert tickets in front of Lucy, raised an inquiring eyebrow, and took a deep sip of the martini.

SIXTY-TWO

From backstage, London could hear the crowd...its rumblings, its clapping, its anticipation. He found that energy exhilarating; a better high than he ever experienced from alcohol or even sex. To know that he was about to take the stage in Radio City Music Hall filled him with an overwhelming sense of pride.

"Amazing, isn't it kid?" Nathan asked, as he took his place beside London. The two of them stared out from backstage on a sea of people. The opening band had finished 15 minutes prior and now the crew was busy setting the stage for London and his band.

"Nate, I can't even express how I feel right now," London replied, knowing that he wouldn't have to try hard to use words. Nate traveled the road to this moment with London; his personal and professional investment in him was always obvious. Now, at the kickoff of a national tour, he was more grateful than ever for Nathan's backing.

"I knew we'd get here, London," Nate told him. "I'm proud of you."

London's eyes welled with tears. His heart felt as if it might explode with love for the man positioned beside him.

"So where's Alex?" Nathan asked, diverting the focus to something less emotional. "I thought for sure she would be here for this."

"She's coming," London replied. He silently wondered what could be delaying his friend. "She probably couldn't decide what to wear." The two friends shared a laugh.

"I'm sure that's it," Nathan replied. "Damn women."

London glanced at the clock on the wall. In about 10 minutes, he would be standing on the stage he had dreamed of playing his whole life. He has seen all of his favorites on that stage. He decided to send Alex a text.

"Hey, honey," he messaged. *"You OK?"*

His phone buzzed back in response.

"On my way, sweetie," Alex told him. *"Don't worry. I wouldn't miss this for the world...just parked the car."*

"Use back door entrance," London texted back again. *"Your name is on the list."*

"Show off," she replied, with a little smiley face.

He laughed out loud. Alex was so unaffected by his new found fame. She remained constant and grounded. More than ever, he appreciated that. Then unexpectedly, his mind went to a memory of his grandmother. As he gazed out on Radio City Music Hall, he remembered how his grandmother would sit in a lawn chair in their garage while he played his guitar. She would get up and dance while he and three other boys stumbled through song after song. No matter their mistakes, his grandmother would keep dancing, love filling her eyes. As a boy strumming a guitar, he would imagine that she was looking at him as he walked up the steps in Radio City to accept his first Grammy Award.

Alex was indeed parking her car. She squeezed her sedan in between two large trucks in what was no more than an alley and decided that the risk of being towed was worth watching London take the stage in Radio City Music Hall. When she arrived at the backstage door, a tall, muscular man greeted her with a less than friendly disposition.

"Alexandra Henny," she told the man, who flipped over a page on a clipboard.

"ID?" he asked without looking up from the page.

"Oh good God," she muttered out loud, not making the doorman's disposition any sweeter. Realizing she was just creating trouble, she quickly followed her expression with something more appropriate. "I mean, you think I'd have that out already, right?"

The man lifted his eyes toward her and nodded his head. His eyes quickly darted down to the open button on her blouse and then back up to her face. He extended his hand to take the ID that she now offered for his inspection.

She shifted back and forth impatiently.

"Have a nice night," the man said to Alex as he opened the door.

She exhaled and moved quicker now. She could hear the opening chords of *Found* and knew that London was just seconds from taking the stage.

"London!" she yelled just as he took his guitar from a roadie. He stopped and turned toward her. He smiled and without a word, she was in his embrace, the guitar squashed between them.

"I love you, London. You're gonna be amazing," she whispered in his ear.

Once he was on stage, the Radio City crowd did not disappoint. Women in the front row held signs up over their heads with his name on them. One made no delay in throwing a stuffed teddy bear at his feet. In between his first and second song, he crouched down to pick up the bear, kissed its furry head, and threw it back to the woman. She laughed hysterically, tears flowing over her flushed cheeks.

Alex remained backstage, but watched the crowd. When five of the 11 songs on London's set list were over, she began to feel nervous that Katorah wouldn't show. The seats she had reserved for her were still empty. She checked her phone for a text. Nothing. She began running excuses in her head. *Maybe Katorah was lost?* Not likely since she knew the city pretty well, especially around the music venues. *Maybe she couldn't find parking?* More probable, but even Alex wasn't sold on that excuse. *Maybe she had just not convinced her to come.* The last scenario was more of a statement than a question in Alex's head. She thought she had been pretty convincing. But Alex really didn't know Katorah very well. What she did know was London's temper. And, if he had scared Katorah the way he described, maybe it was just too much for Katorah to overlook. She began to feel disappointed.

London now began to strum his guitar...the opening of the sixth song. He spoke over the soft notes of the guitar.

"New York, I am so glad you are spending the evening with me," he said and the crowd cheered. "But I am blessed in more than one way tonight," he continued. The crowd cheered again. Alex laughed. It seemed he could say just about anything and they would respond. She imagined London saying *I love grilled cheese sandwiches* and the whole audience clapping and screaming. The thought made her laugh.

"Not only do I get you," London said, extending his arms out to the crowd, "but I am also joined on this stage by my good friend and the finest guitar player around, Mr. Jon Keebler."

A woman in the crowd shared London's admiration for Jon and screamed, "I love you, Jon." Jon turned red and London nudged his friend closer to the front of the stage.

"And on top of all that," London told the crowd, "my best friend in the world...a woman who I could never really introduce...is with us backstage." Alex opened her eyes wide at London and mouthed for him to stop. "I bet," he continued, "that if we all clap for her, she might just come out here and say hello." She was mortified, but the screams of the prompted crowd demanded her on stage. She looked at Nathan for help.

"Sorry, babe, you know I can't control him!" Nathan said and laughed. "You might as well get it over with."

Realizing she had no choice, she stepped reluctantly onto the stage. London moved closer to the curtain to meet her, took her hand, and led her out under the spotlight. She smiled out into the crowd who was mostly blurred by the stage lights. Then, in the typical way she took charge of a situation, she took the microphone from London's hands. "He really is amazing, isn't he?" she asked the crowd. Cheers got louder. London smiled at Alex and leaned over to kiss her cheek.

"Enjoy the rest of the show," she said into the microphone before returning it to London. "They're all yours," she said to him and turned to exit the stage.

Halfway back to the curtain, she noticed movement in the second row. People were making way for someone to join them. She raised her hand up over her eyes to block some of the spotlights and saw Katorah and another woman squeezing into the seats held for them.

Katorah hesitantly raised a hand to wave at her and offered a coy smile as if to say, *Yeah. OK. I'm here. Happy now?* Alex returned the smile and continued backstage.

OK, she thought to herself with a deep exhale. *The rest is up to them.*

SIXTY-THREE

"Let's slow it down a little," London said to the crowd and began the opening chords of *Remember Me*. His producer had been right about this song. It had been an instant hit on the radio and the crowd needed only a second to recognize it. They cheered and then lifted a sea of lit cell phone screens into the air. He smiled at his fans and then closed his eyes to sing. The venue hushed and just listened. When he sang the line, *I will always catch you when you fall*, for the first time, a 20-something in the front row – directly in front of Katorah – screamed out, "Catch me, London! Catch me!"

He stopped strumming his guitar and moved closer to the edge of the stage. He was never one to miss a chance to make a concert really special for a fan.

"Hold on, hold on," he said and stopped strumming the guitar. The crowd again burst out in cheers and whistles. "I have to see who this is," he laughed. The crowd laughed along with him. A man next to the young woman lifted her up onto his shoulders and she extended her arms toward the stage. London looked directly down at her, noting her tiny frame.

"I wondered where you were falling from," he joked. "But now I see," he said and pointed down at the man holding her. The girl waved her arms at London, extending a single red rose in his direction. "Is she heavy?" he joked again with the man. The crowd laughed again.

London moved closer to the edge of the stage and accepted the rose from his fan. Then he leaned over the speaker and puckered his lips to kiss her cheek. When she stretched to reach him, she wobbled on the shoulders of the man who held her. He reached up and clenched her hips.

"Thanks, sweetheart," London said into the microphone. "Now how about you get down from there and I'll sing this song?" At the prompt, the girl happily wiggled back down into the crowd. London paused to make sure both her feet were securely on the ground. Once down, the row being blocked by her elevated stance could now be seen. In the second row... could it be? London blinked. His eyes met Katorah's. And without words, the two were communicating. *Hello*, she seemed to whisper with her eyes.

He felt as though the whole world disappeared. He couldn't believe she was there. He wanted to just stop the show and jump down onto the floor to embrace her. *How is this happening?* he thought.

"London, I love you!" screamed a girl from the other side of the stage. Katorah's eyes shifted to the crowd and then back to his.

He took three steps back and found a stool on the stage. He moved clumsily to find his seat. Then he raised the guitar to his knee, shook his head in happy disbelief, and again began to sing the song from the beginning.

By the time he finished, tears stained Katorah's cheeks. She hadn't really been sure about coming; about seeing him again like this. But she was glad she did. She saw him more clearly through his music than anyone. It was the heart of him; where he began and ended. There was no confusion in his lyrics about who he was or what he wanted.

The crowd erupted in cheers and applause at the end of the song, giving him time to catch his breath. From the stage, he could see Alex watching. He looked at her with wide eyes and petitioned her to look out in the crowd. Alex shook her head as if to say, *I know, London. I know.*

He finished what remained of his set list in 30 minutes. He found himself constantly migrating toward Katorah's side of the stage; afraid that if he stopped looking, she might just disappear. She did not. She sang along, danced with Lucy in the crowd, and cheered. Her joy made him happy. If nothing else came of this, he was glad that his last memories of her would be happy ones.

The last song on his set list was *Breakdown*. It had been the biggest radio hit London had, still on the charts. When the haunt of the electric guitar began, the stage was dark. He stood in the background, his head dropped, his heart pounding. *This is her song*, he thought to himself. *My apology to her. I hope she can forgive me.* He moved to the microphone, a single illuminated image on the dark stage. Only when he sang the opening line did he raise his face to the light.

"Forgive me, girl..."

Screams, louder than before, filled the space.

He continued singing, but he found it hard to open his eyes. The pain in the song was again so new. The apology he had so often wanted to offer the last few months was there, exposed and bleeding out of him.

The dark stage now shown in bright lights and from each side of the stage, a gospel choir marched into view, filling the air with a sweet church-like harmony. Once in position, choir members in bright white robes swayed back and forth in unison. The crowd raised its hands into the air, almost professing a shared need for forgiveness. Katorah stood motionless and listened to his voice. The music overwhelmed her; the sentiment in the song was even stronger than it had been on the CD. She didn't know what to do with this emotion. Finally, he fell to his knees and sang the song's closing line: "Save me from the breakdown."

The arena went dark and again exploded into noise.

"Jesus Christ," London said to Alex backstage and ran a small white towel over his hair. "Can you believe that she's here?" he asked.

"Yeah, I can!" Alex replied.

He paused and looked at his friend. "What did you do?" he asked.

"I did nothing," Alex replied, barely able to keep a straight face. "We take care of each other, right? It's what we do."

Just then, Nathan walked up to him. "Let's get this wrapped up!" he said with enthusiasm. "Get out there and leave them wanting more!" he laughed. "Give them that moment they'll remember."

London danced around with nervous energy, peeking around Nathan to see the stage curtain.

"London," Alex directed. "She's not going anywhere. She stayed this long, right?"

He knew Alex was right. She was right to keep him focused on finishing the show. He was so glad to be there...in Radio City...with her and Nathan and Jon beside him.

"Would you listen to them?" Nathan asked with a grin wider than his face. "That crowd can't get enough of you, man. This is awesome!"

He listened. It was pretty amazing. "Call my mother," he said to Alex. "Can you get her on the phone?"

When his mother answered the call, he simply said, "Listen, Momma." He stood right behind the curtain and pushed the phone through an open slit. He held it there for several seconds. "Can you hear them?" he asked her.

"Hear them?" his mother asked sarcastically. "I bet if I go outside and listen, I will hear them from here, honey! I am so, so proud of you, baby." His eyes welled with tears. "Thanks, Mom. I love you," he muttered.

"Love you more," she said.

He handed the phone back to Alex. Nathan offered him a bottle of water and then put his hands on London's shoulders. "This is the night you've been working for, London," he said proudly. "And this is only the beginning of many, many great nights."

London embraced Nathan. "Thanks, man," he said. "Thanks for always, always believing in me...even when I didn't believe in myself." Then he motioned to Jon. "Ready to finish this?" he asked. "Just me and you out there, man...like it's always been."

Two minutes later, he was back on a dark stage for his encore. On the screen behind him, clouds swirled on a stormy colored screen. The roar of thunder could be heard and the sound of rain echoed through the sound system. Jon began strumming a ukulele. London hoped that when the lights came back up, he would still see Katorah in the audience.

The clouds continued swirling behind him; his silhouette juxtaposed in front of them. Then, the screen began to lighten and the clouds split, seemingly evaporating off the screen. The sound of rain stopped and colors of a rainbow began to emerge, tiny paint spots staining the screen until a full spectrum rainbow stretched from one side of the screen to the other. Stage lights brightened and London stood before the crowd.

There she was. Still there. His heart skipped a beat.

"This is for all of you, for making my dreams come true," he said and began singing the words to an old and familiar song:

"Somewhere over the rainbow, way up high
There's a land that I've heard of once in a lullaby.
Somewhere over the rainbow, skies are blue
And the dreams that you dare to dream
Really do come true."

He looked down at Katorah and continued singing, even stronger than he had in the first verse.

"Someday I'll wish upon a star..." he sang.

Words to the song began to scroll on the screen behind him. The crowd began to sing along, slow at first and then filling the room with voices. He struggled to continue, overwhelmed with gratitude and emotion.

"If happy little bluebirds fly beyond the rainbow
Why, oh why can't I?"

Jon kept strumming the ukulele for London to repeat the last verse. But as London moved to the very edge of the stage, he looked Katorah directly in the eye and revised his last line for her. The crowd hushed as he sang his closing lines.

"If happy little bluebirds fly beyond the rainbow
Why, oh why can't WE?" he ended.

Katorah smiled tenderly at him and nodded her head. The room again went black, except for four letters that illuminated the screen, one at a time: H – O – P – E.

Made in the USA
Charleston, SC
03 November 2013